Single Girl in the City

A Funny, Feel Good, Grumpy Boss, Romantic Comedy

Also by Marina Adair

The Eastons
Chasing I Do
Definitely, Maybe Love
Summer Affair
Single Girl in the City
Four First Dates and a Forever
(coming 2022)

Romcom Novels
Situationship
(coming 2022)
RomeAntically Challenged
Hopeless Romantic
Romance on Tap (novella)

Sweet Plains, Texas series
Tucker's Crossing
Blame it on the Mistletoe (novella)

Nashville Heights series
Promise Me You

Sequoia Lake series
It Started with A Kiss
Every Little Kiss

Destiny Bay series
Last Kiss of Summer
Like the First Time

Heroes of St. Helena series
Need You for Keeps
Need You for Always
Need You for Mine

St. Helena Vineyard series
Kissing Under the Mistletoe
Summer in Napa
Autumn in the Vineyard
Be Mine Forever
From the Moment We Met

Sugar, Georgia series
Sugar's Twice as Sweet
Sugar on Top
A Taste of Sugar

Single Girl in the City

The Eastons

Marina Adair

This is a work of fiction. Names, characters, organizations, places, events, and incidents are either products of the author's imagination or are used fictitiously.

ISBN: 978-1-947591-21-9
Cover design by Lucy Rhodes of Render Compose
http://www.rendercompose.com
Headshot by Tosh Tanaka

To

Table of Contents

Chapter One

Happy Things:
~~*Snickers bar*~~
King-sized Snickers bar

Abilene Woods had barely secured her Good Samaritan hat and already she was having a crisis of faith.

It wasn't that Abi didn't know how to perform a random act of kindness. She was terrified that she'd do it wrong. After everything that had happened, after the two terrible tragedies she was partially responsible for, screwing this up wasn't an option. Which was why she'd been searching for signs ever since moving from Alabama back to Portland.

She wasn't sure what she'd imagined they'd look like. So when no shooting star lit the way and no kaleidoscope of monarch butterflies took flight, Abi did what any good former kindergarten teacher would do: she flipped the universe the big one, then crafted a NEED A GOOD DEED? sign-up sheet and posted it on the bulletin board at the tea shop where she worked.

Miracle of miracles, when she arrived at Sip Me that morning, she'd found not one, not two, but three posted wishes waiting to be granted—and not a one began with *For a good time call…*

So today, Abi was going to make a few lives a little easier. Not bad for her first day in the saddle.

Spring had finally arrived with a light drizzle and a gentle breeze, which carried the scent of dogwood blossom from the surrounding trees. Abi's first stop was at Food Hub and Grub, where she loaded her cart with all the wish-making essentials. She cruised the chip aisle, rescuing a bag of Cheetos, and rounded a display of pecans, which read WARM ROASTED NUTS, before turning down the self-care aisle where she found the last item on her list.

Palms sweaty, heart racing, she glanced right, then left, then up at the security camera overhead. Crossing her fingers that a security guard wasn't zeroed in on her aisle, she snatched the box and shoved it into the cart, sure to hide it beneath the HAPPY BIRTHDAY confetti.

She was reaching for another box and that's when she saw him. The one man she'd come to Portland to meet and had spent the past month avoiding.

Owen Easton. The biggest wrong she had to right. And the biggest flirt on the western seaboard. Dressed in faded jeans and a navy peacoat, he looked like an underwear model and an MMA champion collided, making him one hell of a sexy bad boy. And his smile–*oh lordy*—that smile, which was impossible to ignore, did things to her insides. Dangerous things that worried her.

He glanced her way, making direct eye contact.

Pretending she didn't see him, which only made his smile bigger, she crouched down low like a soldier crossing through enemy territory and dashed toward the cash register—the six birthday balloons floating overhead acting as a homing beacon that followed her every move.

She considered ditching the cart and running for the hills, but then she'd blow her first chance to make a real difference. A chance to help a stranger in need and, hopefully, bring some much-needed balance to her out-of-control world and prove that she was moving in the right direction so Karma would get off her back.

Telling herself to pull up those big-girl panties and there was nothing to be embarrassed about, she loaded up the conveyor belt. Tossing in a king-sized Snickers for strength, she kept her eyes glued to the person in front of her. When it was her turn, she waited impatiently for the cashier to scan each item. Then it happened, the moment she'd spent the past ten minutes obsessing over and stressing about. The cashier stopped when she got to the box of condoms and glanced up when she saw the second.

Abi flashed a bright smile. The cashier lifted a judgy brow, holding Abi hostage with a single look. The woman wore her silver hair in a twist, a Food Hub and Grub apron with PATRICE embroidered across the top, a magenta tracksuit that was bright enough to be seen from the Ozarks, and an expression that had Abi shifting in her shoes.

"You looking to get lucky?" Patrice asked.

Abi felt her face heat. "Excuse me?"

"The lottery's up to thirty million." She scanned the condoms. "You going to buy a lotto ticket?"

"No, ma'am. Just the items in my cart."

"You sure?"

Abi craned her neck, looking for *him*, relieved when he was nowhere in sight. "I'm sure."

"You got thirty million dollars?" Before Abi could answer, the clerk said, "Didn't think so. How many tickets?"

Abi shifted her weight from foot to foot. She had been short on patience her entire adult life, a sentiment she shared with her pint-sized students. Her need to be in constant motion stemmed from a childhood of waiting on everyone else and going nowhere fast. Today's impatience was more of a desperation born from an innate, life-or-death need to escape before Owen located her.

"I'll take one," she said, and then because she was Southern born and bred, she added a honey-sweet, "please."

This seemed to pacify Patrice. "What numbers, missy?"

"Whatever numbers the machine spits out will be fine, ma'am."

Patrice gasped, a horrified hand clutching her chest. "You can't live your life by chance. You've gotta take charge."

Something Abi was quickly learning. There were a lot of missed meant-to-bes in Abi's life. In fact, her life was apparently one big missed meant-to-be.

She rattled off her best friend's birthday, the day they met, and the number of words from the title of her favorite NSYNC song, which was the number three for "Bye, Bye, Bye"—but Patrice wasn't listening. She was too busy turning over the lip gloss tube, which Abi had bought as a special treat to herself for her upcoming do-gooder deeds.

The cashier read the color posted on the bottom. "Cream puff. My favorite pastry."

Abi sighed. Cream puff was also the name of Jenny's cat—a reminder so painful it made Abi want to cry, then devour the entire king-sized Snickers in one sitting.

"I hear you loud and clear, Jens," she whispered to her best friend, who Abi imagined was giving her two thumbs up from the big playground in the sky. "I hope you're happy because I love that color and it's the last one."

Patrice handed Abi the lip gloss and instead of bagging it, like she had the rest of her items, Abi held it out to the clerk. "It's for you. I think the shade would look great with your complexion," she said, doing her best Jenny impersonation. This immediately brought on a wave of guilt because

Jenny was the real deal, a from-the-heart, shirt-off-her-back kind of do-gooder, which was not Abby's first instinct, nor was it her second or third.

Patrice placed a hand over her mouth and her eyes went misty in a way that had Abi's heart growing just a tiny bit. "Oh my. Aren't you an angel?"

She didn't know about that, but the genuine appreciation in the older woman's expression ignited some feeling Abi had thought shattered in the accident.

"Champagne, lipstick, and condoms," a very sexy and unwelcomed voice said from behind. "You must be throwing one hell of a party."

Abi looked up and nearly swallowed her tongue whole. Because there he stood, her reason of reasons looking like sex on a stick. She'd caught glimpses of him over the past month, but always from a distance. A purposeful choice. Now she was close enough to smell his body wash and she realized just how big he was. Tall, broad shouldered, and I-bench-press-kegs-for-fun fit. And he was staring at her with amusement in those heart-stopping blue eyes.

Abi wished to disappear, but unfortunately whoever was granting wishes wasn't listening because how else could this moment come while she was dressed like a singing telegram?

It wasn't often that an amateur do-gooder got to face down her reason for do-gooding on her first day as a practicing Samaritan. By practicing, she meant stumbling, and Abi had stumbled right into the son of the man whose life she had inadvertently destroyed.

As she stood there, dressed in a red nose, clown shoes, and a unicorn headband while buying a giant box of condoms, a shot of guilt mixed with swelling panic caused the secret that she'd held for over a decade to stick in her throat.

People were defined by their choices and while Teen Abi had chosen to do something stupid, she hadn't been the only guilty party in the equation. Sadly, Owen hadn't chosen any of it, yet it was clear by what she'd surmised over the past several weeks that he was the one paying the price.

"Nice shoes," he commented.

"I'm doing a birthday party later."

He glanced at the condoms on the conveyor belt. "Those for the balloon animals?"

"Those are none of your business."

"Isn't that a shame?"

It was more than that. She was still riding the high from completing the first random act of kindness in Jenny's honor, but now she had to delete a point, bringing her back to square one. Because she was about to lie to a man who deserved the truth, the whole truth, and nothing but the truth.

"Do you have a habit of harassing strangers in grocery stores?"

His lip quirked. "Stranger, huh? We're playing that game? I see you at the tea shop all the time."

"No game. Just a fact."

Abi was terrible at secrets and even worse at lying, which was why she avoided it at all costs. But sometimes one did something that—even though it was the right thing to do—warranted secrecy.

For a self-proclaimed good girl, Abi had a lot to atone for. Which was why, after a decade of avoidance, she'd come back to Portland, the place she'd spent every summer while growing up, to right the first of very many wrongs. She was hoping to make up for her most recent wrong that had ended in a terrible tragedy. She'd learned the hard way that every decision had far-reaching consequences, like a single drop of rain on a still lake sending ripples in every direction.

Abi's ripples were powerful enough to tilt her world so far off axis that the only way to atone was to face her mistakes head-on. Even if it was in baby steps.

Recommitting herself to the task at hand, she tossed the condoms in her bag and glanced at the exit, then pulled out her credit card in preparation for a speedy escape.

"ID," Patrice asked loudly.

Distractedly, Abi glanced at the cashier. "What?"

"You belong to AARP?" she asked, and Abi shook her head. "Then if you want the booze, I have to scan your ID."

Aware of Owen peeking right over her shoulder, she stealthily took her ID from her wallet and held it out to Patrice, who studied it.

"Abilene Josephine Marie." She looked up. "And that's just your first name."

"I thought you only needed to scan it." Abi snatched it back.

"Abilene, huh?" Owen asked, the humor thick in his tone.

She ignored him. "I really need to go."

"Is the party leaving the station?"

"Yes, and before you ask, it's a private party."

He rested a casual hip against the counter and leaned in close. A breathe-too-deeply-and-you'll-brush-his-chest kind of close that made her sweat in uncomfortable places. "My favorite kind," he whispered.

Not touching that with a ten-foot pole, she paid for her things and, ignoring the Do Not Enter sign, the drizzle, and the amused chuckle behind her, she raced out of the store and headed toward her bike. Not a motorbike, not even a ten-speed.

Nope, the closest Abi came to transportation these days was Jenny's old lemon-yellow beach cruiser, with a kitty seat cover, and white basket on the handlebars.

She was almost in the clear when her phone buzzed. Her nerves said to keep moving but her guilt told her to check the text to make sure it wasn't an emergency. She glanced at the screen and sighed. It was her sister.

Dotti: IT'S AN EMERGENCY.

Everything in Dotti's world was an emergency. Abi shifted her bags to one hand, wincing when the weight of the wine bottles grazed the still-healing sore spot on her wrist from the accident, then quickly swiped off a return text.

Abi: Are we talking zombies or the Four Horsemen kind of emergency?

Dotti: Hank had to leave for work early and they've outnumbered me.

By *they*, Dotti meant her Irish twin toddlers, Lemon-Marie and Koi, who might just be the biggest emotional vampires this side of the Mississippi. Their objective was world domination, their weapon of choice, temper tantrums.

Abi: You ran emergency dispatch for a decade, surely you can handle your children. Which you planned and begged the universe for, BTW. Remember all the times you said, "All I want to be is a mom"? Well, guess what? You got your wish so suck it up.

Dotti: They found your stash of doughnuts. There's enough powdered sugar on the floor to make snow angels and mutiny is on the horizon.

Abi winced. She'd hidden her stash on the top shelf in the coat closet, shoved all the way to the back and stuffed in a Skechers box. Who knew two travel-sized tots could scale a coat rack? Regardless, it left her with two options: leave Dotti to fend for herself or be late for work. Reminding herself that her new lease on life was about doing the right thing, even when it was the hard thing, she texted:

Abi: Hide the permanent markers and finger paints. I'll be home as soon as I can.

Abi began to pocket her phone when she heard footsteps behind her. "You need help with those bags?"

"You need a bell," she mumbled, and she could have sworn he grinned. She glanced up and nearly rolled her eyes. He stood there easily balancing two bags on one arm, his bicep flexing her way.

Whatever bad juju she'd accumulated throughout her life was coming at her with a vengeance.

"Can I give you a ride?" he asked.

"I'm fine."

She unlocked her Huffy from the bike rack. Still pretending like he was nothing more than a figment of her ridiculously vivid imagination, she loaded up her bike, the balloons floating from her handlebars, the champagne bottles taking up the entire basket. No matter how many times she rearranged her items they didn't fit—the story of her life.

"Why do I have the feeling that's your mantra," he said as she stepped onto her bike. "Where are you going?"

Holding the lighter bag, Abi put one foot on the pedal. "The opposite direction of wherever you're going."

"Funny, your bike's pointed in the exact direction of my work and therefore your work, which happens to be next door to my bar."

She looked down at her clown shoes and lifted a brow. "Does it look like I'm headed into work?"

"Who knows, it could be dress-up day. You are wearing a tie and lace-up shoes." He reached out and tugged her oversized tie, then pinched her nose. It honked.

"Didn't your mama tell you it's rude to give someone a good honk?"

"So it was good for you too?"

She snorted. "I gotta go. I'm already late."

"Then let me give you a lift." There was no teasing or flirting in his tone, just deep concern. For her.

She'd had a lot of people expressing their concern after the crash. Heck, she was as concerned as they were. How was someone just supposed to pick up the pieces and move on? If Jenny were still alive, she'd tell Abi to put one foot in front of the other. And she'd do it with that bright, heal-the-world smile that Abi would forever miss in her life.

Not wanting to let Jenny down again, Abi started pedaling across the parking lot. Owen easily kept pace. Not surprising since she was moving at a snail's pace.

She looked over her shoulder and the bike wobbled. "Stay in your lane," she said. He slowed down so that he was directly behind her but didn't stop. "Now you're tailgating."

"I must say, I like your tail."

She stopped, put her feet on the concrete, and looked at him over her shoulder. He winked. She groaned. "What will it take for you to go on your way so I can go on mine?"

"Since we're both going the same way, you'd save me the worry of wondering if you made it to your final destination in one piece."

"I wouldn't want to *worry* you." Although secretly she loved the idea that she got to him. "You could be a serial killer."

"You're the one dressed like the guy from *It*."

Abi pulled a business card from her back pocket and handed it over. He read it and laughed out loud, throwing his head back and everything. *Such a handsome prick.* "CEO of Wishes by Abi." She pointed to the subtitle "Professional Good Samaritan."

"Yes, and right now I go by Winkie the Uni-Clown. Part unicorn, part clown. I do parties, weddings, and singing telegrams."

"You sing?"

"Today I do," she said, back to cycling slowly across the lot. Her big shoes were only partly to blame. Until last week, Abi hadn't been on a bike since she was twelve. But it was faster than walking and less deadly than other forms of transportation. "Move before I call the cops and tell them a strange man wanted to pinch my nose."

"So, you're still going with the not knowing each other game, Tea Girl?"

She came to a hard stop. "Fine. Darjeeling oolong, loose-leaf tea, six ounces of water, 180 degrees, with a splash of soy. We may have crossed paths professionally." He lifted a brow. "I didn't mean it like that."

"I don't know. The condoms, memorizing my order." He shoved his hands in his pockets and rocked back on his feet, clearly validated. "Is that barista for, 'What's your number?'"

"It's barista for, 'Your drink is lame.' If you ask me, the splash of soy is an amateur move."

As she attempted to leave, he reached for her handlebar, holding her in place. Or maybe it was his intense blue eyes that made her feet feel like she was pedaling through wet cement.

"Since we've ruled out serial killer and you know who I am, please let me give you a ride," he said. "I can put your bike in the back of my truck and drop you off anywhere."

"Anywhere?" she asked.

"Think of me as your own personal rideshare driver." She steadied her bike and he backed away slightly, but she could tell he didn't like it. "Come on, Abi, there's no sidewalk and this is a highway."

She was more than aware of that. Her heart had started thumping painfully in her chest the moment she locked eyes on the heavy traffic and endless line of headlights glowing in the mist. "Really, I'm—"

A bus blew past, the draft knocking her back a step. The smell of the exhaust and the sound of the gears downshifting took her breath away, until her lungs began to burn and her eyes began to water.

Shaken by the memory of the collision, she lost balance and went down to one knee, letting go of her bike in the process. It crashed against the ground, toppling the bottles of bubbly, the glass shattering on impact. The sound brought Abi right back to that day on the bus. Back to the nightmares she'd spent the past few months trying to get out of her head.

She gasped for air. Once, twice, but her lungs weren't cooperating. Neither was her head. She reminded herself that she was safe, that she was on steady ground, and that if she didn't get herself under control she would embarrass herself in front of the sexiest man alive. That was enough to break through the fear.

Too bad it was too late. She'd already lost her footing and she landed ass-backward in a puddle with teeth-jarring force.

Pain shot through her right leg, which had scraped against the bike's chain. Cold wetness seeped through her leggings and spilled into the shoes she'd rented from Costume Palooza and Pawn Shop. Her pride took a nosedive and the balloons bobbed above her like a buoy in the middle of the ocean.

"Shit," she said, experiencing her second collision in as many months. She looked up at the clouds and glared at whoever was beyond. "Shit, shit, shit!" If she hadn't been raised right, she would have said another four-letter word, but her grandma would come down from the heavens and stick a bar of soap in Abi's mouth. She did, however, smack her hands in the puddle like her niece in the middle of a tantrum. "How's that for calm and tranquil?"

When no one answered, she tried to roll over and groaned. Nothing was broken, but she was definitely bruised. She pushed herself to her knees and started to stand when a hand with a sexy tattoo running up the forearm gently wrapped around her elbow. An unexpected *snap* and *crackle* popped between them. She shrugged him off. "I'm fine."

"Give yourself a minute to make sure you're okay," her shadow said. "Where does it hurt?"

Everywhere. "Just a little rattled is all." He offered her his hand again and stubbornly she didn't want to take it, but she was too afraid she wouldn't be able to stand back up on her own. Common sense won out.

His big, masculine hand ran down her arm to take her hand. He was just trying to help her up, but at the simple contact, the air sparked. He looked at her for a long, heated moment, then his face went carefully blank.

"It looked like you went down pretty hard."

"I'm fine," she said again, this time with a bright smile. Her heart was racing, her head spinning, her hands tingling—and it had nothing to do with the fall. When he didn't believe her or move to release her hand, she assured him, "Really, I'm fine. But thank you for asking."

"The cast on your wrist suggests otherwise."

"It's a brace, not a cast." She unvelcroed and velcroed it as proof.

"Disappointing. I was going to ask if I could sign it. Write, 'You should see the other guy' or 'Stay cool, Tea Girl.' Or maybe leave my number."

She ignored this and began to right her bike when she noticed it. Her purse had toppled over, scattering the contents in every which direction— her notebook in the middle, displayed for the world to see. Even worse it was open to *his* page.

Not that it said *Owen*, Abi was too visual for that. But it had enough doodles and sketches, not to mention a swirly O and a drawing of his family's bar to paint a clear picture.

She bent down to grab it, but he was faster. In the end, they each held the notebook like a game of tug o' war, and she was on the losing end.

"You must be a fan of Stout. Funny, I've never seen you in there."

And with good reason. "I'm not really a bar kind of person."

"Then we have that in common."

She blinked. "But you own a bar."

"My family owns the bar, I only run it. Big difference."

Another mysterious clue to be filed away in her ever-growing O folder. "If you say so."

"I say so," he said, not letting go. "Seriously though, I just want to help."

She still held tight, studying him to access his current level of curiosity. "No questions or cute comments?"

"Not a one. Scout's honor." He held up a little two-finger salute and she let go. She even let him load up her bags and hold her bike.

She brushed her hands down her pants and then gave up. There was no point. She was soaked straight through to her bozo-bloomers.

Thanks." She mounted her bike, and a dull pain covered her entire backside. She came to a hard stop and maybe even winced a bit.

"Now, how about that ride?"

She looked at the busy street and then back to Owen. She'd finally found that kaleidoscope of monarchs she'd been searching for. Annoyingly, they were in her belly. And if that wasn't sign enough that this moment was Jenny-ordained, the sky opened and big droplets of rain hit her like ticks on a hound dog.

"Fine." She held up a halting finger. "But if it says twenty-five remember that's the limit, so we go twenty-five." Because limits were meant to keep people safe.

"It's actually safer to go with the flow of traffic."

"Isn't that a fun fact? Twenty-five or no deal."

With a smile, which she had to admit was sexy as all get out, he took her bike and led her to his truck. It was a classic. 1970s. Big cab, bigger tires, and cream with a brown stripe down the side. It was a giant truck for a giant of a man.

He opened the passenger door, and she froze. She looked at the cab and up at him, then, like her meditation app taught her, she closed her eyes and took in a deep breath.

"That is a battle for another day. Today it's about calm and tranquility."

She said it three more times until her heart was back to normal speed. She looked up to find him looking back.

There was a long pause and she braced for the onslaught of questions about her meltdown. He surprised her by not asking a single one, which was the nicest thing someone had done for her since Jenny offered to take her seat at the front of the bus with a couple of hellraisers who had put a fake spider on a fishing line and tugged it down the aisle, causing mass hysterics from the other students.

It ended up being the last good deed Jenny ever did.

Chapter Two

Happy Things:
*The phrase "Sh*t show."*

Owen had made a tactical error.

Touching Abi had been a bad idea because it only confirmed what he'd suspected since they'd first locked eyes over the tea shop counter—their sexual chemistry was off the chart. Following up on the awareness was dangerous for a guy whose days—and nights—consisted of keeping the world spinning for a lot of people. But when she'd tried to dodge him in the store, curiosity had won out.

Now it was a concern. Whatever went down in the parking lot had her rattled. Not that it was any of his business.

He had exactly one hour before he was needed at his family's bar. Deliveries started at nine thirty and the cook staff showed up at ten to prep for the day, and he had two applicants coming in to interview for the open bartender position, leaving him with just enough time to chauffeur a sexy woman around town, one who was as much a contradiction as she was a mystery. Like friendly fire or a cuddly porcupine.

His goal had been to call her on avoiding interacting with him, then swing by his mom's for breakfast, and head to work. Only she'd taken a spill. A small one but a spill all the same, which ended with trembling hands and what he was pretty sure were the beginnings of a panic attack. Then there were the dark circles under her eyes that advertised more than just a lack of sleep. He'd noticed them before when he'd stopped in at the tea shop for his morning fix.

Sometimes she looked sad and other times, like right then, she looked as if life had chewed her up whole. Oh, she always had a smile for customers, but there was a sorrow deep beneath the surface that resonated with him.

"I could walk faster than this," she said, that Southern drawl scrambling his brain. Ever since college, he'd had a thing for Southern women. And Abi was as Southern as they came. She was also as stubborn as they came.

"Noted." He started his truck, and she squeezed her eyes shut. He considered asking her if she was okay, but he already knew the answer. *Fine, fine, and if-you-ask-one-more-time-I'm-hopping-out-of-this-truck fine.* So instead, he said, "Where to?"

Avoiding his gaze, she shoved her phone in his face, which had the directions to their destination. "Nob Hill," she said.

"Nob Hill it is." He pulled out of the lot, sure to keep it at a steady twenty-five. Even then she sat rigidly, ass hanging off the bench seat, clinging to the oh-shit handle as if it were her lifeline.

Following the dictated directions, he turned right, then left, avoiding the highway or any thoroughfares by sticking to city streets. The sound of the wipers and raindrops hitting the windshield created a sense of intimacy.

Abi sat with her eyes slammed shut, whispering "Calm and tranquility," over and over, the stress in her tone growing exponentially.

"You might want to scoot over before you suffocate or get helium poisoning," he suggested, patting the spot next to him.

"Not going to happen," she said primly, moving the balloons between them like the Great Wall of China. Every time he shifted gears the balloons went every which way, blocking his vision.

He craned his neck around a giant cupcake-shaped one and shoved it aside. "Then control your balloons," he said, noting that the more pissy she got, the less panicked she sounded.

She choked up on the ribbons until he couldn't see anything but her legs and clown shoes. "My balloons are none of your business."

Wasn't that a shame. He had a lot to say on the topic of her balloons. "We talking the perky ones or the playful ones?" A fist emerged through the wall of balloons and slugged him in the arm. "Ow." He made a big deal of rubbing his shoulder. "Okay, balloons are off-limits. How about why you're posing as a barista in a clown costume?"

Even in that ridiculous costume, she was pretty in the girl-next-door kind of way. Long brown hair pulled up into a ponytail, face fresh, and a couple of freckles across her nose. He'd never been into freckles, but he was beginning to change his mind. Then there were her eyes, warm whiskey brown and as close to bedroom eyes as he'd ever seen.

She was as far from his normal type as a woman could get. Petite, prickly, and pretty as hell. He doubted she'd say the same. Oh, the attraction was more than reciprocated, but she wasn't letting on if she was all that interested in exploring it. Which worked for him since his wasn't in the mindset for anything more than one night and she didn't strike him as a one-night stand kind of woman.

A few years back, he'd tried for more and had his heart ripped out, along with his ability to trust. He thought he'd found the one with Elena. She was sweet, sophisticated, and so damn beautiful, she'd captured his heart. She'd also captured the attention of his best friend and business partner.

If there was one thing Owen hated more than a cheater, it was a liar. And they'd turned out to be both. He'd lost the woman he could see forever in and his business partner all in one fell swoop. That empty ache in his chest never went away, and he was afraid it never would. He'd learned the hard way that everyone had an angle and a secret, which had the power to hurt. He refused to be on the losing end of that equation again.

She took off her bright red nose. "Today is Lauren's eighth birthday and Princess Jasmine canceled last minute."

"That was rude of her."

"The other princesses all have plans, so it's Winkie to the rescue. And before you make some comment about Winkie, know that this was the only costume left."

"Is Lauren your niece?"

"No. My niece is more of a Maleficent or Cruella kind of kid."

"My niece is more of a Sugar Plum Fairy with Angelina Ballerina thrown in. She made all five of us uncles dress up in ballerina costumes for her birthday," he said, and a good portion of that attitude of hers washed away.

"There are five of you?"

Wasn't that a refreshing question? With two rather famous brothers and his oldest brother being the recently elected district attorney, most people in Portland knew more about his family than he did.

"There were six of us, but my younger brother passed away a few years back." The accident had devastated his entire family. All these years later and they were all still reeling. That the accident came on the heels of losing their dad only made the loss harder to digest. Some days, it felt as if Owen were still trying to put his life back together, only he didn't have all the pieces.

"I'm sorry," she said. "Loss is devastating."

"How about you?"

"I have half-siblings. A sister and two brothers," she said, her eyes once again glued out the windshield.

"Are you close?"

For the first time, she looked his way. "Define close?"

He and his brothers were so close sometimes Owen felt suffocated. There was no such thing as privacy or personal space. And keeping a secret was damn near impossible. "My brothers are as pushy and as gossipy as a bunch of biddies at bingo." Not that Owen was exempt from poking his nose into everyone's business. It was almost an Easton family tradition.

"In my family, we try to avoid each other's business. Like the *never mix business with pleasure* kind of relationships."

That sounded—lonely.

"I guess I'm the closest with my older sister," she went on. "She's letting me stay with her until I find my own place."

He looked her way, those light brown eyes locked on his and—*bang*—there was that flicker of attraction. He'd noticed the way she'd abandon the cash register to make his drink every time he came into her shop as if avoiding him. Hell, it was so obvious that everyone noticed, including her coworkers who always rolled their eyes at Abi's disappearing act. Which he found interesting.

"What brought you to Portland?" he asked, and just like that, her shoulders tensed, her eyes skittered away, and she directed all her attention to her phone.

"We're here." She pointed to a painted brownstone on the opposite side of the street. Pink streamers and twinkle lights twisted around the porch railings and a big birthday banner hung on the front door.

He'd barely turned the engine off when she shot out of the car, a flurry of ruffles and balloons. Bending at the waist, she gripped the side of the door like she was about to tumble over. He was pretty sure she was going to be sick. Which made him wonder if she'd really gotten past the panic in the parking lot or if she'd put on some show for his sake.

"You okay?"

She held up a finger, and quietly mumbled, "I love balloons and unicorns and red dahlias. Bouquet of dahlias." He wasn't sure what a dahlia was, but he suspected it was the red flowers lining the yard of the brownstone. "I love solid ground where the speed limit is two miles per hour with no need for grab handles."

"You sure you're okay?"

She looked up and gave a bright, fake-as-shit smile. "Never been better. Oh, and you don't have to wait. I can ride to work from here. Plus, I have to stop by my sister's first."

"I'm a full-service kind of guy."

"Does that line work for you?"

"You tell me, since you're the one blushing."

"It's called frostbite."

"Uh huh."

She glanced at her bike in the bed of his truck and back to him. "You sure you can wait? I get it if you have to go."

What kind of people did she have around her that would let her ride her kiddie bike in the rain? It was as if she expected him to explain that it was too much of a bother to wait. "I'm sure."

She still didn't look convinced. "I'll be just a minute. I promise." She shut the door, then reopened it. "No peeking."

"What's the fun in that?"

"I mean it. This is awkward enough." The door slammed shut. She watched traffic, skipping over three very clear openings, waiting until there were no cars in sight before crossing. By the time she made it to the driveway, her hair was stuck to her face and she was dripping wet.

He reached in the back to grab his coat for when she came back and that's when he noticed it. The notebook that she'd practically kneed him in the nuts to get. It was in her purse, right there for God, Buddha, and Elvis Presley to see. If it was in plain sight, it wasn't exactly snooping, now was it.

There was nothing special about it. Just a plain black-and-white composition book. But on the front, in bold black lettering, read GOOD DEEDS BY ABI. Which was equally as intriguing as it was amusing. It explained a lot, while at the same time evoking more questions than answers.

He wasn't the kind of guy to violate someone's privacy and Abi took her privacy seriously—point in fact that he knew jack shit about her other than he wanted to get her naked.

Telling himself that the contents of that journal were off-limits, he turned his attention back to Abi, who was still standing on the stoop, a few steps away from the front door. Even from across the street he could see her shivering.

He was about to get out of the car and bring her his coat when she walked up the last of the steps and reached the front door. She lifted her hand to knock, then hesitated, as if second-guessing her mission. She looked over her shoulder and he gave her thumbs up.

What the hell? When had he become a 'thumbs up' kind of guy? Next, he'd start saying shit like *BT Dubs* or *Totes.*

With a nervous nod, she turned back around. And just when he thought she was going to bail, she held her chin up, secured her red nose in place, and knocked. A moment passed and she shifted back and forth, but her chin didn't drop. She waited another long minute and turned to leave when the door opened.

He could practically hear her sigh. She gave a cute shimmy with her backside and shuffled her feet as if giving a little tap dance. The startled look on the other woman's face said that Winkie hadn't exactly made the guest list. Abi must have explained things because suddenly a heard of pocket-sized people gathered at the door and Abi launched into a dance act.

As promised, he didn't watch, but he did roll down the window to listen. She was as talented at singing as she was at riding a bike. He could hear her tapping away, singing some mash-up between "Happy Birthday" and "Singin' in the Rain" and, *God help her,* was she adorably awful.

He'd always thought of her as standoffish the mornings he'd seen her at the tea shop, at least with him, but he was beginning to think that maybe he'd gotten it wrong.

When she came back to the truck, looking like Bozo in a car wash, he laughed. An honest-to-god, from-the-gut laugh. And it felt good.

"You promised no peeking."

"You didn't say anything about listening."

Pressing her lips in a firm line, which didn't hide her amused grin, she hopped in. Cranking the heater to full, he pointed the vents at the waterlogged woman shivering beside him. She huddled around the vent, rubbing her hands back and forth.

"There's some tea in that thermos." He pointed his chin to the mug in the console. "It's all yours."

"You sure?" She was eyeballing it like she'd die of frostbite if he said no,.

"You can spot me a tea when I walk you into work."

She picked up the thermos, her hands a little unsteady as she undid the top and moaned at the bittersweet scent filling up the cab of the truck. "Blue jasmine?" She eyed him over the steam rising from the cup. "And soy milk."

Owen shrugged. He didn't care what she thought—one sip and she'd know it was a damn fine way to take tea.

Abi took a tentative sip and closed her eyes. "Okay, it isn't awful."

"Isn't awful?" He lifted a brow. "Care to change your opinion?"

"No," she said, taking another hearty sip.

"Because that would mean admitting I was right?"

She gave a cute little shrug and went back to gulping down his tea. When her fingers were no longer purple and her chattering teeth had quieted to white noise, he heard himself ask, "Where to next?"

"The senior center on Ninth. I have some condoms to deliver."

Chapter Three

Happy Things:
Impeccable BS meter

After eight years of running his own business, Owen had become a master multi-tasker. But today the universe was testing him.

He stood behind the hostess booth of his family's historical gastropub in downtown and let loose a string of choice words beneath his breath when the phone rang. Again. Stout had been open thirty minutes and already the chaos had begun.

It was an all-hands-on-deck situation, where the boat could go under at any moment, and he was ridiculously understaffed, leaving it up to him to man the ship.

In addition to running the front and back of the house, he was playing hostess, since he was an hour late. He was also juggling being a receptionist, a bartender, and playing cheerful owner—all on three hours of sleep.

The line of waiting customers went out the door and the bar seating was already full. He'd over-seated one section, which had Mandy running food like it was an Olympic sport, and under-seated the booth section. Then there were the people calling to get reservations, to ask about restaurant hours, or to find out when one of his famous brothers was supposed to visit—not that he gave out that kind of information.

Stout wasn't just a place his brothers could come for a beer without being hounded, it was the last tie to their late father. The brewpub was known not only for its deal-making environment, working as the official meeting place for politicians, businessmen, and celebrities, but it was the Easton family legacy. It was the place his brothers gathered to hang and catch up. Owen didn't want that to change.

But after the day he'd had, he was at the end of his rope. He wanted nothing more than to go home, take a hot shower, and grab a few hours of shut-eye—maybe even head over to Hardcore Inc, the tattoo shop where Owen rented space. Between work and family obligations, he hadn't managed to break away long enough to be creative in over a month.

He'd just finished seating a party of nine when his hostess, Lake, came rushing in. She pushed her purse under the counter and into the lockbox. "I am so sorry I'm late. My car broke down."

Owen considered telling her she needed a new car since it had broken down three times in the past two weeks. Coincidentally, the problem coincided with her boyfriend comming to town.

"You good?" he asked, pointing to the line.

"Absolutely." Before he could say another word, she was down to business. Lake might be a little flaky, but she was great at her job—when she showed up.

Confident that she had it handled, Owen headed back to the bar, groaning when he spotted three of his brothers sitting on some stools, smug-ass grins on their faces. His middle brother, Rhett, gave him a little wiggle of the fingers. Owen sent him a finger back.

When he reached the roped-off family section, Gage said, "This place is insane."

Gage was one of the best agents in the country, representing everyone from musicians to professional athletes. He was also father to a seven-year-old spitfire, who had her uncles wrapped around her little fingers.

"Welcome to my life," Owen said, giving each brother a fist bump.

"No wonder you can't get laid," Josh, the oldest and—up until a moment ago—his favorite brother, pointed out. He was dressed in his usual uniform of an Italian suit, wool coat, and dress shoes—looking the respectable district attorney that he was.

Before dealing with his brothers, Owen approached a bombshell a few feet over. She was a fiery redhead, all curves and cleavage in a tissue-thin tee, black bra, and enough sexual bravado to catch the eye of every man and woman in the room.

She was Owen's type to a T. Confident, a little cocky and, by the look she was sending, open to a little flirting—and maybe even more. She'd come in a time or two before, chatted him up and let him know she'd be into a little fun.

Owen liked fun.

Resting his hands on the counter, he leaned in. "What can I get you?"

She glanced at his lips, the tattoo encircling his biceps, and back to his lips. "What's on the menu?"

"What's your preference?"

"Tall, dark, and tattooed." *Hot damn,* his day was turning around. The way she held his gaze told him she'd like to scribble her number on his forehead with a permanent marker. "As for the drink?"

"Oh, I remember," he said, showing off his mad memory skills. A party trick that was his ace in the hole for getting laid. "Jack and Coke for your friend. Shot of Patron for you."

Her smile said she was impressed, which was a little misleading of him. Owen worked hard to memorize the orders of regulars—or pretty ladies who came in looking for him. Only now that he had her attention, he found himself glancing through the window at the tea shop next door.

Red looked over her shoulder and followed his gaze. She must have mistaken his lack of eye contact as disinterest because her expression dilated to *your loss.*

"Just the drinks," she said coolly. He was irritated—at himself—but there was also this strange ping of relief that the conversation had come to a standstill.

Wanting to be a gentleman and make up for the misunderstanding, he poured her drinks and slid them across the bar. "On the house."

He watched her walk away, the sway of her hips telling him he'd blown it. Only he wasn't as disappointed as he should be.

"You're losing your touch," Rhett said, laughing annoyingly loud, while Curly and Moe joined in.

Owen ignored them and helped a few other customers who'd been patiently waiting, hoping to take some of the pressure off the solo-flying bartender. He worked his way down half of the bar, ending with a party of women who wanted five cosmos. He did his little Tom Cruise show with the shaker and nearly dropped it.

"Getting a little slow in your old age," Rhett pointed out.

"It's called work fatigue. It happens when someone actually has to work twelve-hour shifts for a living."

Actually, it usually ended up being closer to sixteen hours. Owen started his workday at nine thirty sharp and between paperwork, payroll, making sure the place ran smoothly and his staff was doing their job, he was lucky if he got to bed before midnight. He used to get to bed by ten, but when he caught one of the bartenders skimming money from the till he'd decided if the bar was open, he was working.

Only his body hadn't gotten the memo.

"Maybe it's because you spent yesterday passing out condoms to Mom's friends," Rhett said, and Owen found himself wondering, not for the first time since yesterday, what he'd been thinking.

Not only had he followed Abi inside, something she was not pleased with, he'd also caught her spinning around the dance floor with just about every old geezer there. Seemed Abi was the senior center's activities director and also the ballroom dancing instructor. She'd dumped the clown suit for a flowy Ginger Rogers skirt and looked damn sexy floating around the room. He attempted to take her for a twirl twice, but she'd ignored him.

Or tried to. Every so often she'd glance his way, frowning at him when he'd send her a wink. Enough winks to make him fifteen minutes late.

He thought of her journal and smiled. "Just doing a good deed."

Rhett and Gage laughed it up, but Josh studied him, long and thoroughly.

His brother had this way of sensing when there was more to the story. And being the closest in age, Josh and Owen didn't have many secrets. In fact, as a habit, Owen didn't do secrets. Period. They had this way of tainting everything they touched. He'd learned the hard way how destructive a secret could be—leaving him with an upfront and honesty-mandatory policy when it came to the people in his life.

So it didn't sit right that he had a tiny secret of his own. Okay, not really a secret; it was more of a keep-my-own-confidence situation. Owen was so overwhelmed with work he was having a hard time keeping his head above water. A fact that would only worry his family.

Tattooing was Owen's first passion and the reason he'd chosen art school over business school. He'd been helping run the family bar since he was sixteen, so he understood the backbone needed to run a business, he just wasn't sure anymore that he was running the right business.

In no way did he want to give over management of the bar, but he wouldn't mind some time to himself.

"Good deed? You wouldn't even take Littleshit for a walk yesterday when I was needed in the studio," Rhett said, referring to his ex-wife's dog. Rhett received primary custody in the divorce—and not by choice.

"Like every day, I was busy. Plus, I'm not a dog walker," Owen said as Fancy—aka Littleshit—appeared out of nowhere and lunged at Owen, nearly taking off a finger. "Jesus, she's like a rat-sized honey badger."

"*He's* like a BS detector with needle teeth," Rhett explained calmly. "He can smell a lie from across the street."

"Well, unless your BS meter has a service animal license, he needs to leave."

Rhett reached into his back pocket and pulled out his wallet, quickly revealing an official-looking stamped by the state of Oregon, laminated card and slid it across the bar.

Owen lifted it and read the top. "Are you shitting me? An emotional support dog?"

"What can I say? He keeps me calm on the road."

Owen slid the card back. "Where's your BS meter now?" he asked Fancy, who was too busy licking his doggie bits to be bothered.

"Now that we have that squared away, how about a pitcher of hefeweizen?" Gage asked.

"I've got five other customers ahead of you three and I'm working my ass off. It hasn't let up since opening."

"Whose fault is that?" Josh asked, walking behind the bar to grab three frosted mugs and fill a pitcher. Normally, Owen would blast him for daring to breach his space, but he was just too damn tired.

"Actually, I interviewed two potential bartenders yesterday and someone for the manager's position."

"And?" Josh asked.

"One was a no show and the other's balls hadn't even dropped."

"And the manager?"

"Qualified but not the right fit."

"You mean not Chris," Rhett said, referring to the old manager, who was reliable, trustworthy, and great with the staff. Plus, he and Owen went way back. All the way to high school. "They don't have to have a history with you to be right for the job."

"Maybe, but I'd rather be down a few employees than try to explain to my shareholders," he pointed to the peanut gallery, "why we're losing money."

Owen had bad luck at picking trustworthy employees. In fact, he'd had a long run of hiring people who liked to break the rules and leave him high and dry. His record with women wasn't all that different.

"This is about control," Gage said. "You are a control freak."

"I run a seven thousand square foot pub and grill." While he ran the day-to-day operations, his family all had equal shares with the bar split six ways. A share for each brother and one for his mom, who also inherited Kyle's share after he died. Yet, Owen ran the entire place by himself, down to managing the cleaning crew and overseeing a staff of thirty employees.

Thirty employees who counted on him to make sure everything was in order and ran smoothly and efficiently. So if that took around the clock supervision, then so be it.

"What about Seattle?" Gage asked, then shook his head as if he already knew the answer. "No way. You're seriously going to miss Clay's game?"

No matter how much he wanted to make it, he was strapped to the bar until he found the right manager. That didn't stop the guilt from seeping in. It was the first game of the season and the Seahawks were favored to win. The whole family was road-tripping it to Seattle to watch his baby brother kick ass, and odds were, Owen would have to miss it.

Hell, these days he missed everything.

"You're going," Rhett said. "Even if it means leaving Clive in charge."

Owen paled. Clive was one of his mom's hires. As the nephew of Margo's manicurist, she'd hired him without talking to Owen. With only eight months of managing a coffee truck under his belt—employees numbering three—he'd been brought on as an assistant manager. And while the kid was a hard worker, he didn't know the first thing about overseeing a place with as many moving parts as Stout.

Plus, there was the fact that he was a pushover. He'd rather leave the state than get caught in a confrontation. And confrontation was part of managing—the worst part, but a part all the same.

"He'd crack under the pressure in under two hours." Another reason Owen couldn't afford to lose focus.

Josh leaned in, shoving all that big-brother 'tude in Owen's face. "Then you better find someone else and not just another manager. We're talking an extra bartender or two."

Owen stared him down. Josh might be two years older, but Owen had three inches and a good thirty pounds on all his brothers. With his buzzed head, more tattoos than fingers, and sheer size, people often mistook Owen for the bouncer rather than the owner.

And that went with women as well. While he wouldn't mind finding a sweet girl like his brothers had, it was usually the bolder barflies who flocked to him.

Tonight was Ladies' Night, and usually he'd look forward to getting his flirt on. How funny was it that the only hot girl he wanted to flirt with would rather ride her bike in the rain than be in a car with him?

He must be losing his touch, he decided. He never had a hard time attracting women. He loved women. But after being with Abi yesterday, flirting with other women didn't sound so appealing. Case in point, Red.

Nope, all he wanted was more time with Abi rather than surface banter with a one-night stand.

After watching his brothers find their person one by one, he'd begun to wonder if that would ever happen for him. Which was a ridiculous thought since he didn't have the time or interest in being anything other than the king of one-nighters.

"I'd rather hire the right one than hire anyone," he explained.

"He's got a point," Rhett said quietly. "Nothing good comes from rushing into things."

Owen's heart went out to his brother who was no longer talking about the bar. Two years ago, Rhett had a whirlwind marriage with a woman who decided she no longer wanted to go the distance. The ink on the divorce papers wasn't even dry and Stephanie was already seeing someone else.

Rhett didn't talk much about it and Owen was the last person to drag something out of someone who wanted privacy. He just hoped Rhett was talking to someone. Owen knew firsthand what it was like to be walked out on and it was as gut-wrenching as it was isolating.

He wasn't sure if it was the betrayal that hurt so much or the idea of failing at love. His parents had loved so easily. In fact, he and Rhett were the odd guys out when it came to love and relationships. He knew Rhett would find his person, but Owen didn't really see that for himself.

Being vulnerable wasn't exactly in his wheelhouse.

"Then you'd better get a more accurate picker," Gage said. "You've got a month to find the right one."

Chapter Four

Happy Things:
Smiles that hurt your cheeks

Abi would like to say that she hadn't thought about Owen once over the past week. But that would be a lie. A big, fat, pants-on-fire kind of lie that irritated her.

Even standing there in the drizzle, while her hair frizzed to record-breaking status, and waiting for her sister—who was already twenty minutes late—a little smile crept in. A smile that was stupid since it would lead nowhere except Heartbreak Alley. Not that her heart was involved, but other parts of her were bordering on betrayal, the little turncoats.

Instead of smiling, she should be fuming. It was cold and wet, and the beginning stages of frostbite were setting in, but not even Dotti being Dotti could dampen her mood.

Plus, Dotti was technically doing Abi a favor. She didn't have to drive across town in the dark to pick up her kid sister because said kid sister was too scared to step on a bus and too broke to rely on rideshares. But in a way, Dotti owed her.

While both sisters inherited their grandma's house, after Dotti got married she and Hank moved in and moved Abi out. It was as if her sister was trying to prove that possession was nine-tenths of the law since she'd taken over nine-tenths of the house. Which was how Abi wound up teaching in Mobile to begin with. She'd felt so displaced she'd taken a job as far away from Oregon as she could. As it turned out, she'd loved her time being back in the South. It was how she'd met Jenny. But a small part of her, the eight-year-old part who'd been shuffled from one house to the next, hoped that Dotti would have asked her to come back.

Only she hadn't.

Even after the bus crash, Abi had been the one to ask if she could come home to heal in the one place that made her feel safe. Except instead of sleeping in the room she'd spent every summer for over twenty-seven years, she was stuck on the couch. Two of the bedrooms had been turned into her niece's and nephew's rooms, Abi's childhood bedroom was her brother-in-law's home office, and Dotti had overtaken Mee-maw Ruth's room. Leaving Abi an outsider in her own house.

She considered demanding her room back but then decided it wasn't worth the energy since she'd be leaving soon. She wasn't exactly sure what soon meant but she felt it lurking around every corner.

She pulled out her phone and swiped off a text.

Abi: Where are you?

Dotti: I'm otherwise detained.

Abi: The shop closed twenty minutes ago.

Dotti: I'm not your Uber driver.

And just like that the smile vanished, which was for the best since smiling over a guy who was likely to hate her come reckoning day was a bad move.

Abi: No of course not but you knew what time I got off. I've been in the rain waiting for you.

Dotti: And I've been waiting for Hank to get home so I can leave.

As if being slapped around by Mother Nature wasn't enough, no one could ruin her mood quite like Hank. Not only because he was the reason Abi was in the rain after dark, but because he'd never fully appreciated how much Dotti did for the family.

Abi: He knew I was working until closing.

Dotti: You knew I had the kids alone today.

Abi: Fair point.

Abi looked up at the sky, which was glaring back, and calculated just how broke she was. The answer was flat broke. Then she calculated how exhausted her sister must be, which eclipsed how badly Abi's feet ached. This was a clear case of WWJD—what would Jenny do. Jenny would let Dotti off the hook.

Abi: Don't worry. I can catch a ride from—

Her fingers came to an abrupt stop. There was no one. Not really. While she'd made friends at work, she hadn't really *made* friends. The accident had erected new walls around her already impenetrable fortress. Very few people would work their way into Abi's heart—she was going to vet each and every one.

After her parents' divorce, Abi hadn't been in one place long enough to establish deep connections. Being shuffled between houses, Abi wasn't around enough to play with neighborhood kids or go to birthday parties, making it difficult to cement friendships. In fact, Jenny had been her first and only best friend.

They were more than friends. Their relationship fulfilled the kind of bond Abi had always wanted with Dotti. While they were half sisters, they weren't all that close. Not only had there been a big age gap to overcome but they'd always been in different stages of life. Plus, living in Dotti's shadow was hard.

Dotti was outgoing, optimistic, and adored by all. Abi was more of an acquired taste in that class clown kind of way. She had a way of lightening the mood and making people laugh, but she'd been told she could be a lot to take in large doses. Dotti took after their mom whereas Abi was just like her dad, leaving Abi feeling a little like the odd duck in her familial flock.

Then there was the time Dotti had asked Abi for a favor. A simple, easy to execute, no-way-to-mess-it-up favor. Only Abi managed to mess it up.

Hank's company was throwing a family picnic and it was important that Dotti made an appearance. But it was the same day as preschool sign-ups for Koi. It was one of those snooty, glorified daycares for tiny tots that cost as much as college, but it had been important to Dotti. All Abi had to do was get to the school's office by three, stand in line and hand in two forms.

Abi was teaching summer school full-time to get in her student-teacher hours, so she knew that making the cutoff time would be hard. But Dotti never asked for anything, so Abi wanted to come through—she really did. But a parent had been late for pickup and Abi wasn't going to leave a five-year-old alone in an abandoned parking lot, so she'd missed the deadline. Koi didn't get into the preschool, Abi felt like shit, and Dotti never asked her for a favor again. Didn't talk to her either—not for a long time.

While Abi had been trapped in that bus, surrounded by chaos and tragedy, she thought about that day and other days like it and took stock of her life. She revisited the things she was proud of, the things she wished she'd done differently, and imagined the way a person like Jenny would live her life. Only now that she was home, she realized she needed to find some balance with the universe. No one had ever blamed

Abi for switching seats, but Abi blamed herself. A part of her always would, which was why it was so imperative to replace some of the good vibes that vanished the day Jenny died.

Jenny had been on Abi for years to reconnect with her family. And that started with Dotti. This was her chance to push the restart button on her life and she wasn't about to fall back on old habits and run because she was scared.

So she thought to herself, "WWJD?" Jenny would find her own ride home and save an overworked, underappreciated mom of two tantrum-throwing terrorists from leaving her house after bath time.

Abi: Don't worry. I'll figure it out.

She hit Send and then grimaced. Jenny would have done the same, only she wouldn't have laid on the guilt. As if Karma were doling out punishment, the side door of the bar opened and out walked the exact person she'd been avoiding all week.

Owen was dressed in his standard uniform of dark jeans, a black tee that was in a losing battle with his biceps, and a ball cap that had the bar's logo on it—flipped backward. He also wore a dark-blue tradesman jacket and a sexy smile that had her belly quivering.

Not wanting to see him when she looked as if she'd survived the Great Flood, she moved closer to the building, to hide in the shadows. Wrong move since she only brought attention to herself.

He turned around and the light from the lamppost lit his face and that smile. It was warm and real and a little amused, but it softened his entire face. And it made her good parts tingle.

He walked closer, his broad shoulders blocking the light the closer he came. "Why are you lurking in the shadows?"

She shot him a *Don't mess with me* glare. "I'd say I'm lurking to shank you, but I left all the wooden stirrers back in the tea shop."

He took in her white work shirt—her very wet and very see-through work shirt—black work pants, and lack of jacket and then back to her shirt again. She crossed her arms. "They're just boobs, get over it."

"They're never just boobs." As he said it, he shrugged out of his jacket and slid it over her shoulders. Abi opened her mouth to tell him that she was drenched and would get his soft and fuzzy and incredible-smelling jacket wet when masculine hands settled on her arms and gave them a warming rub. Up and down until her body heated to furnace levels.

"You need another ride?"

"Just waiting on my sister. Who should be arriving on her broom any moment."

He studied her and she knew when he figured out that she'd likely be waiting indefinitely. "Then why don't you wait for her inside."

"She's almost here."

He clearly didn't believe her. "Call her," he baited.

With a dramatic eye roll, she pulled out her cell, then turned away so he couldn't hear. "Hey, yeah, it's me," she said to no one. "Oh, you're almost—"

Her phone rang in her ear and when she looked over her shoulder, Owen had a single judgy brow raised.

"We got disconnected," she lied, then answered for real. "What?"

"You don't get to 'What' me. The whole 'I'll work it out' was a S-H-I-T move," Dotti lectured, and Abi could hear her narrowed glare through the phone. "Bless your heart."

"How is this my fault?" Abi whispered. "I would have taken my bike, but you said you were going my way and we both know that a bus isn't happening."

Her sister's car wasn't really happening either. But it was either face her fear or walk home. Something she normally wouldn't have minded since it gave her a chance to clear her head, but it was 40 degrees and raining and her bumblebee galoshes had a hole in the toe.

"Well after tonight, I'm not happening anymore. Oh, and by the way, ran into the landlord, so I need your half of the rent."

"You're the landlord and Grandma left me half the house too."

"What do you want me to do? Draw a line down the middle and move my family to one half?"

"For starters. Then there's keeping my nephew's naked bum off the couch during his 'screen time,' plus being forced to sleep on said couch is an S-H-I-T move."

While she'd had her own room growing up, her belongings were always packed and ready to go at a moment's notice. Unlike Dotti, who lived in one room from birth to graduation, Abi didn't have the most traditional of upbringings. Or the most stable childhood. She spent weekdays with her mom's family and weekends and rotating holidays with her dad, who traveled a lot, leaving her behind with a stepmom and two much older stepbrothers. Her mom's was linen napkins and take your seat please, while her dad's was more of whoever got the TV-tray didn't have to eat on the coffee table.

She never felt like she had a place that was hers. Desperate to be noticed, at home and school, she became the loudest person in the room.

Her dad used to say she was lightning in a bottle. It wasn't until she got older that she realized it wasn't a compliment.

Her parents associated her with a jolt of energy zapping around and crashing into things before crashing into something—or someone—else. It didn't matter how hard she tried, she'd had this uncanny ability to disrupt people's regularly scheduled lives. It wasn't that people didn't like her, she was everyone's fun-time gal, she was just never anyone's real-time gal.

Was that what she was doing here? Falling back on old habits? Maybe she had outstayed her welcome, but she didn't have anywhere else to go.

"Then you need to pay half the mortgage," Dotti said.

She looked over her shoulder to find Owen still there, but he'd turned his back, giving her some privacy. Not that it mattered, the alley had the acoustics of Carnegie Hall, making every one of Dotti's eye rolls audible for miles. Even so, Abi lowered her voice. "You said it was due next week."

"I said that last week."

"I don't have it right now but—"

There was a long, suffocating pause and Abi knew what was coming next. It was the same requirement her sister had given her two months ago when she'd moved in. "I'd settle for you getting big-girl job, Abs."

"I'm trying."

"Try harder," Dotti said, and it took herculean effort to hold back the tears. Abi was trying as hard as she could, but she kept coming up short. All she felt was guilt all the time from every corner of her life. "Otherwise, I'll have the loan sharks come and crack your kneecaps."

"I'll come up with the money and if the loan shark comes, remind her that my kneecap was already cracked." Along with her wrist and two ribs and, well, any hope of making it through a single night without nightmares. "I promise, I'll figure this out." She looked at the ground. "Can you please come get me?"

"You're lucky I love you," Dotti said. "Hank should be home in fifteen minutes, and I'll head out then. But you so owe me."

Begging didn't really fit into Abi's cool as a cucumber persona, which wasn't all that odd since she wasn't really sure who she was anymore.

"Thanks," she whispered, but Dotti was already gone.

Shoving her phone in her pocket, Abi turned to find Owen standing right behind her, holding open the employee entrance. When she didn't move, he said. "Fifteen minutes is a long time to wait in the rain. And I'd hate for you to freeze on my account."

She eyed him. On the one hand, she was one gust from becoming a popsicle. On the other, she'd been avoiding Owen for two reasons. One was that she had this ridiculous crush on him. And reason two was that she had a really big, really awful reason.

A reason that started the day she'd stolen her sister's ID to buy beer and ended with her taking the easy way out, leaving Owen's dad with a hard decision. Fight a ridiculous lawsuit or lose his liquor license and close down his bar. In the end, the bar had made it but that didn't mean the situation hadn't taken its toll on the Easton family.

It all seemed so stupid now, but back then it had been the single most pivotal moment of her young life. Trying to impress the cool kids in the neighborhood, Abi had gone into a liquor store with the intent to buy alcohol—which she'd successfully accomplished. She never imagined that what started as a dare would wind up with her facing charges or working with the police to nail stores that were selling to minors. She'd chosen the second option, which led to a man losing his job and the Easton family nearly losing everything.

She wasn't sure exactly how Owen ended up running the bar, but from what she'd learned, his dad fell ill and was no longer able to run the gastropub full time. And with trust no longer on the menu, Owen walked away from his own full life to take over the family business.

All these years later and he was still there. Which brought her back to the reasons she'd returned to Portland. To heal from the crash and to make Owen's life the kind of life he should have had, had he not assumed the responsibility of his dad's bar. The kind that included having an actual life—a full one with friends and adventure and laughter. And there was no way she'd risk that over a silly, girlhood crush.

The plan was to keep things light yet distant, establish just enough personal contact to discover ways to make his world easier—then walk away.

Between her strong moral compass and a job waiting for her in Thailand, teaching locals English, maintaining emotional distance was key.

"Or we can both stand out here, but if I catch a cold, you'll have to deal with my mom."

"Moms love me."

"You haven't met my mom," he said. She looked over her shoulder at the street and he stepped closer, like he knew she was going to bolt. "Let's start over." He stuck out his hand, which she ignored since she was rubbing hers together to create friction.

"Bless your heart," she said, and he smiled. "I didn't realize we'd started anything to begin with."

"Not realizing and not wanting to admit are two very different things."

"I didn't hear you mention denial."

He burst out laughing and she gave him a smile. Not the usual one she saved for her favorite customers, but a real one. "No hidden agenda, just a friend helping out a friend."

She thought long and hard. Her mission was simple: fix her mess without getting personally invested. The less involved she became with the Eastons, the better the odds for success. Success in making his life easier and success in walking away unscathed when it was over.

"If I go inside, will you promise you won't bring up my sister or have some need to talk it out?"

"Not a problem," he said. "What's it going to be, Angel?"

Blowing into her hands for warmth, she stomped her feet to get the circulation going and pushed out a breath. "Fine, but only because I wouldn't want to worry your mom."

She sucked in a breath as she walked by, so as not to brush any of his good parts. Understanding what she was doing, the corners of his lips twitched. When he didn't budge, except to move a tiny step into her path, she put her hands on his chest to give him a shove. Only her brain malfunctioned and her hands froze—right there on his amazing pecs.

His gaze went from her hands to her eyes—and held steady. The exact opposite of what her heart was doing—which was racing like it was in the Tour de France. But it was what was happening beneath her hands that troubled her.

One touch and it was like steel wool to a battery—sparks.

She expected him to grin, but she saw only genuine surprise in his eyes, quickly followed by a flash of conflict, and she knew he was about as excited over their chemistry as she was.

Chapter Five

Happy Things:
Bulging biceps with tattoos

Abi sat at a stool eyeballing the menu. Wow, she was racking up the lies. She was pretending to study the menu while secretly watching Owen do his thing. And he did it well. So well, nearly every woman in the bar was watching him with rapt focus.

With his easy confidence and charming demeanor, he had them waiting with bated breath. His every move was cataloged, his glances speculated, everyone wondering who would capture his attention—everyone hoping it would be them.

Abi wasn't wondering. In fact, she was doing her best to put that momentary palm-to-pecs lapse in judgment behind her.

For a guy she'd gone out of her way to watch from afar, she was sure getting her up close and personal time with him. Which was why when he looked her way she glanced around the room as if searching for her sister, who was at least another ten minutes out.

The gastropub was large, with a bar taking up one side and dining on the other. The space still had the original exposed brick walls and copper pipes with silver ducting of a turn of the century canning factory. But the bar, with its copper countertop and backlit glass shelving, brought a sleek, modern feel. Then there were massive accordion glass doors that opened onto the street, giving a stunning view of the upscale Pearl District neighborhood.

Next door was Sip Me, the tea shop where Abi worked. The tea shop she'd applied to so she could watch Owen in his natural habitat, gauge how Teen Abi's decision had affected Adult Owen's life. From what she could tell, while he loved his family's bar, he was also exhausted.

"Hello, ladies."

Abi looked over to find Owen taking in a group of women who appeared to be former sorority sisters. With the exception of the bride-to-be, who was in white and a veil, the bridal party was dressed in matching teal sashes that read BRIDAL BRIGADE.

"Congratulations." Owen rested his arms on the bar and leaned in. "There is one lucky bastard out there," he said, and even the bride smiled. "Now, what can I get you ladies. Wait." He turned to address the blonde one who looked like Marilyn Monroe gone wild. Sexy, sultry, a real bombshell with enough curves to make an hourglass jealous. "Let me guess."

"Okay."

"First off, I'm Owen. What's your name?"

"Olivia. Olivia Rhodes." The woman actually giggled.

"Do you go by Olivia or Liv?"

"Olivia by day, Liv by night. Kind of like Batwoman."

"Okay, Liv, I think you're a classic. Elegant and to be savored, like a martini. But you also have a party side that likes to come out and blow off steam." He snapped his fingers as if he were some back-alley magician. "Vodka martini. Extra dirty."

"Oh my god!" Monroe put her hand to her heaving chest and looked to the girls and back to Owen. "How did you know?"

"It's my thing."

Abi snorted. It must have carried from her mouth to Owen's ears because, even though he was filling the shaker, he glanced her way. More like caught her gaze and locked in, holding her hostage. Then he winked. She winked back. Although hers was more of a *puh-lease.*

He laughed and the Bridal Brigade joined in. Not that they knew why they were laughing, they just couldn't help themselves. He was the kind of man who had that effect on women.

Thankfully, Abi was off men.

Back in Mobile, she'd been in a semi-serious relationship when the crash happened. Lance friend-zoned Abi faster than the plaster on her cast had dried, citing that hospitals gave him the willies. Abi cited that he had a small willie and took herself out of the dating game until further notice.

Liv was giving all signs that she was firmly *in* the dating game and gave Owen a blatant onceover. When Owen smiled, showing all his perfect white teeth, she pulled a pen from her purse, scribbled something on a coaster, and slid it across the bar. "In case you want to blow off some steam."

He pocketed the number, then went down the line, pulling his little party trick for each woman, but Abi was too busy glancing over the menu to care.

"Now, what can I get you?" a soft and sexy voice asked.

She rested her elbows on the table and looked right into those mesmerizing blue eyes. "I thought you'd be too busy blowing off steam to get me anything."

He leaned in too, getting uncomfortably close, especially since he was holding her gaze. "Is that an offer?"

"No one likes a bragger, Owen. No one."

"Ah, so we're back to first name basis, Abilene."

"Fun party trick. I read the same article in *Bartender Monthly*, by the way. FIFTEEN CLUES TO ACCURATELY GUESS SOMEONE'S DRINK."

"That's luck. I'm the real deal."

"Really? Then let me break it down for you. Olivia was in a vintage dress, 1920s jewelry, and Mary Janes. Hence the martini. The extra dirty was because she kept looking at the olives as you put them on a toothpick as if wanting more."

He gave a Cheshire grin. "Not bad. Although when I hear Mary Jane I don't think of shoes, but you still haven't figured out how I knew vodka versus gin."

"You had a fifty-fifty chance to get it right and even if she did prefer gin, she'd rather give in to your charm than admit that you didn't accurately guess her."

"You think I'm charming?"

"I think you know how to work a crowd." It was a gift they both shared. There wasn't a room of people Abi couldn't make laugh or party she couldn't crush. It was her superpower, forged from a childhood of being invisible. Nowadays though, she had a hard time being around anyone, let alone sitting in a crowded bar.

The way people accidentally bumped her chair or brushed up against her made her chest tighten and her palms sweat.

"You've tended bar," he said. It was a statement. An accurate one.

"I've done a lot of things. As for the charm, you can turn it off, it doesn't work on me."

"Then it looks like I have to up my game."

"Or you could drop the game altogether. It looks exhausting."

She wasn't sure what she'd said, but his game face cracked a little and his expression went from *How you doin'?* to one of genuine surprise.

"It can be," he admitted, putting a coaster in front of her. "What can I get you?"

Abi studied him, intrigued by how quickly he went from being "on" to just being. It was as if she'd given him permission to slow down and take stock. Then something she wasn't expecting, something beneath that earlier playboy swagger, tugged at her heart. It was a vulnerability, she was learning, that only came to the surface when he was too tired to camouflage it.

"How about a smile." She could tell her answer caught him off guard. Fair, since it had caught her off guard as well.

He flashed her a warm smile that made her insides turn to goo. "Now it's your turn."

She didn't have to try. Just like that, her grin returned big and full.

In a move that was all manly and sexy, he rested his palms on the edge of the bar top, sending his biceps winking her way. "I like your dimples."

"I like yours," she said.

"My dimples? I don't have dimples. Maybe a rugged jawline or chiseled abs." He waggled a brow. "But dimples?" He scratched his chin. "Nah."

She dug through her backpack and pulled out her compact mirror, then held it up for him. "See. Dimples."

He turned his head right, then left. "Okay, I'll bite. What is it about my dimples?"

"They mean your smile's real. When you talk to customers, your smile is big but not always real." She shrugged. "I like real."

His dimples vanished but the warm flicker in his eyes said he was still being real. A signal that maybe it was time for her to be real and honest.

Okay, here it went. The moment of truth—the truth he deserved.

"Owen," she began. "When I came back to Portland, I knew that—"

"We're out of Stella," the other bartender said, breaking the moment. "I'll watch the bar while you grab another keg." He looked between the two of them. "Unless you want to handle the bar and I'll—"

"No, you go," Abi said, but he didn't budge. "Seriously, we wouldn't want to keep your adoring public waiting." He searched her eyes, where she worked hard to erase any trace of nerves and guilt. "It will give me time to go over the menu and figure out what I want."

Again, he hesitated so she turned her attention back to the menu.

She waited until he disappeared out of sight before she allowed herself to take a deep breath. *God,* she was in trouble. And hungry. And broke.

She looked in her wallet and back to the menu and nearly wept. She had exactly enough money to buy a cheeseburger, a side of fries, hot cocoa, and gas money for her sister. Even though Dotti wouldn't ask, Abi wasn't a freeloader.

She set the menu down and waited patiently for the other bartender to come her way. When her stomach rumbled, reminding her that she hadn't eaten since her muffin at lunchtime, Abi stared at the bartender—as if by staring him down he'd look her way. Only instead, a woman met her gaze before quickly skittering away.

She wore a pretty, red dress, bitchin' black night-on-the-town heels, and an embarrassed smile. Then the woman glanced over at the entry three times in three seconds and studied her lap. It was girl speak for "I've been stood up."

"Nope. It's none of your business. Eyes on the prize." That prize being a big, fat bacon and blue cheeseburger with extra bacon. "The last thing she'd want is for you to go and make it even worse."

Then, as if Jenny herself had plopped down on the stool next to Abi, the song that they had always sung at karaoke became the ambient music at the bar. Abi hadn't even been aware that there was music, but now it was crystal clear.

"I knew there'd be someone," she grumbled to herself. She'd felt as if a good deed was right around the corner all day. Then when she'd had that moment with Owen, she assumed it was because it was time to fess up. But Jenny stepped in and saved her from imminent heartache. At least that's what she told herself when Owen reappeared.

"Seriously, you need a bell."

A smile, sans the dimples. "What did you decide on, Angel?"

It took everything she had to let go of the menu but eventually, she set it down and met his gaze. "A hot cocoa and..." she hesitated, looked at the guy next to her chowing down on a big, juicy burger and groaned. "And a martini for the blonde at the end of the bar."

He laughed, a big, guttural laugh that made her want to laugh along with him. "So much makes sense now."

"No. It's just... she looks sad."

He considered this for a long moment. "Is she a friend?"

"No, she's a complete stranger," Dotti said, pulling up a stool next to her. "My sister's trying to save the world one act of kindness at a time, didn't you know?" She stuck out her hand. "Dotti, nice to meet you."

"Owen," he said, taking her hand and Abi could practically feel Dotti shaking her head—in disappointment. Not that Abi had a defense, she should have told him the truth on minute one of day one.

"She's actually really good at it," Owen said, and something warm spread through her chest at the idea that he'd stick up for her. Instead of joining the bandwagon of *let's poop on Abi,* he'd defended her.

"If you're doling out miracles, Angel," he said, "then can you give me one of those Time-Turners from Harry Potter?"

"Someplace else you'd like to be?" Abi asked.

He looked her up and down, then leaned in. "Right now? I'm good."

"What would make you great?" she asked.

"Is this your way of asking me out?"

"I'm being serious. What would make your life easier?"

"The perfect bartender and a night manager to fill my job openings."

"I'll take it." Her sister elbowed her, adding a grim shake of her head. Calling her out on being stupid. Because Dotti knew her secret.

"Sorry, Angel, the job requires more than a ten-speed. Now, how about I add a burger to that order. On the house."

Owen turned to log the order into the computer and Dotti leaned in and whispered, "Owen? *The* Owen? Have you told him?"

"Can you keep it down?"

"I'll take that as a no," Dotti said. "He deserves to know."

Abi looked at Owen, who was done logging in her order and now helping a group of jersey-wearing guys. "I'm getting to it."

"How long are you going to keep this up?"

Wasn't that the question of the hour. "Until I figure out how to make his life easier."

Chapter Six

Happy Things:
Family... sometimes

Owen might come off as a badass but when it came down to it, he was the biggest mama's boy of the family and his brothers knew it—and gave him shit for it. Not that he had a defense. His mom was the most important person in his life—had been since the day his father died.

After the funeral he returned home immediately, leaving behind an equal partnership in a tattoo shop back in Austin. With Josh off at law school and Owen the next eldest, he was left to shoulder a lot of the responsibilities, including his mom's happiness.

Nearly a decade later and she was still working through the loss of her husband. Although lately he got the feeling it was more the loneliness that got to her, and that's where Owen and his brothers took turns filling in some of the gaps. Sometimes it was a partner for her ballroom dance lessons or movie night, and on Wednesdays they had brunch, then there were always Sunday night dinners.

Which brought him to today, their weekly brunch followed by a few rounds of dominoes before Owen headed to work. With a bag of fresh chocolate croissants in hand, he let himself in and headed straight for the kitchen, which was an open concept with a massive table—a Christmas gift from the brothers and big enough to seat the entire Easton clan, with wives and grandkids included. There were a few empty spots to accommodate the ever-growing family—including the recently vacant spot where Rhett's ex-wife used to sit.

"Mom?" he called out.

"On the patio."

Owen walked out onto the back patio where Margo liked to serve tea and gossip with her friends. But when Owen got there, he came to a hard stop.

In all the years since his dad, Benji, passed, Margo had never dated. Never even entertained the idea. Suddenly that had changed, and Owen didn't know how he felt about it. Just like he didn't know how he felt about walking in on his mom and her new "friend" Eddie, sitting on the patio at such an early hour sipping tea and eating chocolate croissants.

He knew about Eddie. All his brothers did. Eddie was a rideshare driver who'd fashioned himself into Margo's personal chauffeur. But according to the PI they'd hired to make sure Eddie was being a gentleman, their relationship hadn't progressed much past *Driving Miss Daisy*.

Clearly, based on his mom's body language, they'd engaged in a hell of a lot more than long drives through the park. Oh, they were both dressed in breakfast appropriate clothing, looking pressed and fresh, but Owen got the distinct impression that there'd been some smooching going on.

While he'd never be able to put that image in a delete folder, he was happy for his mom. She'd been in mourning for over a decade and Eddie was the first man who'd come along and made her smile.

"Well, don't stand there," Margo said. "Come and give your mother a hug."

Owen did as told, shooting Eddie a death glare over his mom's shoulder. To his surprise, Eddie just glared back—an impressive feat since Owen was twice Eddie's height and weight. But the older man didn't seem to be intimidated—which made Owen think the guy had the balls to last.

"I didn't know I needed to bring any extra," Owen said, holding up the bag, still not sure what to do. Sit? Stay? Leave them alone?

Hell no. He sat between them.

"I didn't forget breakfast. I called Eddie for a ride to my Ladies of Portland meeting, and he stopped by early to surprise me with my favorite."

Owen looked down at the table to find two chocolate croissants. "I should have called."

Eddie stood. "I can leave."

Owen waved at the opened French doors. "I have a lot of work to get through." That was the hand-on-the-bible truth of the matter. He had a week's worth of paperwork to get through today before the next week's work began to pile up.

"Nonsense. You work too hard," Margo said, patting his cheek. "I worry."

"Mom, I'm fine."

"Don't fib to me, young man. I heard you're so busy you don't have time to find a date to my birthday party."

Owen stopped. "Who told you that?"

His mom laughed. "I know everything. Being one of my last single sons, you're a topic of conversation with my ladies' group. Then there are your brothers."

"Which ones?" He was going to kill them.

"What's the fun in telling you that?"

"It was the small one," Eddie said, and Owen nearly laughed. None of his brothers could be considered small but, at six-foot-one, Rhett was the smallest—and the one who was looking for a beatdown the next time he and his brothers met at the gym for some good old-fashioned ass-kicking.

"Why aren't you on Rhett about getting a date to the party?"

"He's still in the throes of his divorce." She met Owen's gaze. "You, on the other hand, haven't brought a girl around since Elena."

He'd barely dated since Elena, let alone been at a point with a woman to consider bringing her around his family. He really thought he'd gotten it right with Elena. Which was another reason he avoided strings of any kind. Professional and personal.

"You hated Elena," he pointed out.

"She wasn't for you. But Sydney is perfect for you."

God no. His mom was awful at playing matchmaker. "Who's Sydney?"

"Betty's grandniece. Last week at Bunco we got to talking about my party and Betty reminded me that Sydney was going solo. So we figured that maybe you could go together." Margo leaned in. "A woman like Sydney is perfect for you."

Now he remembered Sydney. She was a recipe blogger who'd posted a review that claimed "Stout is a dive bar posing as a gastropub that believes it's more than it is." She'd said its owner "confused flirting tactics with customer service."

"I don't think I'm her type."

"Of course you are." She cupped his face. "You're smart and hardworking and so handsome, she'd be lucky to date you."

Sydney would disagree and so would Owen. Sydney was no doubt looking for a suit with a high-powered job who would be the second half of her power couple. Owen was more of a bull with a lot of ink who was looking for nothing more than some play-it-fast sex and to catch up on some z's. Not necessarily in that order.

"I think Sydney and I are more of, uh ... we're just looking for different things."

"Maybe different is what you need. Shake things up." Margo gave a shimmy of the shoulders. "Which is why I took the liberty of seating her next to you."

He ran a hand down his face. "Mom, I can find my own date."

"Of course you can." She met Owen's gaze. "But it's just a few weeks away and you're no closer to finding free time than you are a nice girl."

"I date nice girls." Correction, he slept with women who understood the arrangements. Women who didn't have the whole picket fence in their sights.

"Name one."

He blew out a breath. "No one you'd know."

"Or no one who matters?"

He'd like to agree, but suddenly a pretty Samaritan who liked his dimples came to mind. And would you look at that, those dimples were alive and well.

Chapter Seven

Happy Things:
Blueberry cake doughnuts

By the time Abi reached home, she was soaked through and her legs were the consistency of Jell-O, but she considered it a win. She'd ridden her bike eight miles, during peak traffic, and only broke out in a cold sweat once.

Then there'd been the two good deeds she'd accomplished. She'd potted a plant for the front of the tea shop—a good deed for Mother Nature—and gave an introduction class at the senior center on how to use the internet. Then immediately regretted the latter since Ms. Walker crashed the network by streaming too much porn.

Locking her bike to the porch railing, she went to open the front door only to find it locked. She searched her backpack, then searched it again, dumping out every last item.

"Crap." She checked her pockets. "Crappedy, crap crap." She closed her eyes and envisioned the last place she remembered having them. "Crap!"

They were on the counter at work. The third time that week she'd left something she needed at home at work or vice versa. She considered picking the lock, then imagined Dotti calling the cops on a burglar at large and settled for a gentle knock in case the kids were asleep.

They were not. In fact, when the door swung open, Abi watched as a very loud, very naked Koi raced past with their dog, Buster, fast on his heels.

"I poopied," he exclaimed.

"And not in the potty," Dotti added wearily.

Her sister was dressed in the same nightgown she'd been in when Abi had left that morning, with smudges of mascara that reached her cheekbones, and an apron that had spaghetti sauce splattered down the front.

"You're here." Dotti pulled her into her arms as if they hadn't hugged since the internet was invented. "Thank god, you're here." She grabbed Abi by the shoulders and held her back. "You are here, right?"

"Do you need me here?" she asked tentatively.

"Only if you have wine."

"I can go get wine."

Dotti looked over her shoulder right as Koi raced past again, followed by Buster, and then Lemon-Marie who was waving a wand in her hand.

Swoosh swish. "Let it go. Let it go," the song from *Frozen* came out of the wand. *Swoosh swish. "Let it go. Let it go."*

Dottie shook her head and her normally sleek hair was so ratted it didn't move. "But then I'd be alone."

Swoosh swish. "Let it go. Let it go."

"You don't want to be alone?" Abi asked, because Dotti had spent the past two months trying to get Abi out of the house.

"What does that even mean? Alone?"

"Usually it means by one's own self."

"Don't sass me," Dotti said, but she pulled Abi inside and slammed the door, trapping her in a tower of crazy. Abi turned to find the deadbolt fully engaged. "If you even think about leaving, I will cry."

Whoa. Dotti did not cry. Period. End of sentence. She went through thirty-nine hours of labor, no meds, with Koi and never even popped a single tear. "Who are you and what have you done with my perfect sister?"

"Perfect?" She snorted. "I accidentally sent Hank to work with a mayonnaise and cheese sandwich and he's lactose intolerant, Koi said the F-word in class so now the other moms think I'm a bad parent, I lied to Lemon-Marie and said that Anna and Elsa went on vacation so she'd stop playing the stupid movie, the kids' fish died because I'm a murderer, Hank and I haven't had sex in over a month because he thinks I'm fat, and I'm pretty sure I'm pregnant."

"If you haven't had sex, then how are you pregnant?"

"Because Hank's sperm defy science. Or we might have had sex that one night Lemon-Marie slept in her own bed, but I'm so tired I can't be sure."

"You can't be sure if you had sex?"

Dotti snapped her fingers. "Keep up."

Abi was having a hard time focusing because when Lemon-Marie raced past, she was now also naked.

Swoosh swish. "Let it go. Let it go."

"Right. Sperm of steel, singing wands, and you losing your shit," she teased, but the first of many tears slid down Dotti's face.

"I'm losing my shit and you're judging me?"

Abi shifted uncomfortably back and forth on her heels. She wasn't exactly the affectionate type. She'd long wondered if that nurturing, maternal gene had somehow skipped her. But her sister clearly needed some kind of physical connection, so Abi rested a hand on her sister's shoulder and gave it a pat or two, then took a step back.

"Not judging. Just trying to understand so maybe I can help."

Dotti snorted. "How are you going to help, Abs. Besides Christmas, you haven't been home for more than a drive-by in over five years. You barely know your niece and nephew. You pop around from one job to the next, living the life while I'm here making sure everything runs smoothly."

Abi wouldn't go as far as to say she was living the life. More like sticking her head in the sand and hoping that the guilt would pass her by. It hadn't. It had only compounded. She'd come up with every excuse possible, but in the end, it was shame that kept her away.

It was always there, in the back of her mind, the dream of coming home and building a life in Portland. A real life with family close by, a circle of friends, and maybe some romance.

Only it was hard to start fresh with so many past transgressions looming overhead. That was what her good deeds had been about, but standing there watching her sister in tears, she decided that the most important good deeds were for the people in her life.

Taking in her sister's puffy eyes and red nose, Abi pushed down some of the jealousy and resentment that had built up and made room for a healthier and more productive emotion—empathy.

"You're right, Dot. I have been MIA, but I can try to help you now."

"How?" Dotti asked. "Are you going to carry my could-be, most-likely-in-there baby-bean? Are you going to teach my kids to eat more than grilled cheese? Oh, wait last time you cooked you burned the grilled cheese and Hank had to hang up on an important meeting to put out the fire."

"That was Hank!"

"It was?" Dotti shook her head as if loosening some cobwebs from the corner. "Did you give the kids my iPad during bath time?"

"Hank."

"Did you eat the last half of my blueberry cake doughnut from Voodoo Doughnuts or use my lipsticks for drawing a picture of a castle on the sliding glass door?"

"You send Anna and Elsa on holiday and you're going to judge me?"

"The doughnut?"

"Possibly. But I'm so exhausted from sleeping on a couch I can't be sure."

Dotti narrowed her eyes into two judgy slits. "And you want to help!"

"Fine. I did eat the doughnut and as for helping, how about we start small. I take over feeding the fish."

Dotti paused, then shook her head. "I'd rather do it myself than have to flush the fourth fish down the toilet."

"You've killed three? Did the kids freak out?"

"I didn't tell them. I snuck out in the middle of the night, bought a new one, and when they asked why Fishie was smaller, I told them it was because he didn't eat his broccoli. I murdered my kids' first pet and lied about it."

"Are they eating more broccoli?"

"Never miss a night. But I can't have any aquatic funerals and I'm afraid that you'll flake in a few weeks when you forget and kill another Fishie."

That shouldn't have hurt as much as it did. Abi might have been flaky in the past, but she was working hard to make amends. Working hard to be better. So while she could let Dotti's comment start a sister war, she tried to put herself in her sister's shoes. And frankly, it sucked.

"I promise I won't forget. And Dot, you're not a bad mom. You're the best mom I know."

"Really?" Dotti sniffed.

"Really." Abi put her arms around her sister and guided her to the couch. "As for Hank, you know how much he loves you."

He might be lazy and oblivious and lactose intolerant, but he worshiped the ground Dotti walked on. They'd been college sweethearts, the whole sorority girl–fraternity boy romance that Hallmark movies were based on.

"Now, how about you tell me what I need to do now so you can relax in a hot bath."

Dotti looked at Abi like she was speaking ancient Hebrew. "I don't know."

Abi looked at the mountain of dirty dishes, the piece of string cheese stuck to the side of the fridge, and the popsicle stick in a puddle of what must have once been an actual frozen fruit snack. "What if I start with cleaning the dishes and kitchen."

"What about your cast?"

"Brace. And I'll make it work."

Dotti wiped her nose on the back of her hand and nodded. "The kitchen will be good since I think that's where Koi poopied."

Chapter Eight

Happy Things:
Spontaneous kisses

It was barely eight when Owen headed downstairs to work. Living in the apartment above his bar really cut down on his commute time but screwed with his personal life. The separation between work and home was literally a story away, which made it easy to blend the two. Too easy.

Take today for example. It was the last week of March, which meant he needed to make the schedule for the next month. A task that ranked between a root canal and a colonoscopy on the fun scale. Chris used to handle scheduling, but he met, fell for, and followed a woman back to San Diego. And while Owen was hard-pressed to find a replacement, he hadn't met anyone who could handle the job quite like Chris.

Grabbing a coat from the closet, he made his way down the back steps. Halfway toward the entrance, he spotted a woman standing on the sidewalk, working her way down the street while putting coins in parking meters.

She was dressed in running shoes, a pair of denim shorts—big on the short—with a red oversized sweatshirt and a thousand and one leashes locked around her waist. And attached to the leashes were a dogs—lots of dogs—barking and pulling her in every which direction. Big dogs, little dogs and, *would you look at that,* his brother's dog, who was the loudest of the bunch.

"Pup Tart, down," she commanded, but Pup Tart wasn't listening. Nope, the hundred-pound mastiff mix gave Abi a full-fledged hug, two paws on the ground, two paws on Abi's shoulders, his tongue lolling out the side of its mouth. He was nearly as tall as Abi and nearly knocked her over.

"Whoa," Owen said, walking up behind Abi to stabilize her. She nearly jumped out of her skin and reached into her fanny pack, for what he wasn't sure, but his nuts shriveled up all the same. He lifted his hands. "It's just me."

Looking cool and composed, as if the moment hadn't happened, she said, "You nearly got tased."

"You nearly fell over."

"I had it handled." At that exact moment, a chocolate lab decided to make a run for it and yanked—hard. Abi stumbled forward two steps before grabbing the leash and leaning back against the force. Even when outmatched, she was stubborn and tenacious.

"Who owns the horse?"

"The Lebowski sisters. They each inherited a half."

"Which half hired you?"

"I wished it was the front half, because the back half has been smelling up my morning." Her eyes narrowed. "I really need to get you that bell."

Then she surprised him with a smile, a stunning smile that reached her eyes, and his chest stuttered to a halt. Damn, she was beautiful. The kind of beautiful that stopped him in his tracks.

"Are you stalking me now?" she teased.

Hell if he knew. One minute he was headed to work, the next he was walking over to her. "Maybe I am." She seemed to like that answer. "Or maybe you are since there's an entire city and yet you're hanging out in front of my bar."

"I'm not hanging, I'm walking dogs," she said, and started walking. With only two options, follow her or get busy on the schedule, he fell into step beside her. "And the quarters?"

"Making sure people don't get dinged for an expired meter." She walked another car length, reached into her fanny pack, which was hanging at her hips, pulled out another quarter and *cha-ching*.

"Dog walking or good deeding?"

"Why does it matter?"

"Just curious. So what, you woke up this morning, looked at the list and decided, 'Hey, I'm going for a dog walk?'"

"It's called spontaneity. You should try it." While she said it in a teasing tone, he could tell she was serious. And maybe she had the right to be. When was the last time he did something spontaneous?

"Here." She held out a quarter.

"What's this for?"

"A fun way to spend your morning." He took the quarter and dropped it in the next expired meter. "See. Doesn't that make you feel better?"

Yeah, it did. But he was pretty sure it wasn't the quarter that had him smiling like an idiot, it was the do-gooder who.

"Is life one big spontaneous adventure after another for you?"

"Is that a polite way of saying I'm impulsive?" She didn't look his way, just dropped another coin in the meter, but the hurt in her tone told him that she'd been called a lot of things in her lifetime that had left lasting scars. "It's my way of saying I like being in your world. It's new and exciting. To me, this and you are a mystery."

This time she did look at him and she didn't hold back the vulnerability. "The problem with mysteries is that once they're solved there's no point in digging deeper."

She handed him another coin.

Oh, he wanted to dig deeper. He wanted to know more about her, why she was in Portland since it was clear she and her sister weren't all that close, and where her parents were in this whole situation. He had a feeling that the first layer of Abi was hidden in her good deeds. Not the "spontaneous" ones but the ones in that journal. "What else is in your journal?"

She whipped around to stare at him, looking up at him with those big, brown, laser-sharp eyes, which were flickering with deep, deep suspicion. Or maybe it was something else. Fear. "How do you know I have a journal?"

"You dropped it in the parking lot." It was almost as if she sighed, but her body didn't move. "And when you were at Lauren's party, I may have seen that your journal was a good deed list."

She went utterly still. "Did you open it?"

One minute he was petting Pup Tart, the next he was cupping her cheek. "Never. Whatever is in that journal is your business."

She let out a big sigh, like she'd just been told she wasn't going to die. "Thank you. Most people would have looked or at least taken a peek."

Once again he was left to wonder just what kind of people she had around her. Her co-workers came into Stout after work most nights, but she was never with them. In fact, the other night was the first time she'd set foot in his bar. Which brought him to her sister, who didn't seem to be a big Abi supporter.

"I'm not most people."

"I like that about you." He was beginning to like a lot about her, but this was the first time she'd admitted she liked him—or at least liked that he was an honest guy, which was such a simple concept he wondered who had broken her heart so badly that her bar was set so low. "Are you even curious?"

"Hell yes! I mean, singing telegrams, dog walking, ribbed for her pleasure condoms." He wiggled a brow at her when he said condoms and she rolled her eyes. "Sounds like good deeds to me."

"It does, doesn't it." She neither confirmed nor denied and he wondered why she was being so evasive. She studied him one last time, then began walking, not giving two shits if he followed. Which he did.

He shoved his hands into his pockets and easily kept pace with her, taking one stride for her every three, which seemed to tick her off. "Are you paying off a debt?"

Her expression turned serious, and she looked away. He'd touched on a sore spot, but he couldn't imagine what it could be. Most people would own that they were doing random acts of kindness. Then again, he was learning that *she* wasn't most people. She was friendly but closed off, an experienced listener but not a big talker, and she had this vulnerability about her that was in direct conflict with her tough as nails attitude.

"Do you need help?"

"I've got this," she said as a dog yanked her forward a step and dropped into the poop position. And it wasn't any dog, it was Littleshit, Rhett's five-pound fashion accessory, who was dressed in a pink tracksuit and matching booties. The oversized rat dropped a bomb on the sidewalk and Abi groaned. "The grass is literally two feet from you."

Yip, yip, yap! Fancy walked in a circle, proud of his business, then stuck his tail in the air as if flipping them both the bird.

"Why are you walking my brother's dog?"

"He's your brother's? I didn't know. Some lady signed Fancy up on my Need a Good Deed sheet. Stephanie, I think."

"That's his ex."

"Anyway, I posted that I was walking dogs on Thursdays and the response was so great I added another day."

"On top of working at the tea shop and the senior center? That must make for some long days."

She shrugged as if to say, *So what?* "Not any longer than yours." Then Littleshit pulled a total Littleshit move and dropped another nugget.

"Are you kidding me?" she scolded, then looked up at Owen. "What am I doing wrong?"

She sounded so genuinely upset by Fancy's outburst, he brushed his knuckles over hers, careful of her injured arm, in what was supposed to be a comforting gesture between friends. But the second he made contact, friendly was the last thing he felt.

She jerked her hand away as if jolted by 300 million volts of electricity.

"If it makes you feel better, he doesn't listen to anyone. Not even his parents," he assured her.

"Now you tell me." She looked at Fancy's gift and pushed out a breath. "Do you know how much shit I've had to deal with in the past twenty-four hours?" she asked, but she didn't seem to expect an answer since she went on. "Sister shit, kid shit, dog shit, all kinds and flavors of bullshit."

She sounded exhausted.

"That's a big list."

"And it's growing by the second." She pulled a doodie bag out of her pack and, plugging her nose, bent down and nearly toppled over from the strength of the dogs.

"Maybe I can lighten your load a little."

Her smile was chock full of mischief. "Only if I can return the favor."

Without asking, he unhooked her belt and tied it around himself, which was difficult since it was made for a regular-sized person and he was built like Paul Bunyan, but he worked it out.

"Okay, going in." She plugged her nose, gagged a little, then, with the tips of her fingers, tossed the bag into the trash. She shuffled through her pack as if her life depended on it, located and pulled out sanitizing gel, and doused her hands.

"I take it you're not a dog person."

"What makes you say that? Just because I've never had a dog doesn't make me anti-dog. I'm as pro-dog as someone who has never owned one can get." Her face lit in a light-bulb moment. "You should get a dog!"

"Absolutely, positively not happening. I barely have time to run a bar, let alone take care of a dog." Or help pretty women walk through town for no other reason than the fact that he couldn't seem to stay away from her.

"That is the exact reason you need one." She put a little skip in her step. "Yup, you need a dog." She waved a hand toward the dogs heeling by his side. "What's your secret?"

"It's called taking the lead. Letting them know who's the boss."

She snorted. "Says the guy who is hiring inept."

"More choosy than inept. And back to the dog, it isn't practical."

"Studies show that people with pets have a lower stress level and are happier."

He looked over at her and what he saw looking back had him pausing. She wasn't teasing or giving him a hard time, she was serious. "You don't think I'm happy?"

"I don't know. Are you?"

He had to think about it. Besides poker night with his brothers, when was the last time he'd really had fun? Or been on an actual date? Hell, his own mother thought his game was lacking enough that she'd taken to setting him up.

He looked down at the stunning siren next to him and realized that this was the closest thing he'd had to a date in months. "Anyone I know on your list?"

She looked away. "I thought my privacy is my privacy?"

He tilted her chin so she was looking at him. "I'm not prying, Angel. I'm simply curious. Plus, I already know what's on it."

"You do?... Wait up." She sped up since he'd started walking again. "You aren't going to pressure me?"

Her legs had to do double-time to match his pace, but he didn't slow down. He liked how her body moved when she had to put a spring in her step—since everything else springed to perfection.

"You want to kiss me."

He looked over and the pulse at the base of her neck went into hyperdrive. "That's not in my journal," she said.

Her gaze was locked on his mouth, and he could have sworn he spotted a flash of desire there. "Maybe not. But then why are you staring at my lips?"

She didn't say a word, so he stopped, and the dogs immediately heeled. Before she could walk past, he took her hand in his. And while that same *zap* was there, neither let go.

He moved closer, so close he could smell a fresh, herbal scent that made him hard, and spotted a double whammy of heat and hesitation in her gaze. "Abs?"

"Because I do want to kiss you, but I can't."

He cupped her hip and tugged her against him. "What's the problem?"

"For one, I'm leaving."

While he was expecting a lot of reasons, that hadn't even made his top ten. Him being a confirmed commitment-phobe, that they're complete opposites, that he was a notorious flirt. Those he'd been anticipating. But this, this was as good as a green light. He'd been holding back because he wasn't a long-term bet and she was a go-the-distance kind of woman. But if the only problem in her head was that she was leaving, then that was a problem easily solved.

"When?"

She moved closer, placing them face to face. "As soon as I finish a few things."

"That timeline works for me." Cupping her cheek, he ran the bed of his thumb down her jawline to her lips. He slowly lowered his head until they shared a breath, just for a beat but long enough to know that this was happening. He gave her the chance to back away. She didn't. In fact, she moved closer. "I'm going to kiss you now."

"I know," she said, but then surprised him.

She tugged him down by his coat's collar and pressed her mouth to his, sending a pure electrical jolt through his body.

The kiss was deep and slow. One hand was holding his coat, the other on his chest. His hands were doing more wandering than holding—he kept it PG since they were on a street corner, but it bordered on PG-13 when he realized just how warm and curvy she was. So damn curvy, he couldn't keep his hands off her.

The kiss ended way too soon but just as slow and deep as it had started. With one last peck she backed away. "That was a mistake."

Chapter Nine

Happy Things:
When you use up all your sick leave and call in dead

It was Monday night, Oregon State was playing University of Oregon, and with four-dollar drafts, Stout was busting at the seams. Loyalties were drawn, families split down the middle, and tensions were at an all-time high. It was Oregonian sports at its finest.

He and the rest of his brothers had finally managed to all get in the same six square feet. Even his brother Clay had flown in for the night. They'd been there just long enough to finish a pitcher and for their order to arrive. Owen hadn't eaten since before the lunch rush and could already taste his tri-tip sandwich.

He'd just taken his first mouthwatering bite when raised voices sounded. Setting his sandwich down, he hung his head. "Are you kidding me?"

"Doesn't sound like kidding to me," Rhett said, sounding oh so amused with himself. "Sounds like someone needs a bouncer."

"I already showed two assholes the door and warned the six surrounding tables."

"Maybe you should have gone the extra mile and warned that seventh table."

Owen looked up and gave his brother a long, narrowed glare. "You're part owner, you go handle it."

"And damage these hands?" Rhett wiggled his fingers like a little girl playing cat's cradle. "Do you know how much they're insured for?"

"Great, then send your agent in on your behalf."

Gage laughed, big and loud and like that wasn't going to happen anytime soon. Josh was busy studying his plate so as not to meet Owen's gaze. Then there was Clay, sitting back with a stupid grin on his face. And that's when they heard it, the familiar nails on a chalkboard voice that could only belong to one person.

"Cindy," Owen said, and they all groaned. After a fun round of "Not it," ending with Owen the last guy standing, he shoved his plate back and stood.

Cindy was a bit of a regular. The last time the Beavers lost to the Ducks, she'd crawled up on her table and started throwing things at the big screen—starting with her jersey and ending with her thong. She was wearing layers this time—bonus—but she'd already hopped up on the table.

Some of the patrons had blocked off the area around her, but all eyes were on Loose Cannon Cindy to see how far she'd go tonight.

"Bad call, ref," she shouted, jabbing a finger at the big screen nearest her. "Worst call in the history of sports."

And just like that, a brown and orange Beaver jersey went sailing through the air. One of her friends tried to reason with her, but all that did was make Cindy move to the exact center of the table, putting her right out of reach.

What had begun as a one-man mission had quickly morphed into a team effort kind of situation. Owen couldn't get to her without fear that she'd move to the far edge of the table and topple over. And since he couldn't cover four corners all by himself, he needed backup.

He leveled his brothers with a look and they all shoved their hot plates away and begrudgingly stood. They all knew what this meant. If they didn't get there soon, they'd have to deal with a naked chick streaking through their bar. Not only was having a naked woman on the table a health violation, it also violated a few other county and state regulations.

"This is why you need more help," Rhett bitched, hot on Owen's heels. "If you weren't trying to be all things to all people, you might have a bouncer worth his weight."

Owen did have a bouncer. He'd given him the night off, which in retrospect had been a bad call. He knew it would be a busy night but when one of his employees had a good reason for requesting time off Owen usually caved. Even if it meant putting himself out.

"Speaking of employees, any news on the new manager or bartender?" Josh asked.

"Seriously, we've got Cindy on the loose and you want to talk employee records?"

Owen led the way through the crowd, moving the crush by his sheer size. People always tended to give him a wide berth, which as a bar owner came in handy. When they reached the table, Cindy had lost her tank top and right flip-flop. Not wanting things to go any further, the brothers worked out a plan of action.

Rhett, the sweet talker of the group, was first going to try to reason with Cindy so that she'd come down on her own terms. In the case that Cindy wasn't having it, which, based on history, was the likely outcome, then four brothers would take a side and one would lift her off the table. Throughout the entire planning session, Cindy continued to scream vulgarities at the screen, threatening to unman the ref and any other man who thought the Ducks were superior to the Beavers.

"Okay, now put your height to use and go get you some crazy," Josh said to Owen.

"Wait. Why am I the one who has to risk life and limb?"

"We all played roshambo and you had the losing hand," Gage said.

"I didn't even play."

"Don't worry, I played for you. It was a clear case of rock takes scissors." Rhett grinned. "Now get out there and snag you a woman."

Snag was putting it lightly. While his brothers surrounded the table, Owen reached out to grab Cindy, who took a cheap shot to his chin. She might only be a buck twenty, but the woman had a wicked right hook.

"You fight like a girl," Rhett said to Owen and of course Huey, Dewey, and Louie had to laugh at the ha-ha-funny moment.

"If you'd promised to take a selfie with her, none of this would be happening."

"Me in a photo with a drunk, naked girl would do wonders for my career," Rhett explained.

Gage piped in. "Since it would be a media nightmare, I made the official call and kiboshed it."

"Then, when this is over and I need someone to blame, remind me about that so I can kibosh you right out of the bar." Lowering his voice, he said to Cindy, "How about you come down and I'll give you a seat right up front by the big screen. Maybe get you a burger on the house."

"How about you go screw yourself!"

By this time every eyeball and cell phone in the joint was on Owen and Cindy. People were live streaming, placing bets. One of the pools had Owen losing his right nut, another had him losing the left.

Using her jersey as protection, Owen reached across the table and, guarding his boys, wrapped his arms around her. She shoved off the table and the traction knocked Owen back a step.

"You're blocking my view!" Cindy yelled, then wrapped herself around him like a koala clinging to a tree. Her legs were like a vise around his waist, her arms so tight he was suffocating under the pressure, and then there were his brothers—laughing their asses off.

Promising himself that he could kill them all later he said, "Can one of you give me a hand?"

No one moved, except Cindy, who arched backward like she was some MMA fighter trying to take him down to the mat. Clay took out his cell and snapped a selfie, holding a big thumbs up while Owen was turning blue from lack of oxygen.

"That one's going on the wall of fame," Clay said, referring to the large wall at the back of the bar that housed signed photos of celebrities and popular regulars.

Owen managed to get Cindy through the crowd and to the front door. All and all it took five minutes, but Owen would have the bruises for weeks.

By the time he walked back in, his brothers' plates were empty and his was cold. Appetite gone, he cleared the dishes and stood behind the bar.

"Seriously? What happened to all for one and one for all?"

"What happened to hiring more staff? Had there been just one more person working tonight, they would have spotted Cindy sneaking into the bar."

While this was a true statement, it also pissed Owen off. It wasn't that he didn't want more staff. He did. He just didn't want to hire the wrong staff. But he'd given into peer pressure and put up a job posting on the bar's website. He'd gotten a few hits. "I'm interviewing more people tomorrow starting at eleven."

"How about the interview for your date to Mom's birthday?"

Clearing away an empty pitcher, he grabbed a towel and wiped down the bar top. "It's not happening. I called Sydney and she was about as excited over the setup as I was, so she's bringing some guy from work to get our moms off our backs. And before you ask, I'm not bringing anyone."

"Tell that to Mom. She's got your Date 2.0 all picked out," Gage said, and Owen groaned.

"I heard she met her at bible study," Clay said.

Gage laughed. "She's going to take one look at you and run for the hills."

Wasn't that the truth. If his size didn't scare them off, then his tattoos did. Or the fact that he worked around the clock. His job wasn't conducive to building lasting relationships, which was why he didn't bother to look for anything beyond the occasional breakfast in bed.

"I'll go with you," he heard a smoky voice say. He turned and all he saw was gorgeous. Whiskey eyes, full mouth, and a smile that scrambled his brain.

Abi was sitting at the bar, her chin resting on a fist, looking deceptively sweet. She was also looking smoking hot. She had on glossy lips, this thin white sweater, the see-through kind that hinted at the white lace beneath, and that damn wrist brace.

"Hello?" She snapped her fingers in his face.

"What?" He found himself asking, in case he'd misheard because of the volume in the bar.

"I said, I'll be your date," she repeated, as if that wouldn't end in disaster. It was clear as day that their chemistry was off the charts. But they were as compatible as a cactus and a balloon animal. Not to mention she'd obviously been through some kind of trauma. The bruises, the easy way she startled, the sadness behind those big, brown eyes.

Then there was her arm brace, looking like big neon light flashing HANDLE WITH CARE. And if there was one thing Owen knew about himself, it was that he wasn't all that great with the caring for someone part. At least that's what his ex had told him when he'd asked her why she'd cheated.

Nah, Abi had been through something, something bad, and he didn't want to be one other hardship in her life. Kissing had been a mistake. Weren't those the words she'd used? Nope, going on a date was a hard pass. It would only lead to kissing, which would lead to touching and eventually sex, and finally a keg full of complications. Which was why he was going to his mom's party solo.

"Not happening,"

Abi looked down at herself and he could see her bristle. "Why am I not happening?"

He hadn't meant to hurt her feelings. In fact, he was thinking of nothing other than her feelings, and how she might misunderstand what a date to his mom's birthday would entail. It would be a no attachments, no strings, and no breakfast in bed come morning kind of date that would leave her hurt and confused, two things that were already surfacing in her wide eyes.

Shit. He gentled his voice. "I don't need a date is all."

As if this weren't an awkward conversation to begin with, his brothers all burst out laughing. Abi did not. Her eyes narrowed, her lips pursed, and her hands purposefully hung by her side. Maybe it was the electricity caused by the breeze rushing through the bar, or maybe she was some kind of mythical conduit, but she went from jokester to a human lie detector with a single blink of an eye.

"Well, isn't that a steaming pile of malarkey. Take a big whiff, boys." She made a big deal about sniffing. "Can't you smell it? That's the smell of a cornered mama's boy."

"Here I thought it was Bengay," Rhett said, all kinds of amused. And that's when Owen noticed it, the easy way she fit in with his brothers. They were tall and gregarious in big crowds, which can be intimidating.

Not this spitfire. She could give as well as she took. And handle his brothers like a pro. Still, handling his brothers at the bar was a far cry from bringing her home for a family meal, something he hadn't done since Elena and something he hadn't planned on doing for a long while.

Plus, stronger men had come before and their wives had barely lived to tell the tale. Why put them through all the stress since she was leaving for Asia soon?

"Clearly by the conversations you have going on with yourself, you do. Don't worry, I'll bring a purse big enough to hide your Depends and when people ask me what that Bengay scent is, I'll blame it on my breath mints."

"Will you bring your journal too?" he asked, and her face reddened with embarrassment, leaving him feeling like a class-A jerk. "I just don't want to be one of your Goodwill Toward Men cases."

"Why not?" she challenged. "You're good and maybe you deserve something good in your life right now."

Owen studied her, waiting for the punch line, except she didn't crack even the tiniest of smiles. She looked as if she meant it.

"Fine. I'm not your type." She shrugged. "Maybe the pretty brunette at the end of the bar is. Hang on." She got up and walked across the room, ignoring the way Owen was chasing her from the other side of the bar top. Before he could stop her, she stuck out her right hand. "Hi, I'm Abi and this handsome guy here is my friend Owen."

"Hi, Owen, I'm Jennifer."

"Of course you are," Abi said, then mumbled something that sounded a lot like, "Are you happy now?"

"Hey, Jenny. Can you excuse us for a moment?" he said to the woman, then took Abi by the elbow and dragged her around the side of the bar and behind it. But when he got her there, he couldn't seem to let go of her. She didn't seem to be in any rush to move either.

His grip loosened and he slid his fingers down her arm to her good hand. He was practically lacing fingers when she jerked back.

"Mistake, remember?"

Oh, he remembered. "Can you not ask random women at my bar if they'd like to go on a date with me?"

"Afraid I'll scare off a prospect?"

"No, she's just not my type."

"Then what is your type?"

If he were pressed at that moment to describe his perfect type it would, hands down, be Abi. But hell if he would admit that. She was already walking all over him and that kind of turned him on.

"Why? You interested?"

"My offer was strictly professional."

That made him smile. "So you're a professional dater. Isn't there a name for that?"

"It was a courtesy from one friend to another. Nothing more."

"Are we friends?" he asked, genuinely wanting to know where she stood on the matter. He knew where he stood, and it wasn't anywhere near friendly.

"Never mind," she said, starting to turn away. She paused. "You know, since the universe is enjoying screwing with my life, I thought I would use my powers for good instead of evil. So, in the sake of time, it would help to know what your type is."

"Not Jennifer," was all he said.

"Well, Jennifer isn't all that interested either."

Chapter Ten

Happy Things:
Mee-maw Ruth's Blue Ribbon chili

Abi wasn't a fool. She knew that the way to a man's heart wasn't through his stomach—it was a little further south of the Mason-Dixon line. But since she wasn't looking to crawl into his heart or his bed, she'd decided to go with his brain.

Owen was the most logical person she knew, which meant she'd have to find stealthy ways to help him that he couldn't argue with—and she was going to start by carving out a little downtime for him. So while she'd been avoiding him after that kiss—a kiss that could go nowhere—because a) she was leaving, b) she was in his life under false pretenses, and c) it was a really, really good kiss—she owed it to herself, and to Owen, to finish what she came here to do. And it had nothing to do with his magical lips.

Reminding herself that she'd become a ninja do-gooder, she decided the best course of action when it came to a prideful control freak was a good ol' bait and switch. To keep all her do-gooder plans to herself, then *bang*! He wouldn't know what hit him.

Backpack slung over her shoulder, she entered Stout and made her way to the bar. At the far end sat Owen, interviewing a potential bartender, who was tall, leggy, and had a few strategically placed tattoos. Her smile was sexy and sultry in a way Abi could never pull off—and aimed right at Owen. She looked as if she were interviewing to be his next girlfriend, like she'd swiped right and managed to land on a winner of a man.

Abi hated to admit it because she was supposed to be impartial, but he was a winner. Honest, smart, and handsome as all get out. Then there was his heart that was so big and warm it made Abi want to believe in things she'd never known existed. Things she would never have if she continued to push people away. Then again, other people were the ones who pushed her away first. For her parents, she was a reminder of a difficult time. Treating her differently wasn't a conscious decision, but feeling invisible left marks that would forever shape her life. Even now, they were so busy with their own lives that they didn't see Abi was in pain. There was no invitation, no offer to help Abi through a heart-wrenching and traumatic time. There was only a short visit, then back to their regularly scheduled life. And Dotti, who tried so hard but couldn't quite understand what Abi was going through.

Then there was Owen, strong and steady Owen, who continued to check in on her even though it wasn't his job. Which was how she could feel a few cracks forming around her inner wall. It would only lead to heartache when her time was up and she moved on.

Even still, Abi was unable to stop from inserting herself into his world, finding ways to be around him. She told herself it was the only way to uncover new strategies to make his life easier, to find the perfect time to spill the beans, but that would be a lie. She wanted to be in his life because his world had things she'd never had. Stability, support, a tight-knit family, and an openness that was a little intimidating. There was also a loneliness deep beneath the surface that she wanted to heal.

But her time here had an expiration date, a ticking clock that activated the moment she and Jenny had accepted that job in Asia. A job which started in a little under two months. Jenny had mapped out their whole trip, working in Thailand, a yoga retreat in Malaysia, and sailing through Halong Bay. It was meant to be three months of teaching, travel, and self-exploration. Which meant she needed to get her hustle going so she could move on and live the adventure she and Jenny had dreamed about.

Beyond Asia, she didn't know where life would take her. Maybe to San Diego, maybe Cambodia, but someplace far from Portland and the memories. Someplace as far away from the blast radius as possible. Another reason to stay firmly in her lane. Changing direction this late in the game wouldn't be fair to anyone—especially Owen.

Nope, she had a plan and the faster this place was in her rearview mirror, the safer her heart would be.

Owen turned to Abi. His eyes flickered, first with surprise, then with something that made her stomach do a funny little dance. *What are you doing here?* he mouthed.

Interviewing, she mouthed back, and he grinned.

Sorry, you have to reach the bar to apply.

I come with my own step stool.

He laughed and Legs followed his gaze. When she spotted Abi, she reached across the counter and said something to Owen. It took a moment for him to drag his gaze away, but when he did, he must have said something to Legs, who laughed like he was Jimmy Fallon, then handed him her card and shook him an enthusiastic goodbye.

Before he could even catch his breath, the next candidate walked through the door. She was tall, with an hourglass figure, the top of that glass being at least double Ds. She was sure of herself, stunning, and even flirtier than the first.

Owen, on the other hand, kept things straightforward, effortlessly riding that fine line between personal and professional until he glanced down the bar and locked eyes with Abi and all that sexual intensity was directed at her. This felt genuine. It wasn't some act that he used to put people at ease, it was the real deal. He was the real deal.

She was a fraud.

She tried to smile back but the weight of what she'd done to him and his family, the deceit in her reasons for being there, suddenly turned to lead in her chest. What would he say when he learned the *Why him?* Why she'd chosen to focus on Owen rather than any of the other family members. Would he understand that it was because his brothers had moved on and were living their best lives and he was stuck in the past?

Owen must have seen right through her smile because his expression softened, and he tilted his head in concern.

You okay? he mouthed.

She nodded. But she so wasn't. Her stomach was in knots, her heart sick with anticipation, and the idea of coming clean made her hands tremble. But she tried at another smile, this one brighter but he wasn't buying it, so she looked away.

She smoothed the edges of her résumé, which she'd taken hours the night before to assemble. On paper, she was experienced, a top-notch candidate for any job. But she only wanted to land one job.

When she looked up next, Owen had placed three bottles on the bar top with a tumbler. The woman studied the bottles for a moment as if recalling the recipe from a flashcard she'd made for a high school exam. It took her a long moment, the kind of long that would leave three customers in the queue, then Double Ds measured out the liquid into the tumbler, shook it and poured it into a glass that she then slid across the bar.

Owen dipped a cocktail straw in the glass and took a sip. He gave a *not bad* kind of smile and replaced the bottles. He quizzed her for a couple more drinks, each causing her to pause and think. She made the right combinations each time, but Abi could tell it was a mediocre finish. Not that it mattered. A woman who looked like that could upsell just about any man and keep the tips flowing with her sex appeal alone—that smile would offset her lack of finesse.

Double Ds dug through her purse for something, giving Owen the chance to, once again, look Abi's way. Not wanting to drag him down with her, she perked up and looked at her boobs, giving a light-bulb moment smile.

Ah. She traced her hands over her much smaller hourglass. *My boobs aren't big enough.*

This time when he laughed, she could hear it. She could also see how some of the stress he'd been carrying since she'd arrived dissipated. Abi might not have an abundance of Victoria's secrets, but she could make him laugh. Making people laugh was the easy part—it came almost as natural as baking Mee-maw's cornbread. It was the going deeper that took a kind of finesse Abi didn't seem to possess. At least that was the one commonality between her exes.

No longer the center of his attention, Double Ds reached across the bar top and touched Owen's hand. She left it there while she told him something, most likely her number.

After a few other pleasantries, he said goodbye and ushered her to the door. Abi watched as he interviewed three more candidates and when the last one left, instead of walking behind the bar, he stalked toward her. Five steps out and she could see the signs of exhaustion. She didn't know how many people he'd interviewed prior, but he looked spent. And he still had a full twelve hours of work ahead of him—at least.

"You trying to sabotage me?" he asked.

"Nope, just being neighborly."

She sat back and crossed her legs as his gaze wandered. She was in a blue blouse, black skirt, and the dressiest cowgirl boots she owned. She wasn't glammed out like Legs, but she wasn't there for the bartender job.

He took the seat next to her, turning so they were facing. "What does 'neighborly' entail?"

Oh boy. Her nipples rebelled, reaching out to show him exactly how neighborly they wanted to get. He seemed to be on board because when his eyes met hers, they were full of heat and want. Even after a parade of stunning women, he wanted her.

Just as quickly as his eyes flashed, they went carefully blank. "Job's taken."

"Ah, then Double Ds was a blind date?"

"Potential bartender."

"I thought the position was filled?"

"Just finishing off the last of the interviews for today." Which meant he had more earlier in the week.

He leaned back and crossed his arms over his chest, making his biceps bulge. He flexed. Twice. And when she looked up, he winked because, as she was coming to learn, he knew when her mind had taken a different direction. Refusing to give him the satisfaction, she shrugged as if unimpressed.

"Great." She slid her résumé across the table. "Then I'll see you in," she looked at a pretend watch, "thirty minutes."

He didn't budge. "You're not on my schedule."

"Oh, I signed up online." She showed him her phone with the confirmed appointment time. "Even uploaded my résumé."

He tilted his chin toward her three pages, printed on heavy stock and clipped with a Seahawks-green paperclip. "Then what's that?"

"Me being thorough. Plus, you look like a dinosaur, so I went old school and printed it."

When he still didn't take it, she tucked it between his crossed arms and chest.

Amused, he picked it up and noncommittally flipped through. The longer he perused, the smugger her smile became. She knew what he saw. Top of her class, earning a master's in leadership and administration, and three years' experience managing a wine bar while in grad school. She was also the elementary school representative for the PTA and a bond oversight committee and that's not even mentioning the jobs she'd done overseas teaching English to locals.

"You can't lift trays with your hand," he reasoned.

"I'm here for the manager position."

She'd caught him off-guard. "You're leaving."

"Not for another ah…" How long was she staying? She didn't want to lie to him, but she also didn't want to overcommit. "month or two."

"The answer's still no."

"Hang on, before you get stubborn, think of me as an interim manager. A temporary independent contractor of sorts, whose main purpose is to find, hire, and train a new manager. I can take on the responsibility of hiring new bartenders. It's a win-win. You get to free yourself of a job you suck at, and I get some extra cash."

"Texas A&M, then Duke for graduate school." He eyed her. "You're overqualified."

"I work at a tea shop."

He set down the résumé. "I know. Why?"

"Circumstances." Like needing a job she could do in her sleep since after the accident she'd become short on sleep. "That I don't want to talk about, but I can talk about how perfect for this job I am."

"I'd still have to train you."

"I'm a quick learner. Plus, I'm personal, reliable, more than capable." She lowered her voice. "And I'd never abuse your trust. Never."

The last part seemed to have him reconsidering. He went quiet and gave her résumé another pass, this time really seeing what she'd accomplished since that night. He looked at her over the paper. At the unexpected rush of nerves racing through her body, she uncrossed and crossed her legs three times.

"I'm an asshole of a boss. You'd hate working for me."

"You're a pushover, which is part of the problem. You're also overworked and on the verge of burnout. This shouldn't be a hard decision."

Again, he studied her and again that rush of nerves got the best of her. She knew he'd be a hard sell, but the longer he stared at her, the more uncertain she became. She knew she was, hands down, the most qualified person he'd interviewed. Knew she'd rock the job. So why the hesitation?

Was he that big of a commitment-phobe that a two-month agreement with a pretty face made him itchy? Or was it because of the situation she'd put him in all those years back?

"You don't have to answer now. In fact, my mee-maw used to say decisions were best made on a full stomach." She unpacked her backpack, placing a container of cornbread and a thermos of chili in front of him.

He looked at the setting, complete with a napkin and plastic utensils, and grinned. "What's this?"

"Lunch."

"You do know that I own a bar *and* grill."

"Which doesn't serve my mee-maw Ruth's blue-ribbon chili." She opened the thermos and wafted the steam his way. "If you ask my neighbors back home, it's about as close to heaven as one can get."

"And where is back home?" He gently tapped her cowgirl boots with his foot. "Texas?"

"How did you know?" Being born in Texas, then raised all across the South made her accent thick as molasses yet ambiguously Southern.

"You had on a Longhorns sweatshirt the other day. Then there's the way you say your I's like 'ahh' and your E's like 'ay.'"

"That could be anywhere in the South."

"Abilene is a pretty distinctive name."

"My dad moved around a lot when I was little. I saw nearly every major city in the South. When the nurse asked for my name for the birth certificate, my mama picked the name of my hometown. She wanted to give me a sense of where I came from."

He went silent for a moment, absorbing that information. "Military brat?"

"Nope. Shipping logistics. My dad moved where they sent him. Usually port towns."

"And your mee-maw's chili?"

"Portland by way of Abilene." Which was how Abi had spent every summer in Portland. Ruth followed husband number two to Oregon. After he passed, she chose to stay. She said that while her roots would always be in Texas, her heart was in Portland.

"Did she make this?"

"No, sir." Her grandma passed a few years back and Abi missed her sorely. "Her recipe, my kitchen."

Owen took a sniff and lifted a brow. "Is this as good as it smells?"

"You'll never know unless you give it a taste." A little whisper said she wanted him to give her a taste. But no matter how delicious she found him, romantically he was off-limits. It was bad enough that she'd kissed him, she didn't want to complicate the situation any further.

"I'm not looking for a taste." His gaze ran down her body and back up, her belly giving a little quiver. "I'm looking for a little more."

Her heart pinched with bitter disappointment. Abi couldn't give more than what she'd written down in her Good Deed Journal. Plus, her time there was almost up, so acting on their attraction would be a disaster.

"I'm just here to help with interviews."

He studied her, then leaned in until they were so close she could smell the testosterone wafting off him. "Is this about your list?"

She moved back and his lips quirked at the corners. "It's clear that you hate interviewing, Owen. I, on the other hand, am an excellent judge of character. Five years as a kindergarten teacher, I can spot a turd a mile away."

"Turd?"

"I can't call a five-year-old an asshat, now can I?"

He burst out laughing and she decided that Jenny had steered her to the right place. She'd been avoiding her big project until she'd worked up the knack of Good Samaritan, but apparently Jenny thought she'd had enough practice and it was time to get down to business. The clock had ticked down to that final second and she knew that the jig was up.

She had to tell him the truth.

"About my list," she began, her voice shaking slightly. God, she knew it would be hard, but she never imagined it'd be this hard. She wished Jenny were there to help her with the aftermath. But she was out of wishes.

"The real reason I want this job is—"

A loud crash sounded from behind, immediately followed by glass shattering.

Abi's heart screamed into her throat and a shot of adrenaline hollowed out her stomach. She instinctively ducked and covered her head. Shards of ceramic rebounded off the concrete flooring, pegging her in the calf. A bang split through the air and rattled her skull. Her heart dropped, defying gravity, ricocheting painfully against her ribs. Panic barreled down like a freight train.

Her fight-or-flight instincts kicked in, making her want to fight and flight all the same time. As soon as the thought entered her mind, another bang echoed, the sound restricting her airways, leaving her dizzy and embarrassingly close to tears.

It's just a panic attack, she reassured herself. But no amount of reassuring could hide the truth. Abi was broken to her core, and she didn't know if she'd ever be able to gather the shards of her life that had been left beside the road that day.

And in about two minutes everyone in that bar would know it. Including Owen. They'd know that she was losing her mind.

No, no, no. She was going to be sick.

Nausea roiled, a cold sheen beaded on her forehead, and her body instinctively curled in on itself. It felt like she was slowly suffocating. The counter closed in, pressing her back against the stool and further constricting her airway. She slid off the seat but when she reached the floor it seemed to slide right out from under her.

Then it flashed all around her, the crunching of shoes on rocky ground, the crackling of bending steel, and the screams of twenty kids who were looking at Abi to hold them, to protect them, to make it all better.

Only she couldn't move, she was stuck, trapped by fate and by fear. Breathless and disoriented, she took a single step forward looking for, she didn't know what until she bumped into it.

Her anchor in the storm.

Chapter Eleven

Happy Things:
Hugs

As Owen drew Abi in, he could feel her body trembling and hear her whispering to herself. One minute they'd been flirting, the next she'd leaped right out of her skin, and it hadn't all been from the dropped tray. Nope, she'd nearly collapsed to her knees with fear, just like in the parking lot.

It bothered him then and it bothered him now.

He ran his hands up and down her back, his heart breaking a little while she clung to him as though she needed him more than she needed her next breath. And speaking of breath, hers were coming in short, hard, concerning puffs.

"Cornbread. Honey butter. Mee-maw's chili." She sniffled. "Mee-maw's hugs. Mee-maw."

He tightened his hold and rested his cheek on the top of her head, trying to soothe away the tremors quaking beneath his hands. "You're going to be okay."

"That's usually my line," she murmured into his chest. "I just got startled." She started to back away, but he held on. She looked up. "Really, I'm okay."

She wasn't. He rubbed his thumb down her tear streaks and she pushed his hand aside to embarrassedly wipe at her cheeks. But to his surprise, instead of pushing *him* aside, she rested her forehead back against his chest. Her breathing was still labored and her stance wobbly as if she might keel over at any moment.

"I know you are." Just like he knew she needed to sit down until her breathing slowed.

She straightened and began to sway. "I think I might be sick."

"Your mind is just tricking your body that it's in trouble. But I promise you're safe. I'll make sure you're safe."

"I never know if I can trust my mind," she admitted, her voice so fragile he slid his arm around her waist.

"Then trust me. Can you do that?"

He knew he was asking a lot. Trust didn't seem to come easy for Abi. After hearing about her childhood, he couldn't blame her. Owen had benefited from a strong family support system and sense of community. Moving around as much as she had must have been hard on her, but there was more behind her panic. Something awful happened to her. Something that he was certain he wouldn't like.

"If I say yes, will you make fun of me?"

"Not today." That earned him an ever so quiet little laugh. Grabbing a cold bottle of water from behind the bar, he slid his arm around her shoulder to stabilize her and guided her into his office, where he sat her on the couch.

He went down on his haunches, taking her hand and placing it over his heart. He held it there. "Just take deep breaths. In and out. You got this."

He watched as her heartbeat slowed and her breathing regulated. He didn't let go of her hand, keeping it pressed to his chest. "Can you tell me what's going on?"

"I was just startled."

"You already said that. You should never play poker. Your bullshit face is crap."

"I'll have you know I'm a card shark."

Not today she wasn't. Today she was fragile and expressive, every emotion flashing through her eyes.

His voice dipped low. "Is someone hurting you?"

She looked up, surprise in her eyes. He'd noticed the bruise on her side when she'd reached for a new box of stir sticks last week at the tea shop. Then there was her wrist and the way she held herself as if it hurt to be upright for too long. "It's not what you think."

"Then can you tell me what it is before this image of what I think happened makes me hunt down whoever hurt you." He ran the pad of his finger over the bruise that disappeared beneath her brace.

"I'm a kindergarten teacher. Or I was."

That explained a lot. Wiseass notwithstanding, she had this uncanny ability to nurture just about anyone, including him. He could picture her corralling a class of pint-sized people with her patience and gentle hand—and it made him smile. The way she spoke of it in the past tense and the sadness there made him want to pull her into his arms again.

"I read that in your résumé." An impressive résumé. The best he'd seen all day. But stellar applicant or not, it wasn't happening. "Tell me what wasn't there."

"Three months ago, I was in an accident. A bus accident," she began, her voice threadbare, her eyes on the floor. "We were going to the museum for a field trip and some guy decided to down some whiskey, then get behind the wheel. He T-boned the bus. We went off the road and flipped over."

"Jesus," he whispered. It explained her fear of anything with more than two wheels and why she startled at even the slightest of noises. "How badly were you hurt?" Bad enough that she was still bruised three months later.

She met his gaze and new tears swam in her eyes. "I lived."

Which meant others had not. He didn't even want to know what her world must have looked like in that moment or how one even came back from that kind of event. He wondered if that's what her sexy Samaritan act was all about. Her way of finding balance in a world that had run right over her.

Needing to be closer, he sat next to her on the couch and held her hand between his. "You're shaking."

She looked at him strangely. "That's you."

Jesus, it was him and he had no idea why. But she was looking at him as if she'd never really seen him before and he was seeing a side of Abi that he'd spent the past few weeks trying to uncover. Soft and open, she was letting him in, even if just a tiny bit.

"Thank you for not judging me," she whispered, as if someone else had. "But I don't want to talk about it anymore. I talk when I get upset, but when I talk, I get more upset."

He'd let it go—for now. Until then, he was going to have to earn her trust. If she didn't want to talk about the accident, then he'd get to know her another way. "Let's talk about something else."

"You mean your terrible interview skills?"

He laughed, and it must have been contagious because the corner of her eyes crinkled a smidge. "We already went over that and they aren't that bad."

"First off, the man-bun guy. Women come to bars to look for a sexy face. Man buns aren't sexy."

"Is that why you come into the bar? Sexy guys? Maybe sexy guys with tattoos?" The way her face flushed told him all he needed to know. And that fun fact piqued his curiosity even more.

"I come for the burgers."

"Uh huh."

"Then there's the mafia dropout–looking guy who didn't know the difference between an IPA and a hefeweizen. And Miss Phi Pi can't even make a cosmo without checking her phone for the recipe."

"She can learn."

"Ten to one, she chokes on the first game night," Abi said with that smart-ass tone that told him she was back on her game.

"And what about the blonde?"

"Her double Ds are going to get between her and the bar top. How will she ever reach the tap?"

She sat back and crossed her legs, that black skirt riding up her thigh just enough to give him a glimpse of those toned legs. And her sexy as hell bright red cowgirl boots. Man, the second she'd walked into the bar he couldn't look away. Oh, he hadn't let on that he saw her, but it was as if his body recognized hers from across the space.

"You jealous, Angel?"

"Just more qualified than anyone you've interviewed. I've tended bar." She ticked off a finger. Then another. "Managed a wine bar, as you already know. And headed up boards full of helicopter parents and high-strung soccer moms. So, don't you worry, me and my Bs can handle your bar just fine."

"Now you're just trying to make me blush," he said. "And I love your Bs, but I have a reason for not wanting to hire you. It has nothing to do with your skills, and everything to do with this."

He knew kissing her could obliterate any friendship they might have, but while his brain knew that, his dick was slow on the uptake. It was her eyes, he decided. They'd sucked him in from the first time he'd seen her at the tea shop. But her mouth—*god*, her mouth.

Staring at it was only asking for trouble because he started making a list of exactly how many things he'd like to do to those lips.

Lord help him. He was going to kiss her. He wanted to kiss her. Which made not one ounce of sense, because she was definitely not his type. Okay, with her killer body, lush mouth, and sex-soaked eyes, she was every man's type.

What really got to him? Her smile. It was sweet and sad and so damn determined, it broke his heart—and drew him in. Every time. And Owen couldn't afford to be drawn in. There wasn't room in his life for a smile like that.

But his brain misfired. Maybe it was the way their thighs were plastered to each other, and their hips were touching. He didn't have to go far when he cupped her face and brought her closer and then he did something incredibly stupid. He kissed her.

It started out gentle and soft, his mouth slowly moving against hers as he gauged her interest. Which must have been tracking his because she took it to the next step, sliding her hands in his hair and holding him to her.

She was a great kisser—a real girl-next-door meets sex-goddess combo that was enduringly hot. Speaking of hot, her second pass radiated a surface-of-the-sun kind of heat that slayed him. After the third kiss, he was a goner.

Endless possibilities rushed through him instead of good sense.

She pulled back just enough to look up at him. Her eyes dazed, mouth wet, breathing erratic. "We shouldn't." But even as she said it, she was kissing him again.

He moved down to her neck and lower. She released a little moan when he kissed the curve where her shoulder met her throat. "You taste good."

"Like honey butter?"

He lifted his head. "Like sex."

She held his gaze, and he could see the indecision in her eyes, but he could also see the desire. Stupid idea or not, she was in this as badly as he was. "Maybe just one more," she said.

She took his mouth and gave him not one, not two, but four more until she was pressed all the way against him, officially scrambling his brain. But when he felt things taking a hot and feverish turn, he pulled back. It killed him, but he needed to slow things down. When they went there—and that kiss confirmed they would—it wouldn't be some on-a-whim decision on his office couch.

Resting his forehead against hers, he said, "You see my problem?"

"It must be contagious."

Chapter Twelve

Happy Things:
Sleeping in past noon

The best thing about owning his own bar was that Owen didn't have to answer to anyone—anyone except his over-achieving self.

He'd awoken before six, tidied the loft, made himself a breakfast of poached eggs and bacon—double the bacon—and hit the gym where he and his brothers beat the shit out of each other for fun. Now he was sitting behind his desk shuffling through a giant stack of applications—and that was just yesterday's pile. He had a dozen more interviews today and another ten on Monday. It was barely after breakfast and he already wanted to go back to bed.

And if things weren't stressful enough, the door opened and in walked Rhett and Josh. Without a hello, Rhett plopped down on the couch and Josh in the chair.

"Come back for another beating?" Owen asked, smiling at the memory, then wincing slightly when he reopened the crack on his split lip. Rhett had taken a cheap shot when Josh had distracted Owen. It was the classic Follow the Queen card game, only instead of losing ten bucks, Owen lost a bet and won a right hook to the face.

"Just coming to collect my money," Rhett said. "Pay up."

Owen split an annoyed look between his two brothers. "You and me," he said to Rhett. "One on one, next week at our usual time and channel, double or nothing, loser has to drive Mom to her lady-doctor appointment."

His brothers groaned and Owen threw up in his mouth a little. No one should have to sit in a gynecologist's waiting room with their mother. But Owen had drawn the short straw.

Like his favorite new applicant, Margo wasn't big on driving. Ever since she sideswiped the center divider on the highway, neither were her sons. So they split the workload, leaving Owen with more than his fair share.

"No need," Josh said. "Eddie offered to drive her."

"And we're okay with that?" he asked, wondering what the hell was going on. His brother was more protective of their mom than Owen. "You do remember their shared breakfast on the patio?"

"Ah, that." Josh waved him off. "Clay put the fear of God into the guy. I doubt he'd even hold her hand after that."

Clay was a running back for the Seattle Seahawks and not much smaller than Owen. Which meant he was built like a rhino with bricks for fists. Owen knew because he'd experienced them firsthand. Clay was also living with and in love with Eddie's great-grand-niece and her eight-year-old son, Sammy. So if anyone had the upper hand, it was Eddie. Sex made men do stupid things, like overlook what alone time could transpire into.

Just look at him and his little do-gooder. A single ride to the senior center and he couldn't stop thinking about her—or kissing her.

A month sounded like just the right amount of time to get her out of his system. Had she not applied. Whether she got the job or not, it could be seen as personal preference playing into his decision. It wasn't just a great way to get sued, it was unethical.

"How's the interviewing going?" Josh asked

Owen didn't bother to reply, just pointed to the never-ending stack of résumés.

"Who prints out applications?" Rhett asked.

Dinosaurs, he thought, his mind flashing back to Abi. And that kiss. Two days later and he could smell her perfume on his skin, feel her lips on his.

Damn, he was in trouble.

"I did. It's easier to see the whole picture."

"Who's this?" Rhett asked, picking up the résumé that sat in a pile of its own on the upper corner of his desk. It was also in a class of its own. "Wait. Is this the girl from the other night? The one who offered to be your date and you choked."

"Put it back." Owen grabbed for the paper, but Rhett held it out of reach. He handed it to Josh and laughed.

Josh looked it over. "It is. You've always had a soft spot for Southern girls."

"Just because I dated a few in college doesn't mean that's my type."

Correction. There was one Southern girl who had redefined his type right down to the sweet, sexy drawl. And while he'd brought only one Southern girl home, he'd dated his fair share of debutantes. Although most of them were just looking for a fun time with a bad boy. And who was he to disappoint? So he played the part, which had a ninety-nine percent chance of his getting laid. It also had a ninety-nine percent chance that they weren't looking for anything serious.

At first, it hadn't bothered him. Hell, he was a horny college guy looking to hook up and head on to other pastures.

But the older he got, the older playing the field became. Then he'd met Elena and fell fast and hard, so fast he didn't see the red flags.

It wasn't until she'd called him by another dude's name while in bed that he realized there was a problem. He hadn't even gotten off her before she'd turned it around on him.

"What did you expect?" she'd said. "You're at the bar all the time. You work all the time. There's barely room for us in your life let alone room for me."

"But Luke?" he spat, referring to the only guy who, besides Owen's brothers, he'd trusted with his life. He and Luke had gone back so far, he was like another brother to Owen.

Owen confronted Luke—with his fist—and by the time he got home to talk with Elena, to admit to his part in their problems, she had already packed up and moved out—moved on. To Luke.

Six months later they were married and three months after that they'd had a baby. Now they lived in Denver in a family-ready house with a white picket fence.

It had taken a broken heart and four more years before Owen had learned his lesson. And there he was, searching for red flags in every woman he met. Although he hadn't been able to find a single thing in Abi that gave him pause. She was all the things she'd said the other day and he'd be an idiot to miss an opportunity to get to know her better.

"Wow, impressive." Josh paused for a moment, recognition flickering in his expression.

Owen stilled. "What?"

"Nothing, just that you'd be an idiot to pass."

Truer words had never been spoken. She was not only the most qualified person for the job, she was smart and sharp, and had the right temperament to train a new manager. Plus, he trusted her. Only she wasn't sticking around more than a couple months, just long enough to get under his skin and then be on her way. While that worked great for the bar, he wasn't so sure how that would affect him. Or his next steps.

Owen's first rule of business was never mix the two Ps. Professional and personal. He took it as far as passing on social events with his employees. Oh, they occasionally invited him to some after-hours fun, but he always declined. It was a bad decision to cross that line. And he worked hard to avoid bad decisions.

Rhett flashed a grin. "You don't want to hire her because you like her."

He didn't want to hire her because then he couldn't sleep with her. And when he looked at it that way, he was a jackass. He knew she needed the money and he needed a manager, even if it was just a temporary fix.

"What, is this third grade?" he asked. "I'm just being thorough. Making sure she's the right fit." She was the perfect fit—in more ways than one.

"Then why does her résumé look like you've mooned over it?" Rhett set it back on the desk. "And since when do you dodge a woman?"

"Since, if I hired her, she'd be working for me."

"So, you essentially cockblocked yourself by procrastination," Rhett said, a big grin from ear to ear. Owen sliced a glare at Rhett out of the corner of his eye, which only made the asshole laugh harder. "What? Had you hired someone when we first talked about it, you wouldn't be in this situation."

No, he wouldn't be. So there he was, neck deep in a problem of his own making. He liked problems almost as much as he liked complications. His work life was complicated enough without adding his personal life into the mix.

In fact every time his personal life even smelled a complication, he broke out in hives.

"Have you called her references?" Josh asked, saving Rhett from a punch to the face.

"Every one. All glowing reviews." All eleven of them.

It seemed as if Abi hadn't gotten over her tumbleweed of a childhood. Besides her teaching job, which she'd been at for four years, she'd hopped from state to state, job to job, never seeming to stick in one place for very long.

It answered the question of why, if her sister was here, she'd want to move on so quickly. If he'd been in an accident, his family would rally around him, even cuffing him to a chair if he tried to bail before he'd fully recovered. And while Abi's body would be healed, the scars inside would take a lot longer.

"What does your gut say?" Josh asked.

"That I'd be an idiot to pass."

Chapter Thirteen

Happy Things:
Unexpected adventures

A scream thundered and Abi jerked up straight on the couch, her heart racing as if she'd just finished a two-day sex-a-thon with her potential new boss. Not that she'd been dreaming of Owen. It had been that nightmare. The same damn nightmare that had haunted her for the past few months.

Abi had thought that coming home would keep the horror at bay, but it had followed her from Mobile. She was beginning to fear it would follow her wherever she landed.

"Let go of your sister, young man," she heard Dotti say. "She is not a toy to be dragged around."

By the frequency and pitch of the wails, Lemon-Marie agreed.

Lemon-Marie!

Abi leaped up off the couch. She'd promised to make the kids breakfast and get them ready for daycare. And it was after seven. She must have slept through her alarm. Surprising, since she didn't sleep more than an hour in any one stretch.

Nightmares weren't just for sleep. They lurked around every corner of Abi's world, which was getting smaller and smaller. In the past Abi had been big on adventures and travel, teaching English in Costa Rica and yoga in Fiji. She'd also seen a good chunk of the states. But her world had shrunk to three square miles. If she couldn't get there by bike, then it wasn't happening.

Abi raced into the kitchen to find Dotti standing at the counter. She was wearing fluffy socks, baggy sweats, and a Y'ALL GONNA MAKE ME LOSE MY MIND T-shirt that had dried pancake batter on the hem. Instead of being smooth and styled, her blonde hair was doing a duster impersonation and her expression said the zombie apocalypse had arrived and she'd been turned.

"I am so sorry I slept in," Abi said.

"I kept them quiet as long as I could," Dotti explained, like she was the one who'd been at fault. "I took Koi's pull–fire engine away so he's takin' to pulling around his sister. How has this become my life?"

"It will get better," Abi promised.

"When?" Dotti looked near tears, so Abi did what she hadn't done since she was little and she took her sister's hand. And to her surprise, Dotti fell into her arms.

"Honestly, I don't know." She gave her sister's back an awkward pat. "But I do know this is a phase."

Dotti wiped her nose on Abi's shirt. "I just need another cup of coffee. Then I'll be on my A game."

Abi took the empty coffee pot and held it up. "Was this full this morning?"

She looked in her empty cup. "I don't know."

"I have some good news. I got another job so I can have my half of the mortgage by the end of the week."

Dotti sat at the island, arms folded on the countertop, head resting on her hands. "Only strippers make that kind of money in a week. And you don't have the skills, so what is this new job?"

"I'm a substitute."

"And what kind of substitute makes a grand in one week?"

"A substitute manager slash bartender slash businesswoman extraordinaire?"

"Did you put a question mark at the end of that?"

Abi picked up a rag and started doing the piles of dishes. "Because I haven't officially landed it, but I know I will."

Dotti lifted her head and shot a look Abi's way that had her shifting her weight. "Would this manager slash bartender slash businesswoman extraordinaire be at Stout, working for a man who has no idea who you are?"

Even though she had been a stupid seventeen-year-old, she made a decision that altered an entire family's world. And all for selfish reasons.

"When are you going to tell him?" Dotti asked.

She should have told him right away; it would have been easier. Now she'd dug a deeper hole and she knew that the moment she admitted the truth he'd kick her out of his life and then how would she make his world easier?

The countdown had already begun. Abi was leaving at the end of next month for Thailand, where she'd hopefully find her footing in teaching again, so what was the harm in waiting another few weeks?

"I need to get right with the universe first."

As if Fate herself had come down and given Abi a high-five to the forehead, there was a knock at the door. Without even peeking through the window, she knew who it was.

"Aren't you going to answer that?" Dotti asked.

"You're closer," she accused.

When she didn't move, Dotti rolled her eyes, then went to look out the peephole. "The universe is telling you that it's time to spill the beans."

Abi backed away from the door. "I like my beans just where they're at. In a can. And everyone knows what happens when you open a can of beans."

"It's worms. A can of worms."

"To-may-to, to-mah-to."

"I can hear you," a voice came through the door. A panty-melting voice that was laced with humor. "I know you have work at the tea shop in an hour. I can wait you out or you can answer the door."

Before Abi could climb out the window, Dotti swung open the door. "Morning. I guess I'll leave you two to it." And Dotti walked away, disappearing into the burrow of the house while Koi followed, dragging Lemon-Marie around like a caveman. Leaving Abi alone with Owen.

"Cute kids."

"You should ee them during a sugar rush."

He was looking fine in a pair of jeans that hugged his muscular thighs, a fitted black shirt that had the bar's logo on the front and EASTON across the back like a jersey, and a ball cap pulled low on his head. She, on the other hand, was in bare feet, bedhead, and an oversized T-shirt. No bra. No bottoms.

He seemed a little edgy and a little conflicted, and just looking at him got her hot and bothered in places she shouldn't be hot and bothered.

His gaze tracked from her eyes to her toes, and she knew when he figured out she wasn't wearing a bra. She crossed her arms over her chest.

"You just made my morning," he said, and she glanced down to see that her shirt had stretched over her respectable Bs, showcasing that her nipples were hard.

"It's cold."

"If you say so."

Aware that the house was small and the walls were paper-thin, Abi stepped out onto the stoop and closed the door behind her. "What do you want?"

"To offer you the job."

"I'm hired?" Her heart leaped and fell at the same time. On the one hand, she was going to be able to take some of the responsibility off his shoulders. On the other, she'd have to see him every day, knowing she was keeping a secret.

"I can train you faster than anyone else."

"And you're okay with me leaving at the end of next month?"

"That works for me." As he said it, her heart gave a little ping of sadness. She knew she was leaving, knew he was right to think that way, but he was okay with her leaving, even going as far as to say it worked for him. It was ridiculous to feel a slip of rejection, but she felt it all the same. "I train you, then you help me find and train a replacement."

Her replacement.

"You know, you don't *have* to hire me." Why was she backpedaling? This was what she'd been working toward. "I won't stop being your friend or anything."

He took that in for a moment. "Is that what we are? Just friends?"

"I hope so," she said quietly, ignoring the "just" part. After that kiss, she wanted more. But wanting and doing were no longer going to exist in the same realm in her life.

He studied her for a long moment, his eyes warm and soft. "I want to hire you. I should have said that the moment I read your résumé."

"Thank you," she whispered.

"But there are conditions."

She swallowed. "What kind of conditions?"

"If you come to work for me, we have to keep it friends only."

"You mean no benefits?"

His gaze fell to her lips. "No kissing, no touching, no benefits."

"No benefits then," she agreed, shifting closer.

"I don't want to complicate things." His voice said he wanted to get all kinds of complicated with her and what was beneath her shirt.

"No complications." She moved even closer as if being sucked into his sexy vortex. "I have some conditions too."

H grinned. "You do?"

"It's only fair that I get one."

His lips quirked. "Is this a shakedown?"

"No, this is me adding my own addendum to the agreement."

"That's fair."

"When our time is up and I leave, I want you to remember that we were friends." Man, that was a selfish request. When she told him the truth, he'd have every right to walk away and never talk to her again. But she just hoped that a small part of him would think back to this moment, and all the moments they'd shared, before the extent of her deceit was aired.

"I'll remember everything about you."

"Including why you hired me, which is because I make your life easier." She needed to hear him say it so that no matter what, he'd remember at least that part.

"I'm hiring you because I trust you and I trust your judgment."

As if someone had entered her into the Ice Bucket Challenge, she pulled back. Because if that wasn't a sign to fess up, then she didn't know what was. Owen was all about trust and honesty and, while she hadn't lied, she'd been keeping things from him.

Things that would end their "just" friendship. A friendship she didn't deserve. Not even a tiny bit. This was it, the time she'd been both anticipating and dreading, the time to come clean. Only before she could say anything, he cupped her face and made her look at him. She couldn't remember her name let alone the million and one reasons why kissing him again was a no-no. But then his eyes softened and his touch was ever so gentle, making her feel like she was the most precious thing in his whole world.

"I'm going to kiss you now."

"What happened to just friends?" she whispered—to his mouth.

"You don't start until Monday." He lowered his head and when he was a breath away, he said, "Unless you've changed your mind."

She'd known that he'd eventually hire her because no matter how crazy she drove him, he needed her. Bad. Almost as bad as she needed to make this right between them. "I won't."

"My conditions still stand."

"So do mine."

He gave a single, short nod and she sucked in a breath. His expression was purposefully blank, his attitude dialed to easygoing, but there was an edge to him now.

He cupped her hips and tugged her closer. "Your contract ends a week before you leave."

"Why?"

"Because that's how long we're going to test this 'just friends' theory of yours."

Her heart skipped a beat. "And when the week is up?"

He hesitated, just long enough to send her mind into a spiral. "You're leaving; I'm not in a place where I can commit to more. A week is all I can handle."

She knew this. But hearing it still sent a ping of disappointment cascading through her body. Hearing that it was all he could handle was a painful throwback to comments her parents had made over the years. Logically she knew he didn't mean it that way, but her heart said differently.

"Me too. After I finish things here I'm going to Thailand," she said. Her job in Asia was supposed to be a self-imposed expiration date that insured her ability to maintain emotional distance. A fail-safe to prevent her from making a stupid decision—like giving into a seven-day sex-cation with the man she was crushing on.

The smart thing to do would be to walk away with her heart intact. Only she wasn't thinking all that smart right then. In fact, she wasn't thinking at all when she said, "A week it is."

"I am going to use every spare moment getting to know each and every inch of your body," he said, all confidence and swagger.

And he had every reason to be confident. He was a kissing god. Skilled and practiced, he delivered slow, panty-melting kisses, each one lasting an eternity. Each one making it harder to let go.

As she saw it, a conflict of interest plus an expiration date equated to one epically bad idea, but she was feeling a little naughty right then, so she slid her arms around his neck and, even though she knew she'd flash the neighborhood her cheeky-cut undies, she kissed the hell out of Owen Easton.

Chapter Fourteen

Happy Things:
Holding hands

Abi stood on a rose-lined path looking across the massive green lawn which was speckled with yellow leaves from the turning maples. It was hard to imagine that someplace so beautiful could bring on such sadness.

The last time Abi had visited a cemetery was six years ago for her grandmother's funeral. Now she was back, but Ruth wasn't the only reason Abi had come. She was there to pay respects to someone she'd never met.

When Abi showed up for her morning shift at Sip Me yesterday, there had been a name and number on her sign-up sheet, the wish unspecified. So Abi had called the number, reaching an elderly woman named simply Ms. S, who had a story as heartwarming as it was heart-wrenching. And it hit a little too close to home for Abi's liking. Which was why she'd been standing on the pathway for the past ten minutes staring at Mr. S's grave from afar.

Abi had become a pro procrastinator.

Even the drizzle hadn't lit a fire under her. She was cold and shivering and still hadn't made a move. She knew that today's good deed would be the hardest one thus far. It was going to be an emotional gut punch.

Abi pulled her coat tighter. Actually, it was Owen's coat that he'd lent her, and she'd *forgotten* to return. And when she turned upwind his manly scent teased her, making her wet in places that had zilch to do with Portland's seasonal rainfall.

Ms. S was a widow who'd lost her husband and soulmate over a decade ago. In their fifty-three-year marriage they'd never spent a single night apart. She still lived in the same Victorian Mr. S had surprised her with on their wedding day and still set his place around the dinner table. And on Saturday, without fail, she'd revisit how they used to sit on the front porch, hold hands, split a cold beer, and share the happenings of their week.

After his passing, Ms. S simply moved the location to the cemetery so she could be with him. She'd bring a beer, just one, and drink exactly half, watering his grave with the leftover.

Only today, Ms. S was unable to make the trip. After last week's hip surgery she was housebound, which was how Abi ended up with the enduring task of paying Mr. S a visit.

Armed with a beer and a letter that Ms. S had prepared, Abi had walked the three blocks to the cemetery. Her mission was simple—share a beer with Mr. S. She didn't need to open the letter to know that the contents were private and personal, a love letter between two people who had found the real deal.

The whole ordeal made Abi feel like a fake. There she was at the cemetery to talk to a man she'd never met, take part in a cherished ceremony, yet she'd never made it to Jenny's grave. The closest she'd come was sending a bouquet to Jenny's parents the week of the funeral. Abi had been in the hospital when Jenny had been buried and she had promised herself that she'd go visit Jenny as soon as she was better.

And while Abi was up and walking, she didn't feel better. Not one bit. Certainly not well enough to face her role in her best friend's death. Which was why today was so hard.

Unsure what to do, she approached the grave site and looked up at the sky as if expecting to find some answers in the clouds. Answers? Not a one. Sheets of rain? There were plenty.

Uncertainty gripped her around the throat, leaving her a little shaky and off balance. Was she supposed to leave the letter on the headstone or sit in the wet grass and share a beer with a man she'd never met? And if the wish was to ensure that Mr. S wasn't alone, then Abi would have to do some sharing of her own. And that scared her more than being surrounded by dead people.

"You'd know what to do," she whispered to the heavens. Not only would Jenny know what to do, she'd have found a way to bring Ms. S to the cemetery. It wasn't like Abi could balance the older woman on her handlebars and getting into a rideshare with her hip wasn't an option.

Which left Abi all by her lonesome with no other choice than to pull up a piece of grass and share her week with a stranger.

Heart heavy, she took a step toward the headstone, only her brain must have misfired because she ended up moving backward. She tried again with the same results. On the third step she was about to admit defeat when she bumped into a strong, unwavering wall.

Even before she looked up, she knew who'd be looking back. Owen. They were front to back, thigh to thigh, and everything in between.

Oh boy.

She wasn't sure if she was grateful for the company or embarrassed, because now he knew, that on top of everything else, she was a coward. She calculated just how fast she could run if she took off at a dead sprint, then remembered the half-marathon she'd spent hyperventilating behind the Mommy Marathon group and sighed.

She prepared herself for a tsunami of sexy and turned. *Sweet baby Jesus,* sexy didn't cover it. He was big and wet and wearing nothing more than athletic shorts, a black T-shirt, and tattoos. Lots of muscles with strategically placed tattoos.

And a smile. A warm and encouraging smile. She considered all the things he could possibly say, but not a single scenario involved, "Nice coat."

"Huh?"

Amusement danced in those big blue pools. "Nice coat."

"Right." She slid down the zipper. "I was meaning to return it." She started to take it off when his hands covered hers, stilling them, then zipping her up tight.

"It looks better on you." His gaze ran the length of her, which admittedly wasn't very far since she barely reached his chest. "What are you doing standing in the rain?"

"Procrastinating. Apparently, it's what I'm good at."

His blue eyes were soft, his expression warm. "You could have asked for a ride."

Well, if that didn't make her heart go *pitter-patter.* "I'm still practicing my cycling skills. At this rate, I'll be ready to do my first Iron Man by Christmas."

"Or be inducted into the Good Samaritan Hall of Fame."

Or the Big Fat Liars Club. "How did you know I was here?"

"I have my ways," he said mysteriously. "Actually, it was the sign-up sheet at Sip Me. When you weren't working this morning, I glanced at the list. Picked the one I thought would speak to you the most."

She blinked in surprise. "And you found me?"

"I was stuck between either helping someone named Fred, who needed you to transport a case of lube across state lines, or helping Marcy, who wanted someone to laugh really loud from the front row at her stand-up routine, when your coworker told me where you went."

"Mary," Abi groaned. "I can't believe she told you."

"I can be very persuasive."

Didn't she know it.

"Am I right? Is this another Good Deed by Abi?"

She narrowed her eyes at him. "Are you fishing for information from my coworkers?"

"I thought about it, and while I was tempted, I decided I'd rather learn about you from you."

She looked up at him. His eyes were assessing, his lashes spiked with rain, and his damp shirt stuck to his impressive chest. It was wet and cold and yet he'd come to find her. "What do you want to know?"

"Whatever you're willing to share."

She wasn't sure what she wanted to share but she wanted it to be real.

She'd never met anyone like Owen. Abi's life had always been on other people's terms. Starting with her family and the way she was moved back and forth like some kind of timeshare kid.

With older kids of her own, her stepmom didn't have much interest in stepmom-ing a younger child, so on the days Abi was at her dad's she was responsible for herself. She started walking to school in kindergarten, making her lunches by first grade, and sweet-talking other kids' parents for rides to school when it rained before she was tall enough to see over the counter at the grog shop where she'd buy her dad's cigarettes.

Because of the constant inconsistency in her life, Abi didn't have the chance until high school to be a part of the thousand-and-one extracurricular activities Dotti and her brother had access to. But by that time all the other kids already formed their "activity" cliques, so Abi found herself once again struggling to be a part of something important.

The more frequent the handoffs, the more Abi got lost in the shuffle, the louder she became until it was just background noise. She was just background noise. Then there were the men of boyfriends past, who were drawn to Abi's larger than life personality, only to say she was a *too much too soon* kind of gal. Which made her nervous about showing Owen all her cards.

She didn't want to be too much to handle but she also didn't want to be glossed over. She'd like to think that with age she'd learned that she didn't need to be the center of attention, she just wanted to be the center of one person's world.

"I'm nervous about opening this." She held up the letter. "And I'm tempted to call Ms. S back and lie that I can't do it today. Or tomorrow. Or any of the days." Man, that was hard to admit. She looked up at the sky and groaned. "I swear that I didn't use to be a coward."

"I don't think you're a coward," he said softly.

She met his gaze. "You don't?" Because she did.

"You've had a rough few months. No one would fault you for wanting a little easy in your life. Especially me."

"You don't take the easy way out."

The resignation in his eyes broke her heart. "I can't. Family. You understand."

But she didn't—not really. Her family was more of a make your own path sort than a tight-knit unit. Every family had their issues, but when it came to Abi and her parents, their relationship was fractured. She was different from her siblings, a product of an affair. Her mom and stepdad worked through it, putting the betrayal in the past, but Abi was a reminder of that painful time. Her parents had never said that, but Abi always felt the tension follow her. After graduation, Abi went her own way. Her parents called it moxie.

Abi called it self-preservation.

"You could take the easy way out," she said quietly. "But you choose not to. For your family. I like that about you."

"I like a lot about you." He took her hand and placed the gentlest of kisses on her palm, then laced their fingers.

"This 'just friends' thing is going to be hard."

"Everything about this makes me hard," he teased, and she laughed. She realized that was his intention when his lips quirked. "You can still change your mind about the job."

"And choose the easy way out? What's the fun in that?"

She didn't know how he did it, but one minute she was near tears and the next she was laughing. Even taking the hard way with him was fun.

"Fair enough. Then how about you tell me what our good deed is for the day."

"*Our?* As in some superhero team that saves the world one good deed at a time?" The thought made her heart skip a beat.

"As long as I get to wear the cape and you wear those tight pants, I'm game."

Chapter Fifteen

Happy Things:
Knowing that if plan A fails,
there are 25 more letters in the alphabet

Monday morning Abi stood outside Stout feeling a mix of emotions. She had woken at five to make sure the kids could watch their morning shows and Hank could move about the house freely. That he did it in his boxers was his passive-aggressive way of voicing his opinion on Abi overstaying her welcome.

She did her best to ignore him or the way it made her feel and focus her energy on the day ahead. It was the official start of her time as Stout's independent contractor tasked with hiring new staff and fixing Owen's life. Not that his life was broken, but it definitely had fractures.

Wanting to make a good first impression, she dressed the part. In a pair of pressed black pants, a light-pink blouse, and her dressiest cowgirl boots, she looked like a proper training manager. She'd even done her hair and makeup, brushing on a little mascara and lip gloss, before begging Dotti for a ride. The last thing she wanted was to show up to work looking as if she's just ridden in a BMX championship.

Even with all the preparation, Abi was almost late. Oh, Dotti had dropped her at the curb fifteen minutes ago, but

Abi was still standing under the bar's awning, contemplating turning tail. But Jenny had other plans, sending a pair of kamikaze hummingbirds Abi's way. They buzzed her head twice, the third time going for the jugular.

They were setting up house in a light fixture near the back door and wouldn't leave Abi alone, forcing her to go through the entrance and into the bar. Which was how she found herself at the doorway to Owen's office.

He sat behind his desk, a pair of glasses perched on his nose. His lips were in a hard line and his attention was laser-focused on his laptop screen. His shirt was wrinkled, his hair stood on end as if he'd been worrying his hands through it, and the scruff on his jaw made Abi wonder if he'd slept at all last night.

Her heart went out to him. He might not want to admit it, but he needed her.

"I was wondering how long you were going to stand in the morning fog," he said moments before their eyes locked and held.

"You were watching me?"

"It's a growing problem." He looked at her as if the whole situation was her fault, which made her want to laugh. Maybe it had been a few weeks ago, but after that third kiss, he was as much to blame as she. She considered explaining how this whole two-sided attraction thing worked, but instead she studied him, surprised to realize that she threw him completely off-kilter.

Not sure what to do with that information, she pulled a bag out of her backpack. "I brought freshly made apple spice muffins." She set the bag on his desk. He opened it, peeked inside, and then the most amazing thing happened.

He grinned. A boyish grin that completely transformed his face. "Portland by way of Abilene?"

"Stout by way of Sip Me," she admitted, and he laughed. A real one. "But they are the best in the city, I promise."

He popped a chunk into his mouth and groaned in ecstasy. She wondered if that's what he sounded like in bed. As if sensing where her mind was headed, he held out his next bite. "Want a piece?"

Yes. Yes, she did and, damn the man, he knew it. "I already ate," she said primly.

"You're here early. I wasn't expecting you until later."

Which explained the state of the office.

"Interviews start tomorrow so I need to begin calling and scheduling people. Plus, I wanted to get a picture of what I was looking at."

She looked around the room. Besides the desk, which had more piles than surface space, there were two chairs, a masculine leather couch, which was outdated but cared for, and a massive cabinet housing a vintage beer stein collection. The walls were lined with autographed photos of famous people smiling with an older man. In fact, other than his desk and three tea mugs, which were scattered around in different states of emptiness, the office was actually fairly clean and tidy.

She walked over to get a closer look at the photos. There was everyone from Johnny Cash to Adam Levine to the Jonas Brothers, and in each one was a man of various ages, with a warm and welcoming smile. Owen's smile.

"Is that your dad?" she asked.

"Yeah." He stood and walked up behind her. "He had this open way about him that made people feel special. He knew every regular by name, knew about their family, their struggles. I'm surprised he managed to keep the bar running with his on-the-house habit. Everyone loved Benji Easton."

"I'd heard that famous people played here, but I had no idea."

"My dad was intimidatingly large and could command the room. But he had this generous spirit about him, this amazing capacity for kindness that drew people to him."

Like father like son, she thought.

"He could sweet-talk just about anyone to play a set, then pair nobodies with somebodies in hopes of giving up-and-comers their first big chance. It was the same with other people in his life, always handing out second and third opportunities to get it right. He never gave up on others. Ever. 'Everyone makes mistakes, son. But not everyone gets a second chance,' he used to say."

"Do you believe that?"

He let out a rough breath before answering. "I hope so. I mean, one time he caught one of his oldest employees selling stolen booze out of the back of the bar, and you know what he said? That the guy needed the money more than we did."

"Did he fire him?"

"No, he gave the guy a raise." Owen chuckled. "He always believed the best in people, even when they didn't deserve his grace. He went out of his way to make their lives a little easier." He looked down at Abi. "He would have liked you."

"I don't know about that," Abi said. She'd like to think that Benji would have forgiven her for her part in the lawsuit, but she feared that Owen wouldn't extend that same generosity. Not after he discovered it was her deposition that gave the assistant district attorney what he needed to move forward.

Of its own will, her gaze skittered toward the exit, then back to the sexy and insurmountable boulder that stood between her and freedom. She felt her breath hitch—and not in a good way. Her chest tightened ever so slightly, pissing off her lungs. It wasn't panic that had her by the throat, it was a complicated knot of guilt and remorse.

"Abi?" was all he said, but the concern nearly undid her.

So she pushed every stupid emotion down into her DEAL WITH IT LATER box, which hadn't been opened since the summer before her freshman year in high school. When showing off for the football team, she performed a swan dive. Except when she resurfaced, she shot out of the water unaware she'd lost her bikini top. From that day forward she became known as A-Cup Abi.

Before he could ask what was wrong, she plastered a smile on her face. "So, where do you need me?"

He looked at the couch.

"Business not pleasure, remember?"

"So, you didn't change your mind?" he asked.

Her smile faded. "You sound disappointed?"

His eyes raked her body and she let him look. She might be small, but she was curvy and dressed to use it to her advantage. Today she'd carefully chosen her outfit for maximum effect. Seemed Owen approved. "Conflicted but not disappointed."

"Me too," she said quietly, and his gaze jumped to hers. It held for a long, heated beat before he sat back down in the office chair.

"What's your game plan?"

She glanced around and sighed. This good deed wasn't going to be as cut and dry as she'd originally thought. She could run his bar and hire a new staff with her eyes closed. Being in such proximity to Owen, hearing about his life and not falling for him, would take a herculean effort on her part.

"Before I can hand things off to a new manager, we need to get organized."

"Fair enough. Where do you want to start?" he asked.

"How about with this." She waved her hand over his desk where, based on the mountains and mountains of paperwork, she had her work cut out for her.

"I'm working on scheduling interviews."

She moved behind the desk and gave him a shove with her hip. "Now you're working on catching some sleep before opening."

"That's not happening."

"Which part? Your beauty rest or me doing my job?" He opened his mouth. "Be careful with your next words."

"I'm not big on letting someone else do my job."

"You mean you're a control freak," she said, patting him on the shoulder. He defiantly crossed his massive arms and, *sweet mother of God,* his biceps needed their own area code. "Good thing you have me so that you don't have to worry about anything. Now move or I'll have you removed."

This seemed to amuse him because he dug in further until a category five hurricane couldn't budge this man. But she knew what could. "I have your mother's number and I was told to use it if you become difficult."

He blanched. "I don't even want to know how you got my mom's number."

"I'm persuasive," she said, using his words from the day at the cemetery. "And I'm good at my job." She took his hand to pull him to his feet. When he still didn't budge, she said, "Humor me."

He stood but made it clear that his humor was thin, then held out the chair for her. When she moved to sit, they bumped. She shifted the other way and they bumped again, like two magnets unable to stay apart.

No matter where she moved, there he was. His massive body took up the small space and his scent was all over her even though they'd hadn't so much as touched. Normally, she was a personal space kind of person, and after the accident "room to breathe" had taken on a whole new meaning. But being in such close quarters with Owen and his big, beautiful bod brushing hers with nearly every breath had her close to her first public orgasm.

One more strategically placed slide of the body and she'd go off like a firework.

"Now, where do you want me to sit?" she repeated his question from earlier.

"Is that a trick question?" He smiled and she rolled her eyes.

"Let me rephrase. How can I best help you?"

His grin was alive and spreading—all the way to her belly. "Again, not sure how you want me to respond."

"How about you go sit there." She pointed to the couch and waited until he was seated a good five feet from her before she took a seat. She folded her hands on the desktop and glanced over the screen. "You're working out next month's schedule."

"And the software sucks. Hell, if you can fix it, then you're hired."

"I'm already hired. And I have no doubt I can fix it." It was the same software they'd used at the wine bar she'd managed, and it was as user-friendly as programs came.

"If you say so." He leaned back on the couch and stretched out, his legs so long they pushed up against the desk. His head was leaned back, his eyes closed, and his arms were spread across the back of the couch. He looked deceivingly relaxed and comfortable, but she knew he could pounce at any moment.

He wasn't sleeping, more like making a point. Because ten minutes in, when Abi was completely lost, he mumbled, "Problem?" in this know-it-all tone that was like a rough piece of chalk on a blackboard.

Yes, there was an enormous problem, she just wasn't sure how to go about the solution. It wasn't the software, it was a procedure problem.

"Nope." She popped that P. "Just wondering though, what's the company policy on time off." Because as far as she could tell the policy was to write time-off requests on a memo note and stick it to the desk. And there were a lot.

There was a stack of pink slips tacked under a paperweight. Some were future requests, others as old as six months back.

"We're an employee's satisfaction first kind of company." She looked up and, yup, the innuendo was intentional.

"I'm an independent contractor," she pointed out. "Not that it matters."

"Not that it matters."

Tuning him out, she went back to scheduling, and he went back to fake sleeping. "Huh," was all she said.

He cracked open one eye. "Huh, what?"

"Nothing."

He narrowed his gaze and when she didn't elaborate, he stood and walked around the desk, looking at the computer over her shoulder. He was close, too close.

"Go ahead." He bent over her, resting a palm on the desk, his arm brushing her shoulder, his body's heat slipping through her shirt. She nearly groaned. "Explain the 'huh,'" he pressed.

"It's just that your system isn't working as effectively as it could."

"What do you mean, it 'isn't working as effectively as it could'? It's worked fine for thirty years." Which meant he'd adopted his dad's methods of keeping records and managing his employees. With the exception of maintaining the website, Owen had his hand in every pot.

"Your system is to scribble time-off requests and schedule swaps on sticky notes." She held up a cocktail napkin. "I can't even read this one."

He snatched it, then grinned. "This is personal, not business."

She snatched it back and squinted at the cramped writing. "Candy. Call if you want a lick," she read. "Do you think it's her real name?"

"There's only one way to find out." He reached for the office phone, but she pushed the hang-up button. "What happened to never mixing business and pleasure?"

"Just because a beautiful lady gives me her number doesn't mean I'll call."

"You called me."

He laughed, the sound dangerously low. "I did. Then you steamrolled me into hiring you."

She spun the chair until she was facing him. Big mistake. The motion placed her in a precarious situation. She could feel his smile, so she stood. Not that there was room. It was as if his body filled all the space in the room.

Arms crossed, Abi tilted her head back, all the way back until she was certain he could see her glaring.

"Not even Zeus himself could steamroll you."

"Then I guess I have a sweet spot for angels. It must be the sexy halo."

"Angels don't wear sexy."

"Mine does."

She knew he found her attractive, but sexy? That wasn't an adjective normally associated with Abi. This new information ignited a few unwelcomed belly flutters.

Stupid flutters.

"Do you grant every time-off request?" she asked.

"Not every request." He went from flirty to defensive in point-zero-zero-one seconds, telling her everything she needed to know.

"You gave personal time off to Bryce and Jake for the same three-day weekend, leaving Nora behind the bar alone." She held up the scribbled sticky note.

Not that Nora couldn't handle herself. In Abi's opinion, Nora was the front-runner for the new manager position. But she couldn't be sure until she'd finished interviewing, which would take the entire week. The salary alone was enough for people to want to apply.

He shrugged. "They both had reasonable excuses. Plus, if we're short then I can cover."

"You're the owner, your job is to make sure they have what they need to be successful, not do it for them. Plus, you need some Owen time. Which nights are your nights off?" Abi asked and Owen stared at her blankly. "None. Got it. Well, Monday nights are your official night off. You are persona non grata."

He rested a hip against the desk. "Monday night is football. The bar is packed, the line's around the corner, and gets rowdy."

"I can handle rowdy." And she could. One of the benefits of being on her own for so long, Abi could handle herself in almost any situation. She'd backpacked across most of Europe and Asia, sometimes with a tour group, but mostly on her own. And while she'd been alone, she'd never felt lonely—until she'd returned to Portland. But this time things would be different. "Plus, I think I already have a beat on a new manager."

Instead of feeling comforted by the idea, he looked unsettled. "You've been here twenty minutes and already you've solved all my problems."

"Problem," she corrected. "I don't think there's enough time in the world to solve the mystery that is Owen Easton. Hiring a new, capable, trustworthy manager? That I have a handle on."

He glanced at the piles of paper. "You haven't even looked at a single application."

"Don't need to. You've had the perfect person right under your nose."

He grinned. "You?"

"I'm about as close to perfect as Oregon is to Alabama, but thank you for the compliment," she said. "Plus, I don't have enough tattoos to work the front of the house."

"I have enough for the both of us."

She took a beat. "Are you promoting me from independent contractor to manager?"

"You still leaving next month?"

"Yes."

He didn't even consider it. "That doesn't work for me."

Right.

"Me either." This was a get-in, get-out kind of job and she would do well to remember that. Her time here was nothing more than an extended good deed. Didn't mean that his comment didn't feel like a rejection.

He lifted his gaze to her in question. "But Nora works perfectly," she said, referring to the most senior bartender.

He stared at her, his expression one of pure consideration, then he shrugged. "I like Nora."

"Good. She's been here five years, knows the bar almost as well you, and is already interviewing at places across town."

That bit of information had him looking panicked, which was the appropriate response for someone whose business would collapse if he lost one more employee. "How do you know this?"

"She told me."

He didn't appear to believe her. "She just came out and said, 'Oh hey, by the way, I'm entertaining other offers?'"

"Actually, she said she'd just come from an interview at the Whiskey Depository."

He relaxed. "She'd hate it there and she knows it."

"She needs the money," Abi said. "I asked her why she wasn't applying for the manager position, since it was open and she was clearly more than qualified. She mentioned that she'd brought it up to you in passing and you weren't responsive."

"She asked for more responsibility, so I let her close a night or two and…" he broke off and groaned. "And I'm an idiot."

"That was my assessment too."

He ran a hand down his face. "She's never managed before. Do you think you could train her in the time you have?"

"I know I can." She closed the laptop. "Just like I know that overlooking her as a candidate was a mistake. It may have been unintentional, but still a mistake." When he didn't say a word, she nudged his thigh with her hand. "You don't make mistakes." When he didn't deny it, she stood and sat next to him on the desk. "If you don't like running this bar, why don't you sell?"

He froze. "Who says I don't like running the bar?"

"The stress lines around your eyes." She ran a finger down his jaw. "That you don't smile when you talk about it."

"I smile."

"Not the real kind."

This information didn't seem to take him by surprise. He let out a breath. "This was my dad's place. I couldn't stomach selling it."

That was a kick to her heart. "Then why did he leave it to you?"

"He left it to the six of us, but I was the only one available to run it."

"For eight years?" He'd not only sacrificed his time but also his dream of running his own shop.

"As soon as I walk away, my dad will forever be gone. Every last trace."

Abi tried to imagine what it would feel like to be so close to one's family that they were willing to walk away from their dream to keep someone else's dream alive. But she couldn't. Her parents weren't big on dreams, they were more practical, wanting Abi to go into finance or medicine instead of psychology, especially because she wanted to be a teacher not a psychologist. "If you could leave, what would you do?"

"Open my own tattoo shop." He paused. "How about you?"

"Go back to teaching. I have a job waiting for me teaching English to corporate types overseas." Far away from the disappointment of her parents.

"Would you ever consider working with kids again?"

"No." She refused to look at him. "Would you ever consider going back to tattooing?"

"I think about it all the time," he admitted. "That was the big plan when my dad got sick and I had to put it on hold."

It took her a moment to speak through the guilt. It was one thing to feel bad about what she'd done to his dad. It was another to see how Owen had suffered because of it. She'd started this dangerous game of deceit and now she didn't know how to get out of it. "Do you still tattoo?"

He shrugged. "When I can. I rent space across town. But it's been a while."

"Were you an art major?"

"Most people think I was a high school dropout. But yes, I studied in fine arts."

"I've always wanted a tattoo." Something to remember Jenny by.

His eyes tracked down her body and his voice went gruff. "Where?"

With him resting against the desk and her next to him, the space seemed to shrink even further. He didn't move away, which she found interesting—and a bit arousing.

His gaze dropped to her chest.

She laughed. "Not there."

She turned until her back was to him, then tugged her blouse down her shoulder a little, exposing the strip of skin at the base of her neck. "Maybe here." She looked over her shoulder to find his eyes lasered in. She pushed the top further down. "Or here."

Now his gaze was locked on her lips. "Keep going."

"Are you sure?" she breathed, unable to look away.

"No." Even as he said it, his finger traced where hers had touched, then swept her hair to the side. Her heart hitched as his lips brushed gently over her skin. When she thought he was going to kiss lower, he dropped his forehead to her shoulder. "We can't. I can't."

It took her a minute to hear what he was saying. "But we are."

"And I shouldn't have."

"So then why did you?"

He stroked a finger along her cheekbone. "I find you irresistible." He tucked a strand of hair behind her ear, then lingered at her sensitive spot.

She shivered. "Then what's the problem?"

"For starters, you're my employee."

"Correction. I'm an independent contractor."

A very small smile curved his mouth. "I still sign your paycheck."

Dang it, he had her there. "We can work around that. How about you don't pay me? It can be one of those pro-bono projects."

His smile vanished and he stood. "And there's the heart of the problem, Angel. I don't want to be one of your projects."

"Then what do you want to be?" she asked, and so much blood rushed to her ears she thought she might pass out.

"I don't know." He lied. She could tell by the heated look in his eyes that he knew exactly what he wanted from her. And it aligned perfectly with where her mind was at just then. "I guess we're more complicated that I originally thought."

"It doesn't have to be," she said to his sleek, muscled back as he walked out of the room.

Chapter Sixteen

Happy Things:
Giving a standing ovation with one's tallest finger

The following week, Abi was pulling double duty.

Owen had been right, Mondays were crazy. The line was more than around the block and the place was so packed the servers could barely push through the crush. Abi was helping out where she was needed and right then she was needed behind the bar.

With Bryce and Jake enjoying their last night off, Nora was flying solo, handling anything shaken and stirred. So Abi hopped in and took over tap and bottle service. Thankfully she'd lost the wrist brace, but the doctor had given her strict instructions to take it easy. She didn't think holding pitchers of beer would pass as light work, but they were drowning in orders.

"Thanks for believing in me," Nora said. The bartender wore black kick-ass boots, black jeans, a black tank top that read SUCK IT, and the kind of tough-as-knuckles 'tude that could intimidate the leader of a biker gang. She had choppy black hair with blue streaks and was beautiful with an edge. "I thought for sure Owen was going to hire someone with more experience."

"You were the most qualified. You might not have had the title of manager, but you've proven that you can run this bar," Abi said. "Plus, us girls have to stick together."

"Well, I hope you stick with me through all the paperwork end of things. The learning curve is steep."

"You'll get it." And that was the truth. Nora might not have much experience with scheduling and inventory, but she was a quick learner. And Abi had streamlined and worked out most of the kinks in Owen's process. She didn't know if he was happy about it, but he gave her the leeway she needed to make a real change.

"It's like trying to empty the Puget Sound with a straw."

"We're only a week in. You'll get it."

"I hate to interrupt, but Cindy's back," Mandy, the hostess, said. Everyone around Abi groaned.

"Who's Cindy?"

Mandy pointed to a partially naked woman on one of the high tops in the center of the bar, then to a photo of Cindy under a BANNED FOR LIFE sign.

Abi groaned. "I let her in."

Nora, Mandy, and Dale, the bouncer, all looked at each other and said, "Not it." Then three sets of eyes homed in on her, not to mention the eyes of everyone within hearing distance.

"This is your job," she said to Dale.

"Nope. Bar rules. Whoever lets Cindy in has to get Cindy out before the cops come," Dale explained, then mysteriously disappeared. Nora and Mandy were busying themselves with more important matters—like reapplying lipstick. So much for sticking together.

"Fine." Abi tossed her apron beneath the bar and put on her manager in charge smile. She walked under the bar gate and through the crowd. It was a waving sea of jerseys and sports enthusiasts. And tonight, they were enthused because it was the start of basketball season and the Trail Blazers were facing off against their rivals the Los Angeles Lakers.

Even on her tiptoes Abi could barely see over the crowd. Jumping up she caught a glimpse of Cindy and settled on a direction. Ducking beneath people's arms wasn't hard for the five-foot-one substitute-bouncer. She made it in record time, getting there just as Cindy lost her cami top, only leaving her bra and pants. Neither of which Abi wanted to see float through the air.

"Ma'am," Abi said, putting her hands on her hips and standing firm. Cindy didn't even glance her way. Abi cupped her hands over her mouth. "Ma'am, excuse me but you need to come down."

Ma'am didn't give two shits. She reached for her waistband and that's when Abi put her fingers in her lips and blew a whistle loud enough to silence the bar. Even Cindy looked down.

"Ma'am, you have two seconds to decide the direction of your evening. Either you come off the table or I come up."

Cindy welcomed her up, with her middle finger.

"Bless your troublemaking heart." Abi grabbed the back of the chair and climbed up onto the table getting nose to nose with Cindy, which was difficult since the woman had a good five inches on Abi.

She held uncomfortably intense eye contact until Cindy began to squirm a little. Now that she had the woman's attention, Abi said, "Every employee in here is trying hard to do their job and people like you only make it harder. Take me for instance. Tonight is my first night running the bar with my friend Nora over there. We're in a little over our heads, but you don't see me pitchin' a fit."

"You could be in over your head in a kiddie pool."

Abi stretched up to her full height of five-one. "You don't have the market on being the center of attention, you're looking at a champion auctioneer who can outyell you without moving my lips. As for being rude, I have a list for rude people and all you have to do is ask one of my students and they'll tell you it is a list you do not want to be on."

"Ma'am," Cindy purposefully drawled in her best Redneck Abi voice. "Your list can kiss my ass."

"Your choice." Abi looked at the discarded jersey on the floor, then snapped her fingers at Clive, the assistant manager who was afraid of his own shadow. "Can you please hand me that jersey, sir?"

"Um, yes, ma'am."

Clive fetched the jersey and handed it to Abi. She turned to the crowd that had gathered to watch the spectacle that was Cindy. "Show's over, y'all. Go back to your own business." When every single head turned toward the jumbo screens, Abi held up the jersey toward Cindy. "Now, if you don't get off this table and put your clothes back on like a respectable woman, then I will be forced to burn your jersey and mail the ashes back to you in a Ducks box."

Cindy froze. "You can't do that. I'll sue."

"Fine with me. I'll give you all seventy-six dollars that is sitting in my bank account. I bet this jersey cost more."

"It's signed by the last three quarterbacks," Cindy whispered.

"Then maybe you should treat it with better care. Now, it's your call, how is this going to play out, Cindy?" Cindy looked at the rapt crowd and Abi snapped her fingers in front of Cindy's face. "Eyes right here. What's it going to be?"

Cindy looked at her jersey. "I'll get down."

"Ma'am. I'll get down, *ma'am*," Abi corrected.

"I'll get down, ma'am. And I'm sorry for making your night harder."

"Thank you for that." Abi outstretched her hand for a shake and Cindy looked at it like it could bite. "Friends." It took a moment, but Cindy took the olive branch. And when they both got to the floor, Abi said, "Why don't you let me call you an Uber. On me."

"Why?" Cindy asked.

Abi shrugged. "Why not?"

She reached down for her phone, but it was gone. Thinking she left it behind the counter, she backed up and bumped into something solid that smelled amazing. Then two hands settled on her hips.

Oh boy.

"Am I on your list?" Owen whispered into her ear.

She looked up at him and, *bam*, her heart dropped to her toes. "Not that list." She turned but he didn't let go of her hips. "What are you doing here? Tonight is Owen Time."

"How Owen spends Owen Time is decided by Owen, *ma'am*."

She smiled.

"And Owen wanted to come and see how you were doing," he continued.

"I'm managing."

"I can see that." One hand still on her hips, he took her wrist and ran his thumb over the lingering bruise. She cringed, thinking it still looked all kinds of disgusting. "Is it sore?"

She considered lying, then remembered just how bad she was at it. "A little."

"A little like annoying or a little like aching?"

She looked at his chest. "Both. And before you bench me, I'm not doing anything that the doctor didn't clear." He did say light lifting was acceptable and she was holding the pitchers with her good hand. Pouring a glass of wine wasn't heavy lifting, right?

As if seeing right through her, he said, "I still have to finish inventory, do you think you can help me?"

She tugged her hands away, surprised when it moved to his chest. "Absolutely. Tomorrow, when Nora doesn't need me and Owen Time is over, I'd be happy to help."

He didn't seem to like the answer but wisely didn't argue. "Is there anything I can get you?"

She looked from his hand still cupping her hip, then to hers on his pec. "What's on the menu?"

She watched a mirage of emotions cross his face, from desire to horny, ending with honorable. She took a step back and their hands fell to their sides.

"I need to call Cindy an Uber."

"You'd have to actually use your phone to do that," he said, and she gave him a blank look. "I've called you at least a handful of times and all I got was voicemail."

"I must have left it..." She closed her eyes. "I left it in the hands of my niece. She probably called a fascist dictator to plot world domination. That or Elsa from *Frozen* to set up a playdate. Can I use your phone to call Dotti in case she tried to call me? I don't want her to worry."

Owen handed over his phone and Abi texted Dotti that she'd forgotten her phone and if she could bring it to the bar. A manager needed to be available, and that meant making it easy for the owner to get a hold of her.

"Why did you call?" she asked.

"I guess to hear your voice."

Chapter Seventeen

Happy Things:
~~*Puppies.*~~
Litter of puppies

Twenty minutes later, Abi stepped out of the employee entrance that led to the back parking lot. In the near distance, she could see Dotti's car idling. The wind slapped her around, causing her hair to come loose from her ponytail. April had made a showstopping appearance with fog so thick the Tesla's headlights were fuzzy orbs in the distance.

Thinking Dotti would meet her halfway, Abi walked out from under the safety of the overhang and into the drizzle, which made her hair frizz like the tail of a pissed-off cat. Dotti didn't get out of her car, merely drove closer and rolled down her window.

"I so owe you," Abi said when her sister held out Abi's cell phone. Then she looked into the back seat to find her niece and nephew in footsie pajamas, fast asleep in their car seats. "I am so sorry. If I'd known you had the kids, I would have told you not to bother."

"You said it was an emergency," her sister whispered.

"It was," she whispered back. "But… why didn't you just tell me."

"Hank's working late. He's always working late. And now that you're here, he leaves early too. So, I had to wake the kids to bring you your phone. There. Happy?"

No, she wasn't. She felt awful for her part in the fiasco, but Dotti was partly to blame. Her sister did guilt like the president did executive orders—often and with great authority. A fun fact Abi decided to keep to herself, even though all it would have taken was for Dotti to explain the situation. Sometimes, she felt as if Dotti were setting her up to be the bad guy.

Not that Abi needed much help in that department when it came to family. Outsiders though? Abi might not be everyone's cup of tea, but over the years she'd become a master at making friends and influencing people—a side effect of moving from home to home. But while a lot of people considered Abi their best friend, she'd only ever had one best friend.

Jenny.

"Don't worry about picking me up tonight, I'll find a way home," Abi said.

"How? You can't take public transportation. I live too far outside the city for a friend to drop you off. And you can barely afford to pay rent let alone keep taking rideshares. You need to grow up."

"I am a grown-up," she said, having a hard time sounding tough when whispering. "I'm busting my ass to pay my share, which I have." She grimaced. "Or I will when I get my paycheck."

Dotti wiped her eyes and that's when Abi realized her sister was crying. "Oh my god, are you okay? What's wrong?"

"Everything," Dotti said into her hands. "Hank's never home, I feel like a beached whale. I'm in the middle of a hormonal crisis and my emotions are as stable as a nuclear reactor during an earthquake. Why am I having another baby?"

"So you're pregnant?"

"Like a rabbit in spring."

Abi didn't know a lot about being pregnant, other than it made people crazy, but she did know a lot about helping people.

"How about I take tomorrow off. Switch with someone and take the kids to the zoo. I'll even treat you to a spa day, on me. A day to yourself, being pampered, might clear your head."

"While that is sweet, it's only a temporary fix." She handed Abi the cell. "This isn't working, Abs."

"I know," Abi said. "I am so sorry. It won't happen again. I was just in a rush and completely spaced."

She'd spaced because she was spread so thin. She'd covered for Patty at Sip Me, then ran bingo night at the senior center, where she caught Stan and Bertha doing the cupid canoodle in the atrium. She chose not to report it because then she'd have to write a detailed summary of the entire event—and Abi didn't even want to think about Stan's One-Eyed Willie let alone write about it.

Dotti couldn't hold Abi's gaze and a bad feeling lodged itself right between the ribs. "No, I mean the arrangements."

"I don't understand." But Abi was pretty sure did she understand—understand that life was about to kick her in the teeth again. "Are you kicking me out?"

"Don't think of it like that."

"I don't know how else to take it."

"You could get your *own* place. Have your *own* room. Have some space to work things out," Dotti said. "This could be good for you."

"I think this is about what's good for you." Abi heard her breath hitch but didn't feel any tears. Instead of anger she felt lost and this ache deep in her soul. "For me it just means I'll be alone."

Completely alone. She didn't talk about the accident to her family because she knew it upset them. And she didn't have deep enough connections with the friends she had made to burden them with something so depressing. But being around the sounds and energy of Dotti and the kids had been therapeutic.

"I know you're freaked out about having another baby," Abi said. "Let me help out more, take some of the burden off you."

"This isn't just the pregnancy. It's everything." Dotti was never good with confrontation so when her gaze skittered away, Abi braced herself for the impact. "Hank hates how he has to tiptoe around you in the morning while he gets ready for work. The kids have to be quiet until Auntie wakes up, and you come in at all hours."

"I'm working three jobs."

"That's your choice and we both know it."

Abi knew all too well why she was sleeping on her sister's couch, busting her ass working three jobs to live in a city she couldn't afford. And yet she couldn't bring herself to leave—just like she couldn't bring herself to tell Owen the truth.

"Have you even looked at the elementary school teacher job listing that I sent?" Dotti asked, and a sheer, black panic swept through Abi. She hadn't felt this helpless or out of control of her life since she'd been a kid, her life revolving around other people's priorities. She knew that for Dotti, her family would always be her number one, and that was how it should be. But for once, Abi wanted to know what it felt like to come first in someone's eyes. "Please don't do this, Dot."

"What do you want me to do? You just up and moved, then showed up at my door."

"Because I needed to be around people who love me," she whispered painfully. All she'd ever wanted was to be around people who loved all of her. While she knew deep down that her parents loved her, it always felt as if love was on their terms. She never got to choose where she lived or how she spent her weekends. She was just shuttled back and forth.

"I do love you, but it makes things hard when Impulsive Abi takes over." The comment cut deep. "You gave me less than a week's notice, then showed up on my doorstep."

"I didn't think I had to give notice since that doorstep was formally also mine. As for Impulsive Abi, I'm not her anymore." Okay, not all the way true, she sometimes found herself randomly scouring Voodoo Doughnut's display case without prior or proper planning—bless her thighs—but she never bought more than a half dozen at one sitting. Impulsive Abi was a side of her that, when it came to the important stuff, she'd outgrown. "I'm doing the best I can."

"No, the best you can would be to get an actual adult job. Oh, I don't know, maybe teaching. You spent a fortune to go to school, use your degree."

That lump jumped to her throat and constricted her airway. "You know why I can't do that."

Dotti might have lowered her voice, but the judgment was loud and clear. "I know that you think you can't, but if you just reframe the way you think about things you could totally overcome this. I know you can. It's like riding a bike. Remember when I dared you to do the big jump at the bike park and you went over the handlebars? You eventually got back on."

"I didn't skin my knee this time, Dot. I watched my best friend die." The last word stuck in her throat as cold seeped through her shirt and into her chest.

"I know. And I know you're hurting, but it's been four months."

"I'm sorry if I'm not grieving fast enough for you." She hadn't meant to say it so loud but that feeling of being cornered, stuck without an escape, was slowly tying itself around her neck.

"It's more than grieving. It's like you won't let go and it's affecting everyone around you." Dotti softened her tone. "It feels real, but it's your mind playing with you. I mean it's just like when I was afraid of spiders. Hank wasn't home to kill it and it was near Lemon-Marie so I squashed it and my fear."

"This isn't a spider. I suffered a trauma. A really bad trauma." There. She'd said it. Aloud for other people to hear. Except the look on Dotti's face said she didn't care.

"Hank and I both agree. You need to find somewhere else to live."

"I've been nice about everything because I know I'm hard to take in big doses, but it's my house too, Dotti. Grandma left it to both of us. You can't kick me out."

She might have agreed to sleep on the couch so as not to encroach on Hank's space, or to wake up at seven so that her niece can watch her morning shows. But she was done playing nice if Hank tried to kick her out of her own home.

"I spent more time here than you growing up. Every summer I came here to be with Mee-maw so she didn't get lonely. You came, what? Every other summer and only when Mom made you," Abi said.

"Maybe. But we're not kids. There is a mortgage, bills, property tax, the new roof. Who pays for that? Me. You bailed and left for Alabama."

"Because I was being squeezed out. Once Lemon was born and needed her own room, I was asked to move to the guest room, which then became Hank's office and game room, and my only option was to take the living room couch. So I left and went to Mobile."

Dottie took a big breath. "Koi is afraid to go to the bathroom at night, Abi. And Lemon? She's slept the last four nights in bed with us because of your nightmares. The kids are scared to sleep in their own rooms."

Shame and humiliation made a complicated knot in her stomach, pinching tightly until she knew she'd be sick. "I didn't know."

"It's not your fault," Dotti said gently. "But the kids deserve to feel safe in their own home."

Once upon a time, it had been Abi's home too—a place she felt fearless and free. Every summer, Abi would spend a month with her grandma. They'd go to Belle Mont House for a picnic near the pond and watch the geese chase tourists. They'd spend hours in the kitchen, Ruth teaching her how to make pie crust from scratch and her blue-ribbon apple butter.

Those had been some of the best times of Abi's life. If she closed her eyes, she could almost see herself standing on a wooden chair in pigtails, pearls, and a too-big apron, with flour down her front, a whisk in her hand, and a sheer pleasure on her face.

Abi thought that coming back to the last place she'd felt happy and safe would free her from the nightmares, the panic attacks, and give her the power to slay her demons. But that hadn't happened. If anything, the nightmares were coming more frequently and with more detail. She often awoke with Jenny on her mind.

While Mee-maw Ruth wouldn't want Abi to leave, she also wouldn't want her granddaughters to argue. That had been a stipulation of the will. If they couldn't play nice, then they lost their toy—or in this case, the house would go to their cousins. Abi wanted it in the family more than she wanted it to be hers. Even if it meant she'd be a guest in her own home.

"I'll get my things tomorrow."

Dotti looked torn. "You don't have to move out that fast. I know it will take a few days to find a new place."

"Tess at the tea shop said I could crash with her if I ever needed to. I'll call her after my shift ends."

"If we could afford to buy a new place that's bigger, we would. But unless Hank gets this promotion at work, we're priced out of better school districts."

Abi's heart stopped—right there in her chest. "You'd sell Mee-maw's house?"

"We were going to talk to you about it, but there was no point until Hank finds out about the promotion." Dotti stopped. "You know, if we did sell, you'd have a good nugget to buy something of your own. Maybe pay off your college loans. Do something with your life besides working at a bar."

Abi stepped back. "Speaking of, I better get back to work. My break is almost up."

Her sister said something very olive branchy, very Dotti-like, but Abi was in too much pain to listen. So she smiled when she was expected to smile and even waved goodbye when the Tesla pulled out of the parking lot, kept it together until the brake lights blurred in the distant drizzle.

And that's when Abi squatted down and pressed her palms to her eyes, forcing the tears back inside. Her heart felt heavy in her chest like it was dipped in cement. A wave of cortisol, the stress hormone, began to rise like the tide.

"I'm going to focus on things that make me happy to get me through this." She whispered the phrase her app taught her. "I'm going to think of things that make me happy. Ice cream. Doughnuts. The feel of the sand in my toes. Puppies. Litters of puppies. Jenny."

God, Jenny.

"Puppies." Wiping her nose on her sleeve, she ducked under her hoodie. "A golden retriever puppy named Waffles."

"Or Cheddar," an unwelcomed voice said, and Abi sighed. She looked up and what she found looking back left her breathless.

"Everyone knows that waffles are the second-best food on the planet."

"What's the first?"

"My Mee-maw's chili." She turned around. "How much did you hear?"

"Enough."

"She's just under a lot of stress," she heard herself defend her sister, something she'd spent a lifetime doing.

"My brothers and I fight all the time, but we'd never kick someone out."

It was said as if that were the standard for families everywhere and that she deserved to live in a family like his, who had this fierce protective streak when it came to each other. At that moment Abi felt as if it extended to her. And she didn't know what she thought about that.

"Not all families are like yours. In true Woods family tradition, she kicked the bird out of the tree and hoped I knew how to fly."

He stepped out into the drizzle and locked gazes. "Do you?" he asked quietly.

"I used to," she said honestly. "Now I'm lucky if I can put one foot in front of the other without tripping."

"I can name a dozen people just tonight who would disagree."

"Would you be one?" She wanted to know how he saw her. A girl who was scared of her own shadow or a warrior who could slay her own dragons.

"I'd be the biggest one."

She swallowed hard. "Thank you." She didn't know why, but at that moment she needed to hear that. Especially from him.

"There's an apartment upstairs," he began, and she felt the tears threaten again. "Okay, maybe an apartment might be an oversell, but it has a bedroom and bathroom and its own entry. The only thing it shares with my loft is the kitchen. It's yours if you want it."

It took a moment to speak. That he was offering to do something her family couldn't was humbling—and embarrassing.

"Thank you, but Tess from work already offered."

He was quiet for a moment. "I go to Sip Me every morning. There's no Tess working there." She looked up and there was a twinkle of amusement in his eyes. "It's yours if you want it, Angel."

"Thanks, but I'm good."

"Are you?" She was so far from good that when she glanced up, he looked a little blurry. He reached out and, with his thumb, wiped a tear away and that's when she realized she was crying. There was no build-up and no sniffles, just a few tears leaking from her eyes. "My offer is no different than you and your good Samaritan acts."

There was a difference. A big one. She was holding on to a secret, one that would change the way he felt about her, so she didn't deserve his offer.

Chapter Eighteen

Happy Things:
Marathon napping

Later that night, Owen found himself in his office after closing. He hadn't necessarily thought that Abi had been avoiding him all night, but he hadn't caught so much as a glimpse of those sexy boots since the parking lot. Until he walked into his office.

It was well after last call, the night already faded into early morning, and there she was asleep on his couch—or attempting to sleep.

Her eyes were shut and she was quietly snoring, but she hadn't stayed still more than twenty minutes at any one time before rolling over. Which was always followed by a barely audible moan before she'd drift back into a wisp of sleep.

If she'd looked tired in the parking lot, then she looked absolutely exhausted now. The kind of bone-deep exhaustion that came from deep disappointment and heartache. Hell, his heart ached for her and he didn't even know her whole story—only that it would piss him off.

It was rare that Owen found himself on unsure footing. Typically, if something needed to be done, he handled it himself. If there was a problem, he knew the solution. He had a massive problem on his hands and not a single clue as to how to solve it.

He'd spent the past eight years putting his own needs and wants on the back burner. But he wanted Abi. He wanted her safe and he wanted her in his bed. He'd known this deep down the first time he walked into Sip Me and she'd served him with a shy smile.

Oh, there wasn't a shy bone in her body, but that day she'd been shy. The next day she'd been aloof until she'd eventually turned salty. Which only intrigued him more because it meant he got to her just like she got to him. Before long, he'd adjusted his schedule to match hers. She both fascinated and amused him. Tonight, she worried him.

She held her body taut, her face was pinched, and her legs moved restlessly, back and forth as if unable to find a comfortable place to land. That he wanted to be that place surprised him.

She'd already turned down his offer to stay in the apartment and, stubborn as she was, his gut told him she'd turn him down again.

She associated accepting help with being weak and she was determined not to take up too much space in people's lives. The conversation with her sister made that clear. Then he came along and implied that he didn't have the extra space for a relationship. He wasn't looking to commit, he didn't have the bandwidth for that, but he also didn't want to be another person who pushed her aside when her time was up.

Reason number 397 to keep things simple. She had enough to deal with besides some guy who told her he wanted her in his bed but not his life. He'd been on the receiving end of that scenario, and it blew.

As if on cue, Abi stirred, gripping her bad wrist before rolling onto her back. Her eyes squeezed shut with pain, but she remained in this constant state between barely awake and acutely aware. He'd overheard that she was sleeping on her sister's couch and wondered if this was what she suffered through every night.

She was so petite he could have slid on the couch with her, but that didn't make a couch a suitable place to sleep.

Owen had already turned off the overhead lights, just using his desk lamp to see as he put in some time on inventory. Abi had only been there for a week and already she'd streamlined his system, organizing his office so that Nora could eventually pitch in. And as much as that should freak him out, he was surprisingly calm about the whole thing.

Abi did that. She had this way of making things easier. And not just as an employee, but also as a friend. It was in her nature to care—for the people in her life and strangers alike. She was a lot like his dad that way, generous and selfless to a fault. Between the tea shop, working at the senior center, and Stout, her schedule was jam-packed, yet she still found the time to help with her niece and nephew and do kind things for strangers.

He wondered when someone had last done something kind for her. He sure hadn't. He'd been so busy trying to keep her firmly in the friend zone that he'd done more pushing than giving. And that stopped now.

He clicked closed the laptop and walked to the couch, sitting next to her. He tucked her hair behind her ear and quietly said, "Abi?" When she didn't so much as move, he ran a hand down her arm. "Angel?"

Her lashes fluttered open and she blinked sleepily up at him. Her lipstick was long gone, her mascara slightly smudged, and her hair had come undone from its band and was tousled. She looked sexy and fragile as hell.

"Owen?" she asked, her voice rough with exhaustion. "Are you really here?"

Yes, she was sleep drunk and yes, it was understandable that she was unsure of her surroundings, but the question didn't track. He didn't know why, but it inspired questions of its own. "I'm here."

"Oh." She rubbed her eyes with her right hand and grimaced. "I thought I was dreaming."

"While I like the fact that I star in your dreams, how do you feel?"

"A little tired but—" She abruptly sat up, then clutched her ribs. "Ouch."

"You going to let me check on that?" He placed his hand over hers, but she moved back, sidestepping his offer.

"It just smarts a little sometimes."

"How often is sometimes?"

"More than I like." She put her feet on the ground and closed her eyes as if trying to find her sea legs. "I'm really sorry. I didn't mean to fall asleep. My head was just hurting so I laid down." She stood, then straightened her clothes. "I'll get back out there. Nora must be running her ass off handling things on her own."

"Nora handled business."

"Still, I shouldn't have left her high and dry." She smoothed a hand through her hair as if it would help. The only thing it accomplished was to make it stick further on end, in an adorable and enduring way. "I just need a minute to collect myself and I'm good to go."

He noticed she was holding her injured arm to her stomach as if afraid to jar it. Proof that she'd pushed herself too hard. And that was on him. He shouldn't have left her alone to man the place until he had another bartender on the payroll. Hell, he should have sent her home the moment he learned she'd pulled a double shift next door. He couldn't even imagine how her wrist must hurt.

Or her ribs and whatever other injuries she had. She must have suffered severe injuries if they were still giving her problems all this time later. Then there was the argument with her sister, which would have had most employees asking to go home. Not Abi. She was going to push forward so as not to leave anyone in the lurch.

"You don't need to go anywhere except to bed," he said. "A real bed."

"Seriously, after that power nap, I feel so much better. Even my headache is gone."

She turned to leave but he cupped her elbow. "Abi, it's three in the morning."

It was as if his words didn't compute. "That can't be." She looked at the clock over his desk, her eyes squinting in disbelief, then going as wide as kegs. "Oh my god, why didn't you wake me?"

"You looked like you needed the sleep."

"And I also need to pull my weight," she said. "Tonight was supposed to be your night off. Owen Time, remember? I'm really so sorry, this has never happened to me before. I'll just call Dotti to come get me and… oh." Her cheeks burned with what he suspected was remembrance. Then she swallowed hard, and he knew she remembered every hurtful thing that had been said. "I mean I'll, uh, call…"

That was the first time Owen realized that while she was friends with everyone, Abi didn't have any friends of her own. At least none close enough to bail her out in the middle of the night. And that tore him up inside.

"The studio is empty. I even put clean sheets on the bed."

She dropped her gaze to his chest, something he'd come to realize she did when she was embarrassed. "You didn't have to do that."

He put a finger under her chin and brought her face back to his. "I wanted to. You need to sleep in an actual bed, not on someone's couch." He could see her considering this. Even though she didn't have another option, her gaze went to the exit. "If you decide to walk to your sister's place, I'll walk with you and I really would rather not spend my night in the rain."

That earned him a small smile. "Just for tonight. And I insist on paying you."

He wouldn't take a penny from her, but that was an argument for another time. Right then, his only goal was to convince her to stay for as long as she needed.

"It's there for anyone who works for me and needs a place to stay. Nora's slept there a couple times when she was too tired to drive, and Jake crashed there for a few months when he and his girlfriend broke up. I don't see how this is any different."

What he could see was the worry building up. "Are you saying that my sister and I broke up? Is that what it sounded like to you? Because I just thought it was Dot being pregnant and overwhelmed."

He thought it was Dot being a self-centered bitch, but he wasn't going to say that. It was one thing to complain about a family member, it was another to have someone else do it. One of those *protect what's mine* instincts.

"I think she'll..." *What? Come around?* He didn't want to lie to her but there had been a finality to her sister's tone. "I think she regretted what she said the moment she drove off."

Abi's chest fell with relief. "Me too."

God, he wanted to pull her into his arms and hold her. Tell her everything would work out. But he had a sinking feeling that in Abi's family things rarely worked out for her. Take her parents for example. Where the hell were they in the equation?

And why was he feeling as if this were one of those *protect what's mine* situations between him and Abi?

Chapter Nineteen

Happy Things:
Midnight snacks

No matter how tired Owen was, sleep eluded him. He wasn't sure if it was the way Abi clutched her side in pain or the terrified look in her eyes when she thought her sister had walked away for good, but she'd kept him awake all the same. And it wasn't the first time.

In fact, she was either on his mind or in his dreams so much it was as if she'd taken up permanent residence in his bed. Now she *was* sleeping in his bed. Unfortunately, it was the one across the hall.

Since, at present, he couldn't sleep nor could he sleep with a beautiful woman, he went with the next best option—food. He'd skipped dinner and was hungry as hell.

Tossing the sheets back, he padded to the kitchen, which was a few steps from his bed.

Tired of hoofing it back to his apartment after work, a few years ago Owen had renovated the second floor of the bar into a high-end loft with a private deck that overlooked the city. With the exception of the bathroom, no walls separated the living space, allowing the sunlight to shine freely through the entire loft. Since morning was the only time Owen could guarantee he'd be home, he wanted to take advantage of the light and views.

The bedroom took up a good chunk of the back of the loft, but the kitchen was the largest part of his place. With concrete countertops, state-of-the-art range, and open-concept shelves, the kitchen was his favorite area of the loft.

Some people meditated. Owen cooked. It was the only time his brain was completely still. Even when he slept his mind was racing with all of the things he needed to accomplish the next day. But in the kitchen, he felt at home.

Some of his favorite times as a kid were cooking with his old man.

Owen scoured the fridge for what he needed. On tonight's menu was a double-decker Reuben, with extra kraut, homemade Russian dressing, and two slices of Swiss cheese. He'd just pulled out the corned beef when he heard something from across the hall.

He strained his ears and heard it again. A low, distressed moaning. Abandoning his sandwich, he tossed on a pair of jeans and walked into the hallway.

There was silence for a long moment and just when he was about to leave, another sound came from Abi's apartment. Crying.

Growing up with five brothers he didn't know what to do with tears, but he'd also come to know that Abi was one tough cookie, and not brought to tears easily. He considered whether to alert her to his presence or let her go on thinking she was alone. Option one didn't sit well because he respected that she was a private person who'd likely want to work through things on her own. Option two left her with her emotions but it also left her alone. Which brought him to option three, bring her a sandwich because everyone knew that the best way to deal with a problem was on a full stomach.

Plus, when he'd been having a shit time, she'd cooked him chili and the best damn cornbread he'd ever had, which nearly brought him to tears. However, before he could decide the correct direction, he heard a long guttural sob.

Screw it.

"Abi?" He knocked but she didn't answer. He knocked louder, then pressed his ear to the wood. When he didn't hear footsteps, he grabbed the spare key out of the bowl by his front door and let himself in.

He'd rather have her mad at him than run the risk that something was really wrong. And from the sounds coming from the bedroom, something was wrong.

He raced into the room and just like earlier she was shifting back and forth, but this time there was an urgency to it. Panic had his body going into full alert. Then there were the tears and sorrow-filled sounds that tore his chest open.

She was dead asleep, thrashing in her bed as if trying to outrun a ghost. And maybe she was. For the second time that night, he gently brushed a hand down her arm. "Angel?"

Only this time she didn't come gently away, she shot up with a gasp and clutched her chest. Her gaze darted around the room, then at him and her face scrunched as if she were doing her damnedest not to cry.

"Are you okay?" he asked softly, unsure of what his next move should be. Even with his sisters-in-law, he was out of practice with emotional interactions, so he couldn't pinpoint if her expression originated from unease or fear. Whatever it was told him she was spooked.

"No," she whispered, and it was like a punch to the chest. It was the first time she admitted that she was, indeed, not okay. He had a guttural feeling that it was the first time she'd told anyone the truth since the accident.

"Do you want to talk about it?"

She shook her head ever so slightly and, with a shaky hand, pushed her hair back from her sweaty forehead. Not wanting her to feel that she was cornered, he leaned back to give her some space, but instead she crawled right up into his arms so that not a sheet of paper could fit between them.

He wrapped his arms around her and held her to him. "I got you."

She pressed her face into his neck and he heard her breath hitch, could sense when her airway constricted, and feel her every tremble. She was one gasp away from a panic attack. He ran his hand up and down her spine in soothing motions.

"It was just a nightmare."

Her arms tightened around his neck. "I know. They're just so real," she said into the curve of his shoulder.

He knew exactly what she meant. In the months following his dad's passing, Owen had his fair share of nightmares. But nothing as extreme as what he'd just witnessed.

"With each one they get more intense and more vivid to where I start to remember every detail. Sometimes I wake up and I can smell the exhaust from the bus." She pulled back and her eyes were swimming with tears. "I just can't get her eyes out of my head. She was just out of reach. I tried to grab her hand, but I couldn't and by the time the paramedics got there she was gone."

He pulled her all the way onto his lap and pressed a kiss to her temple. "Have you talked to anyone about this?"

She nodded. "My therapist said the dreams would get worse before they get better, but I never knew it would get this bad." She settled against him, feeling soft and vulnerable in his arms. "I think Jenny knew the moment the bus stopped rolling that she was going to die. I didn't know." Her voice broke. "I didn't know until the last minute, but she knew. And the part that gets me is, she was clearly at peace with it." She pulled back to look him in the eye. "How come she was at peace with it, and I can't get over it?"

Using his thumb, he brushed away her tears. "I read in a book that Death doesn't haunt the dead, he haunts the people who loved them and were left behind."

"Her last words to me were to be good."

"Abi," he whispered as she clung to him, making his gut clench.

That, right there, was why she did the things she did and why she was so adamant about helping people. Even when it's hard, like with her sister or Ms. S, she followed through, putting her well-being last.

"I was in the hospital room alone when my dad passed," he heard himself saying. "He was hooked up to a ventilator so he couldn't talk, but he never took his eyes off me."

She pulled back and cupped his jaw. "Where was your family?"

"Everyone had left the room to go to the cafeteria. We wanted my mom to take a break and eat something, so we took shifts staying with Dad. They hadn't been gone more than a minute when he looked at me, took one last breath, and I watched the life drain right out of him. It was as if he were waiting for my mom to leave because he didn't want her to see him die."

"Owen." Concern filled her eyes. "I am so sorry you were alone. At least I had the other teachers. No one should watch a loved one die like that."

"I never knew Death was a tangible thing," he said. "It has an energy of its own that drains the room the second someone dies."

"That's how it felt with Jenny. Like her passing left a void in the world that could never be filled."

"I was thankful that I got to say goodbye, but over time this resentment built up. I was angry at my dad, angry at my brothers. I felt like everyone had left me to deal with the loss alone. We all mourned him, but my family couldn't relate to what I'd gone through. It created this divide, with me on one side and my family on the other. Not that they knew." Jesus, now that he was talking, he couldn't seem to shut up. He'd never admitted how those last few moments affected the entire course of his life to anyone. But talking to Abi about it felt right.

"Is that why you took over the bar?"

He nodded. "I couldn't stop thinking about the way he looked at me, all that love and pride directed at me. None of my brothers were in any position to step up, so I did. There was a reason he waited for it to be me, and I couldn't get it out of my head that maybe that was why."

She ran her fingers through his hair. "Do you regret taking over the bar?"

"No," he said without hesitation.

"Do you ever wonder what your life would have been like if you hadn't taken over?" There was something in her tone that he couldn't quite decipher.

"Every day. Don't get me wrong, I love working at my dad's desk, stepping into his shoes, and watching the thing he was the proudest of grow and succeed."

Her expression went soft. "You were the thing he was the proudest of, Owen. *You.*"

Her words brought on an onslaught of emotions. Complicated and concerning. He'd told himself not to get too involved, to keep things simple, but there was nothing simple about the way he felt. He could not only trust her with the bar, he could trust her with his secrets and that created an intimacy that wouldn't be good for either of them, since he'd already decided to keep things uncomplicated.

"My dad was too trustworthy, and people took advantage of that. So when he got sick, the family decided that someone had to be there to oversee things. That someone was me."

"Sometimes when the house is quiet and I'm alone with my thoughts, there is this overwhelming anger at Jenny for leaving me the way she did. I know rationally that it was no one's fault, but in here," she touched her heart, "I wonder why she didn't fight harder."

That was exactly how he felt about his dad. Why did he wait until it was just him to finally give in to the inevitable? "I don't know if I should be honored my dad chose me or if I should be angry."

"Does it get any easier?" she whispered.

"Honestly? No," he said, and she settled herself against his chest again, resting her head on his shoulder, her feet tucked under her as she sat on his lap. "But eventually the good memories begin to outweigh the bad and the anger fades, but the loss never fully goes away. It just becomes more distant, like a faded memory."

"I don't want it to fade," she whispered. "I'm already starting to forget her voice."

"Sometimes I pull out the emails he sent me while I was away at college just to remember the way he worded things or his sense of humor."

"I'm sorry we share this." This time when she looked at him there was something new in her eyes. Awareness.

Her fingers spanned to cover the place right above his heart and her gaze dropped to his lips. Which was a-okay with him since he was having the same affliction. Then they were both moving closer, their mouths nearly touching. They both went in for the kiss, twice, their lips a breath apart, their eyes locked.

Neither looked away and neither backed away. But when they went in for the third time, he knew he was going to kiss her and they'd end up sleeping together. And that would be a mistake.

And not because she was his employee but because she was scared and vulnerable. And he wasn't going to be *that* guy so he rested his forehead to hers and took in a breath.

She abruptly pulled back. "I didn't mean …"

"I did."

Embarrassment touched her cheeks and before he could tighten his arms, she scrambled off his lap. He could practically see her walls go back up and lock into place.

She crossed her arms over herself. "But you didn't."

"I don't want it to happen this way," he said quietly.

"Me either," she said even quieter. "Things were just emotionally charged."

It was more than that, but he'd let her have it.

He stood and pulled her to her feet, acutely aware that she was in nothing but his shirt and a pair of lace panties. "How about we go somewhere less charged," he suggested. "Are you hungry? I make a mean Reuben."

"Do you have sauerkraut?"

"What kind of question is that?" he teased.

She smiled a real smile and his heart showed its soft underbelly. "Then I guess you can make me a sandwich."

Chapter Twenty

Happy Things:
Chris Hemsworth's butt

After swinging by the bank to drop off yesterday's deposit, Abi took a field trip to the senior center to teach a class on the internet, which the ladies used to search for photos of Chris Hemsworth's butt, before stopping by the doughnut shop where she purchased a dozen doughnuts, inhaling two before she even reached her bike. Then she rode to the duck pond a few minutes from her sister's house.

It was Wednesday and every Wednesday Dotti and the kids spent the morning feeding the ducks. Well, Lemon-Marie sat there in her princess dress and wand while Koi chased the birds around the lake ripping his clothes off until he was down to his pull-up diapers. Dotti didn't seem to care so Abi went with the flow.

But today there were no kids or Dotti. Abi waited an extra twenty minutes, but they were a no-show, which saddened her. She grabbed the pink box of doughnuts, her backpack, and her cold latte and headed to the bike rack to find her Huffy, which was sandwiched between a Spider-Man bike and a tricycle. She considered cutting out and heading into work early but decided that she wasn't going to flake. There were fish to be fed and she was the superhero on duty.

She thought about the six wishes that needed granting on the bulletin board at Sip Me and the listing for a comes-with-a-hot-plate room to rent across town, but didn't give in to the need to procrastinate.

She'd already narrowed down what her good deed for the day would be and no matter how hard Dotti tried, she wasn't going to wreck it. So instead of heading downtown, Abi made a detour to her grandma's house.

She thought about using the key, but decided against it, knocking instead. She heard Dotti look out the peephole and then silence, followed by some heavy breathing. Dotti had a habit of hyperventilating when she was being sneaky.

"I can smell your guilt through the door."

More breathing.

"I have doughnuts," Abi said. "Voodoo doughnuts."

There was a pregnant pause, followed by, "A blueberry cake doughnut?"

"Two blueberry cake doughnuts."

Abi opened the box and wafted the scent through the door. She heard a sniffing come from the other side, then the door opened. Dotti stuck her face through the crack like Jack Nicholson in *The Shining*.

Swoosh swish. "*Let it go, let it go*" played in the background.

Dotti pressed the heel of her hands to her eyes. "I'm being punished by the Mommy gods for giving my kids screen time before the age of three." She looked up. "What are you doing here?"

"Not avoiding you because of a stupid fight."

"It *was* stupid." The door opened. "*I* was stupid and mean."

"And a first-rate bitch," Abi added, sticking her foot in the door just in case Dotti decided to go into ostrich mode.

"That too." Dotti blinked. "Wait. Why are you here?"

"I'm on fish duty."

"Even after our last conversation?"

"Even then." Abi kicked the door with her toe. "Are you going to let me in or have the neighborhood gossip mill take bets on if I've finally lost it or if you've finally kicked me out?"

Abi handed over the box of doughnuts and Dotti stepped back to let Abi enter. "You brought me doughnuts." Dotti snapped the lid shut and her eyes filled with panic. "You brought doughnuts! The kids will sniff out the sugar and destroy the house. Depending on how much icing they eat, they might even burn it down."

"Which is why I bought two plain cake doughnuts. Low in sugar and icing free."

"You're a god among mortals." Dotti put the box on the top of the fridge, but not before taking a big bite of a blueberry cake doughnut. She groaned. "This is the closest I've come to an orgasm since before Lemon-Marie was born. Wait there was the one time we hired a sitter and instead of going to dinner we had sex. In the minivan."

Abi plugged her ears. "Since when do we share personal info like orgasm timelines and soccer mom sex-capades."

Swoosh swish. The music continued repeatedly.

"It's the pregnancy hormones. They make me do terrible things."

"So, it's official? You and Hank are pregnant?"

"*I'm* pregnant. *Hank* is at the golf course for his nine a.m. tee-time." Dotti's eyes filled. "I wish people would have told me before I decided to become a mom, not that I would trade them for the world, well, maybe a dozen blueberry cake doughnuts, but people tend to leave out the hard parts."

"Yeah, I know the feeling," Abi said. "Everyone told me I'd be okay, but they lied."

Dotti froze. "Was I one of those people?"

"You still are." How's that for honest? "And it sucks. Having my sister doubt that what I'm going through is real, sucks. Sleeping on the couch sucks."

Not sure what to say to that, Dotti poured them both a cup of coffee. "I didn't mean what I said last week."

"Yeah, you did. But don't worry, I won't be sleeping on it again."

Dotti's face paled. "You're not coming home?"

"Eventually yes. And I *will* have my bedroom back. All of it or I will stop playing nice guy and burn Hank's office to the ground." Abi wasn't sure where that stood on standing up for herself, but she felt pretty damn proud right then.

"How about tonight?"

"I found a temporary place to stay." Which was as much of a relief as it was a ticking time bomb. Even though she and Owen hadn't kissed, they'd crossed a line that couldn't be undone.

"I tried calling," Dotti said, offering Abi a cup of coffee. She took it and sat at the kitchen counter. "You didn't answer."

"I wasn't ready to talk. I'm still not."

Dotti's face scrunched like she'd eaten a hormone laced lemon and was trying not to cry. She didn't try hard enough because a single tear spilled down her cheek.

"No, no, no. No way. You don't get to do that," Abi snapped. "Not this time."

"Do what?"

"Cry so that I feel bad for you."

"That's not what I'm doing," Dotti said, and Abi lifted a *liar-liar* brow. "Fine, maybe I am. But this time I really do feel bad for kicking you out and for the way I talked to you." She sniffed. "Are you ready to talk now?"

"No." Abi wasn't sure when she'd be able to face what her sister had done, but that wasn't going to stop her from completing her good deed. "I'm here because I promised to help with the fish."

"And the kids? Last time you helped with the kids. And they're staging a mutiny and I'm on the losing end."

"Which is why I brought this." She held up an Anna wig. "I will bring Anna and Elsa home for a one-time visit with Auntie Abi. We will dress up, sing, and then I will puncture my eardrums so as never to hear that song again."

Swoosh swish. "Let it go. Let it go."

Lemon-Marie made a grand appearance in all her princess gear, a mash-up of every Disney princess ever created, with her wand in hand. She waved it and nearly poked Abi's eye out. She raced around the table with her wand dragging the floor, knocking every leg of every chair before ducking beneath the tablecloth.

Swoosh swish. "Let it go. Let it go."

Swoosh swish. "Let it go. Let it go."

A Cinderella shoe came flying out and tagged Abi in the shin. Followed by a second and finally a crown.

"How long will this game of strip princess last?" Abi asked.

Dotti waved a hand. "She'll run out of options before long and then Koi will get in on the action. Only he takes off his Pull-Ups and goes outside and pees on the tree like our neighbor's dog. He's in some kind of *Lord of the Flies* alternate reality. It's super fun." Dotti glanced at the house, which looked like a toy bomb went off, and gave a resigned sigh. "I wouldn't blame you if you turned around and walked out."

"Leaving you with my favorite munchkins?" Abi peeked her head beneath the table and growled, sending Lemon-Marie racing out in a fit of giggles. Abi stood and, with her good arm, swung her niece up over her back into a fireman's hold, Lemon-Marie squealing with glee. "Fee. Fie. Foe. Fum. I smell a diapered bum."

Abi stomped down the hallway with her niece still on her back and when she caught sight of Koi she roared like Godzilla. His little face lit up and he raced into his bedroom looking for a place to hide.

Hide-and-seek lasted all of thirty seconds, followed by a bribe of one doughnut for two hours of playing Big Kid No Talk while they watched *Frozen*. Abi kept the kids entertained until nap time, which was where her time at Casa Dotti came to an end.

Abi tapped on her sister's door, then opened it to find Dotti in bed with her feet elevated.

"The kids are fed, changed, passed out, and probably won't wake until dinner. Oh, and I cleaned the kitchen."

Dotti studied her strangely. "Why are you being so nice?"

"Because you're family. And because I made a promise to someone I loved that I'd do good. And the best way for me to do good today is to be there for the people I love. Regardless of what they did. Plus, I came here for the rest of my things. Well, at least the things that fit in my bike basket."

"I can drive you."

"I know, but I need to figure this out on my own. Plus, you shouldn't have to chauffeur me around. This is another reason I came, to say I'm sorry for taking advantage of you. That wasn't my intention."

"I know," Dotti said.

"I was hoping I could leave the rest in the garage until I move back to Alabama."

Dotti's tears came to an abrupt stop. "You're going back to Alabama?"

"There's something I have to do." Like visiting Jenny's grave and maybe even visiting Jenny's parents. What good was do-gooding if she didn't do things for herself that would make her good with the world?

"When?"

"As soon as I finish my contract at Stout. And before you ask, no I haven't told him. As for why, I want him to feel what it feels like to have his life back before he shuts me out."

"That's actually a good reason."

"Does that mean my old reasons were crap?" she asked, feeling more defensive than she should.

"No, I just... thank you for today."

Chapter Twenty-One

Happy Things:
Light-bulb moments

It had been three weeks since she'd moved into Owen's apartment and a week since any kind of a near-miss kiss.

It had also been three weeks since her last nightmare—go figure. Even so, a ping of guilt ricocheted throughout her body every time she saw him. Taking him up on the offer to stay in his apartment had been about as responsible as it had been intelligent. Yet there she was, living off his generosity while harboring her secret.

Not that she was a freeloader. She paid him rent every Monday. Hhe'd refuse to take her check and she'd hide it in his mail. It had become a fun game. Then there was her plan, a good plan that took all sides into consideration. And while she wanted to blurt out the truth and get it over with, following through on her promise to make his life happier was more important.

It didn't matter, her time there was winding down anyway. Nora was practically running things on her own, Owen's professional life had been streamlined, and Abi was finally on good terms with her sister. Well, "good" might be stretching it. They'd talked the other day when Abi had shown up for fish duty. It wasn't a long conversation, but no one had cried—progress.

Dotti had insisted that Abi move back in, but she'd semi-politely declined. Abi wasn't about to ruin any forward progress they'd made.

"You can always crash with me," Nora offered.

Abi and Nora were in the breakroom hanging a giant whiteboard that had lines and grids in permanent marker and people's names in erasable marker. Nora was holding the board while Abi lined up the screws. "I don't have a spare bed and my roommate smells like saltines and ramen, but I have a sleeping bag and super plush carpet."

Which sounded worse than Dotti's couch. "Thanks, but my contract is almost up."

Abi looked at the calendar on the lunchroom wall and sighed. *Next week!* The days had flown by and it was nearly time to pack up, yet her heart said she wasn't ready to go.

"You're really going to leave?" Nora asked. Today, she was dressed as manager extraordinaire in a pair of black pants and a white button-down, and her hair was pulled back into a complicated knot at the base of her neck. Personal, professional and, with her nose ring, the perfect hint of edginess needed to run a gastropub.

"That's usually what happens when one's contract is up," Abi defended.

"No, what they do when they're as good as you is, they negotiate. Ask for a permanent gig. Demand a raise."

While part of Abi, that part that loved being around Owen, wanted to re-up her contract and maybe ask for something permanent, the sane part of her, who knew how this would play out, warned her that Owen didn't do permanent—at least not in his personal life. And especially not with someone keeping such a huge secret from him.

It didn't take long to uncover that Owen valued loyalty and honesty, two things that shouldn't be all that hard to maintain, but she'd dug herself into a hole and wasn't sure how to dig herself out—at least not without full repelling ropes and a winch. She knew this going in, had made her bed so to speak, and yet her heart sank at the idea of things ending. Because once their week was up, so was the gig.

He'd promised her they'd remain friends and, while she wouldn't blame him if he reneged, she was banking on that promise.

"When it's up, I'll be moving on."

Nora looked at her as if she had something to say, then shook her head. "Everyone was hoping you'd stay on longer. And I mean *everyone*."

"That's sweet."

"Has Owen mentioned anything?" Nora said casually.

"No, he hasn't."

And she didn't think he would. They'd made an agreement and, as long as her work was finished and his life was noticeably simpler, she was going to stick to it.

"You don't need me, you are so ready to do this on your own," she told Nora.

"I know." Nora was about as short on confidence as she was on tattoos. "Doesn't mean we want you to leave. Things have been going so smoothly since you arrived. You've been here, what, a month?"

"Six weeks." Six nerve-racking, unexpected, sexually frustrating, and wonderful weeks.

"The employees are happy, morale is up, it feels like a family again. And bonus, Owen isn't his standard-issue grumpy self."

"He's not grumpy," she argued, and Nora lifted a brow. "I can see how he comes off as grumpy, but he's just stressed. Wouldn't you be? Running a place like this all on your own, knowing that your family was counting on you to make it work?"

"All I'm saying is that he's different when you're around."

Abi nearly dropped the drill. "Different how?"

"Come on, you have to see it. I mean, it's pretty clear he's you know, getting some."

"It is?" she croaked.

"Cut the crap, Abi," Nora said. "How long have you two been boinking?"

Abi laughed but Nora stood there serious as hell.

"We're not 'boinking.'"

"Well, you're something. When you two are together there's so much sexual tension it makes me want to reach out and touch someone. Like my ex who was terrible at monogamy but a god in bed." Nora hung the board from the screws and stepped back to admire their handiwork.

"He's that good?"

Nora fanned herself. "Religious experience."

The last man-made orgasm Abi'd had was, um, never. She didn't know if she picked lazy men or if it was her. Looking at Nora with her piercings and tattoos, Abi decided her friend looked like a woman who demanded her orgasms.

Abi hadn't demanded much out of men except attention. And maybe a date night every so often. Just by his kiss Abi could tell that Owen would be a ladies-first kind of guy, who'd be single-focused, not giving in until Abi had experienced her first with-someone orgasms.

Her nipples chimed in, reconfirming just how mind-blowing sex with Owen would be. What if this was her wake-up call? The universe telling her to grab the bull by the horns? To walk away from something great in hopes of finding something amazing.

"So then what's going on between you and Owen?"

"Honestly? Nothing. A big, fat almost-but-not-quite nothing. He has this boss-employee line he won't cross, which I think is smart and noble, but it's confusing as hell."

Nora pulled a chocolate bar from her lunch bag, broke off half and offered it to Abi, who snatched it right up.

"He learned a hard lesson that made him a by-the-book kind of boss. I heard he used to date one of his employees and she cheated on him and lied about it. She broke his heart and he walked away from his tattoo business over it."

"That's awful," Abi said, getting a clearer picture into Owen Easton. "I had no idea."

Now she understood why honesty and loyalty were so ingrained in him. It's normal for business owners to be wary about being taken advantage of, but Owen had been betrayed by someone he loved.

"So he didn't always live for work?" she asked, hoping beyond hope that maybe her decade-old decision hadn't had as much of an impact as she'd originally thought.

"I don't know. I've been here three years and the guy's always buried himself so deep in work he had paper coming out his ass."

"He's not that bad."

Nora laughed. "But you're not sleeping together?"

"No."

Abi opened her mouth to say more but decided to close it. While she knew his reason, she felt in her gut that there was more to his decision. Her endgame was clear: until she came clean, she wouldn't allow things to progress any further. She hadn't sold alcohol to minors, but she still held herself responsible for part of the event that changed Owen's dad's life.

Abi's body tingled every time she thought about his promise on Dotti's porch. How absolute he'd been in their one-week policy. Only now that it was almost here, a week didn't seem enough. Her heart was saying that it would never be enough and that if she wasn't careful when she left, she'd leave it behind. So while she wanted more, she knew better than to ask.

"We're just friends."

Nora snorted. "Uh huh."

When Nora disappeared, Abi moved on to her first good deed for the day. A good deed for the universe.

She pulled the ladder from the closet and shimmied it to the middle of the room, where she set up shop. She'd spent the entire afternoon yesterday double-checking that all sixty-three light bulbs around the bar had been replaced with eco-friendly ones. All that was left was the breakroom.

Using her servers' apron as a tool belt, she filled up with supplies and started up the ladder. And by up, she meant climbing a single rung.

Ten minutes later, she'd made it to the impressive rung number three. With the light fixture closely overhead, an eco-friendly light bulb in one hand and imaginary prayer beads in the other, she pushed onward and upward.

Onward and upward.

Onward and upward.

Shit.

No matter how long she stood there or how many times she whispered, "That is a battle for another day. Today it's about calm and tranquility," she couldn't gather the courage needed to crawl onward and upward just one more rung.

"You totally have this." Hands clammy, she lifted one foot and then quickly put it back down when she felt the world sway. "You so don't have this."

First busses, then cars, and now heights? The crash had been the gift that kept on giving. At this rate she was bound to enter retirement before she could screw in even a single bulb. Yesterday had been easy, she'd pointed to the light fixture and Clive became hero for the day, swapping out one for the other.

But today was Clive's day off and Abi was too embarrassed to ask anyone else to climb up Rapunzel's hair.

"What are you doing up there?" Owen's silky, sexy voice said from below. Her heart warmed. Along with some other, more pertinent, parts.

"Being environmentally conscious by putting in eco-friendly light bulbs. They last three times longer and use half the energy. Even the universe deserves a little pampering. Only I can't seem to reach the light to swap out the bulbs." She sighed. "Correction. I can't seem to climb any higher to change the bulb."

"And the whiteboard?"

"I figured that if everyone could see the schedule, they'd be less likely to play sick. Knowing they'd literally be leaving their co-workers in the lurch is a great motivator. Plus, if everyone can see who's working then—"

"Everyone can see who's bailing for a day of fun."

"Exactly." She turned around to ask him why he was there, but then she forgot how to speak. Owen had climbed up behind her and perched on the second rung, which brought him eye level. "Smart and sexy."

She opened her mouth, but all the air whooshed out of her lungs and her heart melted faster than a pat of butter on hot cornbread.

The man redefined "sexy." A faded college T-shirt clung to his impressive chest. His hair was a little messy, and his jeans hung dangerously low, giving her a prime view of chiseled abs and lean hips, and highlighting his yummy parts. No ball cap, no pretenses, and no confusion.

Sometimes he'd leave her to enjoy her coffee and other times, like that morning, they'd sit on the patio and talk about everything and nothing, all at the same time.

She learned about his childhood, and she shared small slivers of hers. Usually cracking some kind of joke when things became too serious. She could tell he wanted more, but after hearing about his idyllic childhood, that was all he was going to get. But she did tell him all about Jenny and their time in Mobile and how it was the first place since her grandma passed that felt like home.

Even when they kept things light it was as if they were circling each other, waiting for the other to pounce. But while it was always sex-charged, it was still friendship driven. That was why seven in the morning had become her favorite time of the day. And when she finally left for—she couldn't say greener—other pastures, she'd miss those quiet moments, almost as much as she'd miss him.

And that wasn't even the most tempting part. Nope. The more she saw Owen as a normal, real guy and not the repentance she'd come back to Portland for, the more the boundaries seemed to blur, and the harder he became to resist.

"I suck at boundaries," she rushed out, more for her than him. "For me, they're more of a test than a line in the sand."

"I'm excellent at boundaries." His hand cupped her hip and he leaned closer. "Around you, not so much." His gaze dropped to her lips, his fingers splayed around her waist. "Are you on the clock? Please tell me you're not."

She considered lying, but she'd already racked up her fair share of those. "I just started."

He groaned low in his throat and dropped his head to her shoulder. "That's probably for the best." But his hands stayed right there on her hips, his thumb teasing under the hem of her shirt, making short little passes on her bare skin. "This is becoming harder and harder."

"For me too."

She felt him straighten and a rush of air left his lungs as he pulled back—all the way back. "Now, tell me how I can help?"

She held out the light bulb. "Can you put it in?"

"I've never had a problem putting it in," he said.

"You don't get to do that."

"Do what?" he asked innocently.

"Turn my words into foreplay. You made the rules. Your conditions, remember?"

"Oh, I remember. When Horny Owen finally runs into Responsible Owen, he's going to kick his ass."

Taking the bulb from her apron, his hands grazed her stomach, a feather-light contact, but her lungs went on strike. His gaze locked on hers and held for an eternity. With a wink, he lifted an arm and easily screwed in the bulb.

"Now you're just showing off," she said.

"Is it working?"

"I don't know. I was too busy," *checking out your lips*, "thinking up 'How many friends-without-benefits does it take to screw in a light bulb' jokes."

"I hope the answer is two because I'm a one-woman kind of guy."

Oh boy. Needing a breather, she looked back at the light fixture that was a mile overhead. "This is so stupid." She breathed out the words slowly. "I mean, it's just one silly step."

He ran his thumb along her jawline, then tucked her hair behind her ears. "Sometimes the first step is the hardest." His hand slid down her arm, giving her a little squeeze of support, then let go.

Her heart raced, but for a whole other reason. She felt as if this was a turning point for them, that if she didn't do something now, the moment would pass.

What had been stopping her to begin with? First, it was to keep her distance, which was a joke. She couldn't stay away from him even if she wanted. Which was why she hadn't found a new place to live—because she didn't want a new neighbor. She wanted her current neighbor, who was looking at her as if he could read her every thought.

If so, maybe he could explain what was going on. Explain why she'd been holding back. His bar was running like a well-oiled John Deere at the county fair's annual tractor pull, her job was technically done, yet she was still working there as if there were other things to fix besides light bulbs.

She was afraid that if their relationship changed, she'd lose what they had. But there was a potential amazing on the other side if she was brave enough to go after it.

God, she wished Jenny was there to tell her what to do. Right at that moment, a warm strength filled her chest and she knew what Jenny would say.

"I have a favor to ask," Abi said. "I need a ride somewhere Tuesday night."

He lifted his head and his lips quirked at the corners. "Are we stopping global warming? Saving the dolphins?"

"Something better," she said, knowing what she had to do. "And before you say no, Nora is managing that night and—"

"Yes."

She stopped. "What?"

He stepped up one more rung and everything lined up. Thigh to thigh, shoulder to shoulder and all the good parts in between. His good part was a little bigger than it had been moments ago, which made her nipples hard. He leaned in and, against her ear, whispered, "Anything."

"Even though it's Two-Dollar Tuesday?" Which, with its two-dollar drafts, was almost as packed as game nights.

"Even then."

Chapter Twenty-Two

Happy Things:
A good game of Grab Ass

"What kind of good deed are we talking?" Owen asked as he looked up at the flashing neon sign, which read SADDLE RACK.

The Saddle Rack was a country bar and dance hall that Abi frequented. It was a city take on a country-bred pastime, and a decade past its prime, but it was the closest thing to remembering her roots Abi had found since arriving in Portland. She wasn't a regular, but she tried to make it to Tuesday night Two-Step-Off, where couples showed their moves for a plastic trophy and a free pitcher of Lone Star.

Abi never turned down the opportunity to dance, but she'd turned down plenty of offers for more. Usually she came for the comradery, a chance to feel not so alone. Tonight, she'd come for so much more.

"It's a surprise."

"Are we teaching Delores how to ride the mechanical bull?"

She grinned up at him, which meant she had to tilt her head all the way back. Damn, the man was tall, and big and built and a whole lot of other adjectives that if she listed, she'd be there for hours. "What part of surprise includes me telling you the surprise?"

"The kind of surprise where I know what I'm walking into."

"You're walking into a country bar, where there will be loud music, dancing, drinking, and fun. Lots of fun." He flashed his white teeth and two double-barreled dimples appeared. "Don't you flash those things my way. They won't work on me." They totally worked on her. More than she'd like. And he knew it.

"Then why are you holding my hand?" She looked down and sure enough, she was holding his hand. Before she could snatch hers back, he laced their fingers. "Don't worry, I don't bite. Unless you ask really nicely."

Her body heated to panty-melting hot at his comment. With a knowing squeeze, he led her across the parking lot holding hands as if this were some kind of date. Not a first date. They knew too much about each other for that. But a fresh and exciting date all the same.

"Okay. If you won't tell me the good deed, can you at least tell me who it's for?"

They reached the door and she tugged him to a stop. "Actually. It's you."

The glow from the full moon him from behind, the bill of his hat casting a shadow over his face. But she felt those serious blue eyes catch on hers.

"Me?"

She turned to face him and took both of his hands, wrapping them around her waist and stepping into him. "You," she whispered.

He groaned. "Resisting you is becoming a problem."

"Then don't," she said simply. "Just let tonight be. It's nothing more than you adding a little fun into your life."

He tightened his arms and tugged her closer. "You saying I'm not fun, Angel?"

"I'm saying you need to take some time for yourself. And since I couldn't exactly hijack a tattoo shop, I figured I'd bring you into my world. Maybe even teach you something new."

He looked around the bar, which was packed with men wearing Stetsons and women wearing city-folk cowgirl boots, and laughed. "This isn't my first rodeo. I went to college in Austin and dated my share of Southern belles."

Her smile went a little brittle at the comment. "I might be Southern but I'm as far from a belle as we are from Austin. More of a football fan who worked as the water girl."

"If you'd gone to Portland High, I would have fumbled a lot." He ran a finger down her jaw. "I feel like I keep fumbling with you. I don't always say things the right way or use the right finesse when navigating us, and for that I'm sorry."

"Navigating around a magnet in a metal boat is hard," she said. "And I like that you're straightforward. That way I know where I stand." And that way she could protect her heart.

Oh, who was she kidding? Her heart was so exposed she was surprised he couldn't see it beating. His generous nature, the way he loved his family, and the way he looked at her like she was the kind of woman who deserved someone of her own. Which was a dangerous place to be because once she handed over the letter burning a hole in her purse, their whole relationship would change. The countdown would be activated and she had exactly one week to make him feel for her the way she felt for him.

But that was what she wanted, right? To give up great in the hopes of experiencing amazing?

She felt Owen's eyes on her, carefully assessing as if he had something to say on the matter, but he remained tight-lipped. "Then let's go for a spin around the floor."

"Before we go inside, I have something." With a shaky hand she reached into her purse and pulled out the letter that had the potential to blow up everything. With trembling fingers, she handed him the letter.

"What's this?" He glanced at the one-page, two-paragraph, to-the-point letter, then met her gaze over the paper.

She swallowed—hard. "My resignation."

"I thought I had another week or two." He folded it up and for a moment it looked as if he was going to hand it back. And for a moment, she wished that he had. But she couldn't last another day, let alone week, pretending that the insane connection between them wasn't there.

"We did, but things moved faster than I originally thought." Mainly they did. "Nora is ready, you're fully staffed, even Clive has found his rhythm."

"Clive's rhythm is to hide in the breakroom and hope that whatever problems arise disappear."

"Oh, he's a long way from being ready to handle it alone and Mandy should be working the same shifts as him, but there's hope. He does great with the customers, and he can actually problem-solve easy things."

"What? Like dogsit Littleshit?"

She laughed and it brought out this boyish grin that was equal parts sexy and enduring. "Like give you a little breathing room so you can do what you do best."

He pressed her up against the wall, placing a hand on either side of her, then placed his lips on her ear and whispered, "Changing light bulbs with a beautiful woman?"

She hung her fingers from his belt loops, staying caged between his arms. Her heart gave a loud *boom boom*. "Charm the customers, make them feel like family," she whispered. "You're good at that."

He was good at a lot of things, like making her forget.

"I think that's you. I might be able to charm the patrons, but you're the one who pulled everyone together and created an environment people want to be part of. You have this light that draws people to you, makes them feel a part of something special."

"I just built on what you've already created."

"You didn't 'just' anything. You're special and people can sense that."

She didn't know how to respond to a compliment that was genuine and heartwarming. Her instinct was to make light of the situation, throw out some quippy joke or flirty line. Anything to distract from what she was really feeling. Instead, she said, "You make me feel special."

He sculpted his hands down her sides to her thighs, paying extra attention to her bottom on the trip back. She rested her hands on those biceps she'd been watching all month, so she wouldn't fall over as the air whooshed out of her lungs.

Hell, she'd suffered from severe oxygen deprivation since the minute he'd shown up on her doorstep, wearing dark jeans and a blue button-down that made his eyes look like cobalt.

He'd opened the truck door for her and helped her inside like this was an actual date. While in the truck, they'd talked about their day, the little bits and fun bits, laughing like they'd done this a million times.

"So this starts our week?"

She blinked and realized she'd been staring at his lips. "What?"

Tightening his arms around her, he leaned in and whispered, "Let the games begin."

Abi didn't have a response to that other than to hide her disappointment. This wasn't a game to her, it was so much more. But she knew the conditions going in, had even agreed to them, so she couldn't fault him for sticking to their deal.

A little part of her recognized that one week wasn't going to be enough, but at this moment she was willing to take what he had to offer. And she'd enjoy every single second of it.

"Maybe we should start with that spin around the dance floor," she said.

Spin was the understatement of the year. Owen didn't just spin, he glided. His hand rested confidently at the small of her back, sliding a little lower with each song they danced. Tugging her closer with each step, until she was certain they were engaged in the sexiest display of public foreplay in the history of the world.

Every brush was like a shot of lightning, every touch as dangerous as gasoline on an already smoldering fire. When the music shifted and the line dancing began, they left the floor and headed to the bar.

Owen ordered her a beer and an iced tea for himself. When the bartender left, she turned on her stool to face him, their knees brushing. "Did you ever find that date you were looking for to accompany you to your mom's birthday party?"

He hooked his feet around the legs of her stool, his hands around the back curve of her knees, and tugged her closer. One minute she was facing him, the next she was practically sitting on his lap. And damn he smelled good. Before she could stop herself, she took in a big whiff and sighed.

His hands went to her thighs, rubbing down and back up, moving higher and higher. "You applying, Angel?"

"Is the position still open?"

"Depends on your qualifications," he teased.

"Let's be honest. I'm overqualified."

Those dimples deepened and her mouth watered. "Is that right?"

"Let me list the top five reasons why I'd be the perfect date. One." She held up a finger. "I'm an excellent conversationalist. And my banter is top shelf."

"That was two," he pointed out smugly.

"Three." She held up her third finger, the middle one, and he out-and-out laughed. "I don't take your crap. Four. I'm great with moms. Scratch that. Moms love me."

"As I mentioned earlier, you haven't met my mom. She nearly scared off my two sisters-in-law. They call her Satan's Keeper."

"She hasn't met me."

This time when he ran his hands up, his thumbs went so high her clothes nearly melted right off her body. "And five?"

"Oh, you'll like five. The dress." It wasn't actually *her* dress. It was Dotti's but Abi was confident that with a little Anna and Elsa bribery she could sweet-talk her sister into sole custody for the night.

His gaze heated. "Tell me about this dress. In great detail."

"It's red and a little off the shoulder. It's fitted and goes right below the knee." She took his hands under hers and glided them down to her knees. "It looks respectable from the front, but the back is where things get interesting."

"I like interesting." His voice was low and husky, like tossed gravel.

"There's a slit that goes obscenely high." She ran his hands around to the back of the curve of her knee, then slid them up her thigh.

"We talking thigh-high?"

"Higher." She didn't stop gliding his hands until they were a good two inches from go-time. He made a sound of sheer male appreciation. "Then there's this zipper." She let go to spin on her stool until her back was to him. "It starts at the base of my neck." She touched the spot she was speaking of, then felt his lips on her skin.

Abi wasn't big into PDA, but she didn't feel like they were in public. From the moment he'd taken her hand on the dance floor, it was as if the entire crowd had faded into the background, leaving just her and the man she'd been crushing on for months.

"It goes the entire length of the dress so if someone were to, say, have talented hands, all it would take is a single tug and *poof*." She made little explosions with her fingers.

"You don't have to convince me. I'd be damn lucky to have you on my arm."

"Then what's the holdup?"

"Hell if I know." He kissed her neck. "Why do *you* want to go, Angel?"

She turned back around to lean in all the way until her lips were grazing his ear, "Because you're the sure thing."

He chuckled. "What gives you that idea?"

"The way you're looking at me."

"And how's that?"

She ran her hands up his chest. "The same way I'm looking at you."

Chapter Twenty-Three

Happy Things:
Rain-soaked kisses

They'd been in the dance hall for over two hours, but in that time a small storm had blown in, opening up the sky and dropping enough rain that people were huddled under the awning.

Owen came up from behind and wrapped his arms around her, pulling her back against him—where she got an up-close-and-personal moment with his impressive front.

"We can wait it out," he said.

She melted back into him, her heart doing a little flip of anticipation for what the night would hold. This was what she'd been looking for. And she'd found it. If only for a week.

She tilted her head back, looking up at him and meeting his gaze. "I'm done waiting."

"Thank Christ."

His hands slowly moved over her hip, coming to rest at the small of her back. He guided her across the lot, using his big body to protect her from the worst of the rain. But the water on her face felt fresh and exciting, an unexpected turn of events, and the exact kind of spontaneity Owen needed more of in his life.

Only three steps from his truck, hidden by the tall cab, she tugged him to a stop.

She looked up at the sky and the thousands of droplets reflecting under the moon, like fairy lights twinkling across the night's sky. She opened her mouth to catch some rain, laughing when it tickled like champagne bubbles on the tip of her tongue.

"We're getting drenched."

"That's the point." She looked at him and found him looking back with enough want that her body quivered a scant inch from orgasmic levels.

He was like some Roman god arising from the storm. His shirt clung to his chest, the fabric was nearly see-through across his flat stomach, his canvas of tattoos visible. His hair and lashes were rain-spiked and his lips were wonderfully, temptingly wet.

"I think I'm seeing your point." His eyes couldn't stay above her lips, dipping low enough to tell her that not only had he noticed that her white cami had turned translucent, but she wasn't wearing a bra. "That answered that question."

"Any other questions you need answered?"

"Just one. Do you wear a matching set?"

She twined her fingers in his belt loop and tugged him right up in her space. He smelled like spring nights, rain, testosterone, and all things manly.

"I guess you'll have to find out."

His hands slid into her back pockets and he squeezed her ass. "Then what are we doing standing in the rain?"

She fisted her hands in his shirt collar and tugged him down—with authority. "Not standing. Kissing."

"You sure this is what you want?" he asked.

Did he even have to ask? Maybe her non-verbal communication skills were a bit rusty, but she was shrink-wrapped to his body, her nipples grazing his chest, while she rubbed up against him like a cat in heat.

"Oh, I want." Slowly, ever so slowly, she went up on her toes and whispered against his lips, "What did you say earlier? Oh yeah, 'Let the games begin.'"

That was all she got out before his mouth crashed down on hers. She went in hot, but he had other plans. Long, deep, slow plans that had her body melting against his again and again. All the pent-up chemistry and denied release led to an explosion that rivaled the Big Bang.

She slid her hands over his pecs—what impressive pecs they were—and around his neck, tugging him lower. But it still wasn't low enough. Their difference in height made things a little challenging.

She let out a frustrated huff and he smiled against her mouth.

"This isn't funny." She snagged his lower lip between her teeth and gently bit down. This time he groaned—one of those sheer-male appreciation groans that got her hot. "You're just so big."

"Guilty as charged."

She threaded her fingers into his hair and went up on her tiptoes, but it wasn't still enough. "You need to come down."

"Trust me, I will. But I need a flat surface for that. So for now, you need to come up." He pinned her against the passenger door, placing a hand on either side of her head.

His biceps bulged, his chest expanded, and his lips grazed her chin, moving higher to nip at her earlobe. Their bodies weren't touching and yet it felt as if his hands were all over her.

He rested his forehead against hers, his eyes locked and loaded, tracking hers.

"Wrap your legs around me, Angel," he said, and her bones liquified.

"What?" she asked

"You heard me." She had, and she also heard the animalistic growl in his voice so—even though Abi didn't like to take orders from anyone—she did as she was told.

Her feet left the ground and she was swept up into his arms, his hands cupping her ass, a large palm on each cheek easily holding her weight. She wrapped her legs around his waist and their lips—and other more exciting points—lined up perfectly.

She was smiling so big she knew she looked like a fool, but she couldn't help it. He made her happy. Being around him made her world better. "So much better."

"We're aiming higher than just better."

He gave her a devastating kiss, thorough and slow, building the heat. She tightened her legs, rolling her hips so his hard ridge pressed against her sensitive flesh. He groaned so she did it again.

The rain fell around them, flashes of lightning brightening the inky sky, like embers illuminating the blackness. Their bodies rubbed against each other, their hands grasping for traction, slick from the night's storm. And their connection deepened with every kiss. She could feel it and knew that he felt it too.

She reached for the first button, then the second and he groaned into her mouth. But when she went for the third, he pulled back slightly, not enough for their lips to part but enough to stop the momentum. And that split second gave way to guilt. She couldn't do this. She couldn't pretend that everything was okay and that she wasn't carrying this big secret. He deserved to know who she was and what she'd done before they had sex. And she knew that sex was where they were headed.

This was it, the moment that Abi had been dreading had finally come. Only it had come too early. Regardless, it sounded as if the buzzer had finished its countdown. Her secret had begun to feel like a lie, and Abi never wanted to tell another lie as long as she lived.

Abi felt her face heat and her head go light. "Wait. I have to tell you something."

"Now?"

"Right now." She took a deep breath before continuing. "You know how I kind of make a mess of things? Well, when I was seventeen, I used my sister's ID to buy wine coolers and I got caught."

Owen started laughing. "Babe, I thought you were going to tell me you were married or had a secret fetish for cowboys in just chaps. If so, I can order a pair right now."

"It's not funny, it was awful and scary and I made a selfish decision and a lot of people got into trouble. Good people," she whispered. "The cops roped me into being a snitch on liquor stores who looked the other way on fake IDs."

He rested his forehead to hers. "Hold up. You didn't do anything the rest of us didn't do. You just got caught. Shit happens."

She closed her eyes. "Even if Stout was one of the places I snitched on?"

He held a beat, a long beat where her heart rolled over waiting for the arrow. Instead he cupped her face, ever so gently. "You weren't the only one Brody sold beer to."

Her eyes tingled. "I wasn't?"

"No." He ran a finger down her jaw. "Brody made his decision, that's on him. As for you, you were a minor."

Her eyes glistened and a watery smile curved at her lips. "So you don't hate me?"

"I don't hate you." He kissed her nose. "I could never hate you."

"What about your mom?" she asked. "Your family?"

"I'll handle them," he said quietly, letting her know that they were in this together.

Elation and relief battled for dominance inside her chest. This whole time she'd been carrying around a secret that she thought would tear them apart when, in fact, coming clean had brought them closer.

"You want to hear about the time I got arrested for stealing panties?"

She snorted and it felt good to release some of the pent-up anxiety and fear. "Desperately."

"I came up with this brilliant idea to break into the girls' locker room and raid their lockers. The mission was to make a flag out of panties, only we set off a silent alarm. The cops came in right as I was breaking into Sarah Clark's locker."

"Who was Sarah Clark?"

"The better question is who is her dad. The chief of police."

Abi covered her mouth. "Did you get arrested?"

"No, but I did get a ride home in the back of a patrol car and my mom had to vouch for me. Which she refused to do unless I was given community service. And that was how I spent all summer break volunteering at a nursing home where I saw my fair share of granny panties."

"Did it break your silk and lace fetish?"

His gaze roamed over her body. "If I say no, will you help me overcome it with a fashion show of you in every single thong you own?"

"How about we do a game of you show me yours, I show you mine?"

"Hell yes."

When he didn't move confusion and uncertainty snuck in. "Are we stopping?"

"Angel, I'm six-four which is more than the space of my cab can handle especially if I'm going to show you my best moves."

She kissed his jaw, his neck. "How about you show me your good moves now and then we can get to the best moves later?"

Shifting her to one arm, he brushed back the wet hair from her cheek. "With you they're all going to be my best moves." He kissed her gently and slow. "I don't want this to be some flip decision."

"So you're saying no?"

He spun her around and she was suddenly sitting on the truck's bench; she hadn't heard him open the door. One minute she was in his arms, the next she was in his truck, with him standing between her thighs, which were still wrapped around his waist. "I'm saying until we get back to my place."

She looked at the interior of the truck, then back to the muscled man in front of her. She saw the problem. "Even if you have to go the speed limit?"

He kissed her nose. "Even then."

Chapter Twenty-Four

Happy Things:
Marvin Gaye

Even doing the speed limit they made it back to the loft in record time. Maybe it was luck, maybe it was the gods shining down on him, but his determination to do the right thing had paid off—in spades.

Next to him was the most gorgeous woman he'd ever seen, soaked straight through to her no-bra breasts, which were a miracle of their own. He hadn't even put the car in Park when he was leading her up the flight of steps and through the back door.

"Your place or mine?" he asked.

She didn't answer, just tightened her arms around him and kissed the bejesus out of him.

His place it was.

Mouth still fused to hers, he unlocked the door and they stumbled inside. Before they'd crossed the landing his little multitasker had his shirt unbuttoned and his jeans zipped down. Which was fine with him since his hands had been busy with her jeans, which he'd peeled halfway down her legs.

Their current state of undress made it difficult to navigate his place, making them more of a wrecking ball blasting through. They banged into one wall, then the other, which spoke to their dedication to the cause because there were only four walls in his loft.

She shoved off his shoes, using her feet to pull his jeans the rest of the way off.

"Commando," she said, running her hands down to give him a little nice-to-meet-you stroke.

He did some inspecting of his own. "Thong. Red. Hot as hell."

Then they were back to kissing, hands moving, legs shuffling and then they stumbled right into the kitchen counter.

"Boots," she said against his mouth.

"Love them."

"Unless you want me to really *stumble* into bed, then they need to come off."

Right. He saw the problem. Wet denim and cowgirl boots. Taking her hips, he sat her on the counter. She rested back on her hands, looking like a fine Southern sexpot, then held out one leg. He disposed of the boot, then the other, tugging her jeans off and onto the ground. When all the obstacles were dealt with, he picked her up and whirled her around, which made her laugh—and what an amazing laugh it was.

Genuine, contagious—the kind of laugh that made his chest ache for more than just surviving the day-to-day.

Onto the bed they went, where he plopped her down on the mattress, the movement giving her breasts a little jiggle, an outstanding viewer experience.

Going to his place had been an excellent choice in location. It had a king-sized bed, compared to her twin, and a headboard that could make things interesting. Then there was the kitchen and all the thirteen counters and nooks that they could explore over the next twelve hours. That's a flat surface every hour—and one for good luck. And if—*if*—they happened to run out of places, then they'd go back into the truck and give it a whirl.

Hell, maybe he should have just started in the truck because then she'd be naked and on top of him screaming his name. But then he wouldn't be able to see her on his bed, laid back with her damp hair spread across his pillow, looking up at him like he was going to rock her ever-loving world.

Needing a moment, he stood back to take in the eighth wonder of the world: those perfect tens, which were practically spilling out of her top. The kind of top that had two little straps that were meant to mess with a man's mind. That kind of top.

Tight. White. Wet. And floor bound. Just as soon as he could stop staring.

"You going to keep looking or are you ready to move on to the touching portion of the evening?"

"Just deciding where I want to start."

Identifying his point of entry, he crawled up her body and, making himself right at home between her thighs, he ever so slightly lifted the hem of her top. "Maybe here." He dropped a gentle kiss right above her belly button. Then one right below.

"That's a good place," she breathed.

"I know of an even better place." Spanning his hands around her waist, he tugged her lower and lower down the bed beneath him, nipping at every exposed rib until he reached the undersides of her breasts. He took his time exposing them fully, wanting to watch as they puckered.

She shivered and, hell yeah, it was game on.

"How about here?" He licked one, then the other, moving back and forth to pull her into his mouth until her back was fully arched off the mattress. Her head dropped back, the pulse at the base of her neck pounding erratically.

"Better?"

"Amazing," she moaned.

"We can still work on that." He ran his hands up and over her head, her see-through shirt falling to the mattress. Pressing open-mouthed kisses up her neck, all the way up, he made a detour and captured her mouth.

Most guys went right for the win. Not Owen. To him, the pre-game was as important as the touchdown. Which was why he took his time to explore. And explore he did.

He nipped her lower lip, then went in for several deep, hot kisses that left both panting. As he was kissing her, he rolled onto his side, holding himself up on his elbow. With his free hand, he danced his fingers down her stomach, watching her flesh quiver in his wake. Then, *holy Christ,* he was there—the exact place he'd spent the past two months dreaming about—the place right beneath that thong.

He'd wavered between teal and red since they seemed to be her favorite choice in footwear color and she seemed like a coordinated type of gal. Sure as shit, it was red and lace and the same color as her boots—which were strewn across the floor creating a path from the front door to his bed.

She might not be commando, but her thong didn't rate all that high on concealment. It was so teeny and tiny with see-through lace, she might as well have been naked. Which was his next step.

Then, Abi was totally and completely naked in his bed.

He considered flipping her over or maybe flipping her onto his lap—backward. But while he wanted nothing more than to be inside of her, he also wanted to be gentle. The more he'd uncovered, the more the extent of the accident was visible, and the more committed he was to making this the best experience of her life.

A big order, but, like she'd said, he was a big guy. And he always delivered on his promises.

His hand slipped further down. He listened to her breathing, then not breathing, then making this sexy little release of air. "Ah, what do we have here?"

"The best spot," she said, and then did the hottest thing known to man. She slid her hands down to tangle with his, guiding him lower. "My favorite place is right here, in case you were wondering." She didn't play coy or try to be mysterious; she knew what she wanted and, in no uncertain terms, gave him the green light.

He looked up to find her looking back through her lashes. Their gaze caught and held and, for the life of him, he couldn't look away. Didn't even blink as she slid their fingers inside and her eyes went heavy-lidded and lust-drunk.

He knew how she felt; he was about to explode and she had barely even touched him.

She picked up the pace, their hands disappearing all the way beneath the lace, and the rhythm became frantic and frenzied. She was close, so close. Tightening around him, her hips pumping up as their hands moved deeper. She showed him what she liked and, even sexier, what she loved.

And who was he to deny her any want or need she had. And, apparently, she needed more because she pumped harder, their hands moving faster until… until… *Good god,* the until was going to be spectacular.

"Owen?" she breathed.

"Yes?"

"Owen," she cried out and fell over that edge so fast and hard he could feel her come apart beneath his hand. He stayed with her until she gently came back down.

Not wanting to lose the momentum, Owen was wrapped and ready in *Houston, we made contact* no time flat.

They both gasped at the glorious sensation of finally, *finally,* being in a place to rock her world. She seemed to be on the same wavelength because she started rocking and moving and before he could catch his breath, she was on top straddling him. Her hands were next to his shoulders, her breasts within perfect mouth-to-nipple distance, and her ass in his hands.

It was the holy shit of trifectas that had him thanking Marvin Gaye, ribbed for her pleasure condoms, and every sex god that ever existed.

"I figured this was your favorite place," she teased and then sat upright, bringing him deeper than he'd ever been.

Ah, a multi-tasker indeed, this one. She was rolling her hips while stroking him at the base. It was a double-the-trouble move that had him close to take off. She did it again and then, because he couldn't help himself, he lifted her off him by her hips and rose into her.

"Owen," she whispered.

He did it again and because three time's the charm, he did it yet again.

"Owen?" This time there was a frantic edge to her voice.

"Yeah, Angel?"

She lifted her lids and looked at him through her eyelashes, then gifted him a small smile. "I guess I just like saying your name."

"I like hearing it from you. Especially when you say it all breathy. But I gotta be honest, I love it when you scream my name."

Owen sat up and, gently gripping her waist, maneuvered them so he was upright and she was straddling his lap. He didn't want to crush her and he didn't want to accidentally bump one of her bruises, so he positioned her for maximum penetration and minimal bumping.

She slid her arms around his neck and buried her face into the curve and held tight. They started moving again but this time it wasn't with that mindless urgency, it was with something even better.

An awareness that what was happening between them was special. Their brushes and touches came from someplace deeper, someplace Owen refused to acknowledge.

She felt it too. He knew it. But like him, she was fighting to keep things straightforward, within the parameters that they'd previously agreed to. To him, those parameters were blown to bits the second she'd called out his name. It showed him that this wasn't some one-time, here-now gone-tomorrow kind of connection.

Not that he expected her to change her plans, but it was enough to know that if things were different, if his life had room for more, that she'd be the kind of woman he'd want to be with.

"Owen?" she asked, her eyes filled with concern. "You okay?"

No, he was not okay. This woman had him completely spun up. It was as if they were vibing on the same wavelength; she could sense what direction his emotions were heading. Which was good, since he felt like he was in foreign terrain without a map. But there she was, this bright beacon helping him find his way.

"Owen," she said and this time when she said it, he could hear the confusion in her voice and that's when he realized he'd stopped moving. He just sat there with her in his arms breathing in her scent.

Thrown off-balance, he quickly recovered and single-mindedly focused on Abi and her pleasure.

He brushed her lips when she threaded her fingers into his hair and yanked him. Fusing their mouths, she took it from zero to hotter-than-hell.

Gripping her waist, he moved her up and down as she used her knees for leverage. All it took was a few more deep and even slower thrusts and he was about to get a gold star in holding out. Because he was primed to go but she needed just one more little swirl of the—

"Owen," she cried out and, miracle of all miracles, she went off like a firework, tightening around him so forcefully he could no longer hold back. So he didn't.

He let go in one of the best orgasms of his life. He let the tide drag him out and when it pulled him back in, they were laid back on the bed, Abi was in his arms, and they were both gasping for breath.

After a long moment, Abi curled up next to him, lacing their fingers.

"I think I found *your* favorite place," she teased.

Owen chuckled, deep and low, but it didn't ring true because as far as he was concerned, all the teasing left the building. Because while she had, indeed, found his favorite place, he was starting to think that maybe Abi was his favorite place.

Chapter Twenty-Five

Happy Things:
Finding your big spoon

A long and eventful time later, after they'd covered six of the thirteen flat surfaces, Owen lay on his side with Abi snuggled against him, fast asleep.

His right leg was slung over hers like he was her own personal blanket, and his arm was around her, his hand cupping her breast as if he owned it, while he listened to the gentle rhythm of her heartbeat.

He stared out the window at the soft glow of the streetlight illuminating the room, with a big, goofy grin on his face. He wasn't really a cuddler but there had been a lot of "wasn't really"s in his life since meeting Abi. Like not really ready for a commitment or not ready for a relationship. While he still wasn't sure if he had the space for either of those, he found himself thinking about all the what-ifs.

What if it wasn't all the external things that made a relationship hard? What if he was using that as an excuse because he was afraid of getting hurt again? But the biggest what-if of all was the what if he hurt her. His life was full and she deserved a big, all-encompassing, ride-or-die kind of partner and he wasn't sure he could be that person. But maybe he was willing to give it a try.

But he didn't know where her head was at.

He knew where her body stood, but was her heart still set on moving on after their time was up? He knew her relationship with her sister was strained and she rarely talked about her parents—Abi was on her own. What Owen didn't know was if it was her choice or a life that had been handed to her. He knew practically nothing about her life pre-accident. Hell, he barely knew what happened in the accident.

Her injuries told a horrifying story.

"I can almost hear you thinking," she said, her sleep-roughened voice making him count the footsteps to the kitchen counter. "What's going on in your head?"

He pressed his answer firmly against her butt and she gave a tired chuckle. "The other head."

"You need to specify or he'll think it's go time." He debated whether to even broach the topic of family. First impressions of Abi were that she was a big, friendly, open book. But on closer inspection, there were a lot of layers that she kept locked up tight. It was that part of Abi that he wanted to know. The side of her that she was too afraid to show people. And layers usually start with the past. "Tell me about your parents."

She looked at him over her shoulder as if he'd gone mad. "We're naked and you want to talk about my parents?"

He feathered his fingers down her arm in soothing lines. "I want to know about you."

She took in a deep breath and held it, so long he was certain she'd change the topic with one of her smart-ass jokes, but when she exhaled, he felt her body sink into his. "I'm the surprise baby in a yours-and-mine sandwich."

"So you were the Ours?"

"Not really," she whispered. "My mom and stepdad were going through a rough patch. My mom met my dad at work and, surprise, here I am."

Owen couldn't imagine a situation where either of his parents would stray. They set the bar high for marriage and love. Even a decade later his mom still mourned his dad in her own way.

"How did that work? With your parents?"

"My mom and stepdad eventually pushed through and stayed together, but it was rough. At least Dotti said it was. I was a baby, so I don't remember."

"But Dotti told you how bad it got?"

"Mainly my brother, Steven. He and Michael are my dad's. Dotti's my mom's."

The way she said it, the wistfulness in her voice, told him that while each of her siblings had a parent, Abi had none.

"And your dad?"

She rolled on her back, those gorgeous brown eyes shining up at him. "He was married too, but it didn't last. A couple of years after the affair, he and his wife divorced. She got the house and my brothers lived with her full time. My dad just got them on the weekends, along with me. So I had three siblings. All of them older. Dotti is the closest to me in age and friendship, but we're separated by five years and an opposite-personalities problem."

Jesus, Dotti was her closest sibling? Having met Dotti in public he could only imagine what she was like behind closed doors.

"So, you lived with your dad?"

"My parents could never agree on who got me when, so I spent a lot of time being shuffled back and forth."

Shuffling around had bled into her adult life. He wondered if she even realized why she didn't stay in one place too long and what it would take for her to stick.

He brushed his nose across a big, angry scar that sat below her collarbone, then pressed a kiss there. He'd seen this same scar before, only from the back, right below her shoulder blade.

"The metal casing from the bench seat in front of me tore free. The bus skidded for a few yards, then stopped when it hit the side of a pole. I slid forward and caught on the metal." More like the metal went through and through. She looked at him and, as if knowing where his thoughts were headed, she said, "I didn't feel it. They said I was in shock."

She might have been in shock, but she'd felt it. He could see it in her eyes, the way they skittered away briefly and how she worried her lip. It was her tell.

"I know, I'm a terrible liar."

He knew what she was doing. Humor was her way of avoiding hard topics. But he wasn't going to let her off that easy. "And this?" He ran his hand ever so gently over the yellowing mark on her side.

"I bruised my kidney."

Rolling on his back, he took her hand, studying all the tiny scars and discoloring. He tried to kiss her palm, but she took her hand back. "I don't remember how I got those. The doctor said it's road rash." She turned over to lie on him, resting her cheek over his heart. "It will eventually go away."

He'd bet there was a lot she couldn't remember. Trying to process all of that at a single time would overload anyone's brain. It broke his heart that what she did remember was the image of Jenny and the children.

As for the rest of her injuries, he doubted anyone else knew the extent. Abi wouldn't want to worry anyone or be too much of a burden, it was something he'd noticed around the bar. Abi was always the first to volunteer and the last one to leave. And no matter how crappy her day was, she was always smiling and joking, making sure everyone felt included.

"Where are your parents now?"

"My mom's in Florida and my dad lives with his new family in Connecticut."

He ran his hand down her spine, waiting for her to continue. When she didn't, he asked, "I mean, why aren't they here with you?"

"Dot's house isn't big enough."

"Then why aren't you there with one of them?"

She looked him square in the eye and that's when he saw the emotion lining her lashes. "We're not that kind of family."

He brushed the hair out of her face. "I'm sorry."

"Me too."

Chapter Twenty-Six

Happy Things:
A partner who knows when you're bluffing

The cards were stacked against Abi on this good deed. No matter how skilled she was, the house always won. And this house was about to collapse unless she pulled an ace out of her sleeve.

Darlene from the senior center called earlier in a panic. Tonight was the annual Silver Sharks Poker tournament and she and a host of other residents came down with mononucleosis. Seemed a group of silver singles, who were looking to mingle, snuck out to play a little game of spin the bottle. Darlene landed on a lemon and wound up quarantined and knocked out of the tournament.

Now they were down a venue and one player.

And that was how Abi ended up at Stout sitting across the table from Margo Easton. The oversweet scent of perfume mixed with proprietorship and entitlement was a dead giveaway. Then there was her outfit. Linen pants, a mauve silk blouse, and pearls. Not even Spring could dictate what the woman wore.

Bracing herself to look into the eyes of the woman whom Abi had unintentionally wronged, Abi felt her stomach churn and she froze in place. Margo wasn't so much

Satan's Keeper as she was Medusa, able to turn Abi's feet to concrete, making it impossible to take her seat.

"Who in God's name are you?" Margo asked, and Abi blinked, shaking off the nerves.

You are the Mom Whisperer, she reminded herself. *Moms love you.*

All her exes' moms still kept in touch with her. Her exes, not so much. Usually, when people had had enough, they'd had enough. But she did have a magic touch when it came to moms.

Not with Owen. He embraced her quirky and prickly side. Over the last four days, he seemed to want more of her, not less. They'd had a glorious four days taking dogs for walks, granting wishes, and kissing in the rain. There'd also been nighttime kissing which led to nighttime touching which led to nighttime until daytime sex. Mind-blowing, earth-shattering, life-altering sex.

For the first time in her dating life, sex led to this cosmic connection she didn't know existed. A connection she was likely to be severed from, because if there was one thing she'd learned about Margo it was that she was keen, intuitive, and observant. Employees said she had a stare that could break anyone. She was a human lie detector.

It was rumored that after one of Margo's infamous looks an employee admitted not only that he was stealing kegs but he was behind on his water bill, cheating on his girlfriend, and told his mom he was sick on her birthday when he went to a concert instead. Margo made him call his mother and come clean, then fired him on the spot. He fled the bar in tears.

Abi didn't know if she believed in Margo the Myth; the woman was shorter than Abi, small-boned, and wore linen for the love of God. But she also didn't want to awaken the beast. Because while Abi could turn on that honeyed

Southern charm, she could also go toe to toe with anyone. But this wasn't anyone. This was Owen's mom and Abi wanted to win her over.

"Hi, it's nice to meet y'all." Abi gave a nervous little wave. And then because she was addressing a room full of her elders, she introduced herself properly. "I'm Abilene Woods, and I'm the stand-in tonight."

Margo looked her up and down, then paused and something she swore was recognition flashed in the older woman's eyes. Abi's stomach sank. "What kind of name is Abilene?"

"A special one. But, if you like, you may call me Abi."

She couldn't be sure, but it looked as if Margo's lip twitched, then suddenly her expression went to one of curiosity. "Do we know each other? You seem familiar."

Abi gulped, then looked at the exit. *There's still time to run!* But that would only confirm what Abi had feared as of late—that she was a coward.

She answered as honestly as she could right then. "I don't believe we've ever met, no."

"Huh." Margo didn't seem convinced, but let it go. "Where's Darlene?"

Abi smiled a so-sweet-you'll-get-a-cavity smile that had an unparalleled success rate with mothers of all kinds. "Darlene's under the weather, so she asked me to be her stand-in." She looked around the table and spotted the only single chair—and swallowed.

"Who's my partner?" she asked, but she already knew. Her fate had been sealed before she'd even arrived.

She looked up at the ceiling and glared. *You'd better have one heck of a good reason for this, Jenny.*

All eyes went to Margo. "Right. Well, nice to meet you, partner." Abi stuck out her hand and leaned over the table, and everyone looked her way. It was like a Wimbledon match.

In the end, Margo reached across the table and embraced Abi's gesture. But when Abi started to pull back, Margo held on. She was strong for a woman about to turn seventy. "Do you even know how to play? You look like you're right out of high school. I haven't lost in seven years, and I'm not going to lose because I was paired with a young whippersnapper."

"I was the reigning poker champion at Alpha Epsilon Pi, a fraternity. So we should make a winning pair."

"Big talk for a small girl."

"Bless your heart, you have no idea who you're playing with. Sit back and watch." They were big words since inside she was quaking in her boots.

Abi took the deck of cards and shuffled them like she was a dealer at the largest casino in Vegas and Margo said, "Okay then."

"Ante up," a woman with a teal pantsuit and white orthopedic sneakers said.

Everyone put in their ante and the dealer gave each player two cards. Eventually, the table was ready, and the first game was in play. Abi had a king and queen of spades, a strong start especially since there was a jack of spades on the table.

When all the cards were dealt and the chips were played, the game was called and, *would you look at that,* Abi and Margo won the hand.

Abi collected the cards and gave the deck a good shuffle, casually looking up at Margo, who was staring back. Like her sons, she had these big, blue eyes. Unlike her sons, Abi was pretty sure the woman could shoot lasers from them.

"I stand corrected," Margo said.

"Don't worry about it. It's easy to underestimate me."

People had been doing it her whole life, at least until Owen. But that was going to end in just three days and she didn't know what she'd do after that. Or where she'd go. Thailand sounded so extreme, and she doubted Portland would be a good option for her wellbeing.

Abi was back to handing out the cards when Margo asked, "Are you the Abi dating my Owen?"

Oh boy. Abi choked on air.

"I wouldn't say dating." What would she call what they were doing? It was more than friends with benefits but not quite dating. And in a few days it would come to a close, so what was the point of trying to define or justify anything to anyone. Plus, Abi wasn't the kind of person to kiss and tell. When it came to her personal life, she kept things close to her chest.

"We're spending time together," she decided was the appropriate response. Short. To the point. And open-ended.

Let them think what they want. She wasn't giving anything away. If Owen wanted his mom to know what was going on between them, then that was up to Owen to tell her.

Margo clutched her pearls and ran her nail along the necklace. "Time that dipped into our movie night."

Abi's went chin up and shoulders back. "I apologize for that, ma'am. I thought he needed some fun and to let off some steam."

The table gasped.

"Are you saying I'm not fun?" Margo accused.

Oh shit.

"No, I'm saying that Owen does a lot of things for a lot of people, and I wanted to do something for him."

The older woman stopped stroking her pearls. "I agree," she said, and the room took a collective exhale—including Abi.

"He also needs to have some more balance between work and his personal life."

"And you've convinced him to take time off?" Margo looked beyond impressed.

"I don't think Owen will do anything he doesn't want to do," Abi said. "He's stubborn and a bit of a grump, but I hope he takes advantage of the time that's been freed up by his new staff and managerial guidelines, which have been streamlined so anyone can …"

Abi faded off because everyone was looking over her head and she knew who they were looking at. The stubborn, grumpy guy whose bed she'd left just a few hours ago.

She looked over her shoulder and nearly swallowed her tongue. Today Owen was dressed in business casual, which for him meant dark jeans, a button-down rolled at the sleeves, no tie. He had a meeting with a new beer distributor, which was supposed to have already started.

"What are you doing here?' she whispered.

He rested his hands on the back of the chair and leaned against it. "I could ask you the same." His thumb ran up her spine in a stealth move that only the two of them were aware of. She shivered so he did it again.

"She's partnering me, so don't distract her. We're on a roll," Margo said, and Owen lifted a surprised brow.

"On a roll, huh?"

"I have many talents."

He leaned down and whispered in her ear, "Oh, I know." While Abi was choking on his comment, he walked around the table.

"Hi, Mom." He went over to give his mom a peck on the cheek, but not before he had let Abi know that he was thinking about her. Which was sweet and reassuring.

She might not know where she stood, but he let her know that he was thinking about her as much as she'd been thinking about him.

Margo radiated when Owen was near her. With six sons to her name, she must be drowning in testosterone, but she didn't seem to mind. She took his hand between hers and her entire face transformed, softened, glowing with pride and love. It was as if the bitter, puckered woman disappeared and in her place was a warm and caring mother who adored her kids.

It was such a foreign concept to Abi that she didn't know where to look, so she focused her attention on shuffling the cards. She wondered what it would be like to be on the receiving end of a love like that. To have a bond so strong that it could withstand the worst.

Abi couldn't even get her parents in the same room, let alone be civil to one another. She'd spent her life listening to the worst parts of her parents. As a kid, she always wondered if they talked about her like that behind closed doors.

Heck, she still wondered. They'd called a grand total of three times since she was released from the hospital. Oh, they'd come to visit when she'd been in the hospital, but once she was deemed okay by the doctors, they flew back to their respective lives, leaving Abi alone to figure it out. And there was a lot to figure out.

How to get out of the lease for the apartment she and Jenny shared, where to go, how to manage the pain and physical therapy on her own. How to come back from the worst tragedy of her life.

"Did you all know that my Owen here is an artist," Margo beamed, but Owen was focused on Abi. "He painted every picture in my house and did a mural for Susan."

"The one of the Italian landscape?" one of the women asked, clearly impressed.

There were some *Wows* and *I didn't knows* and an *It's just stunning.*

Owen actually blushed. His cheeks were honest-to-god flushed. She bit back a grin. "I'd love to see the mural. Do you have a photo by chance?"

"Of course I do," Margo preened. She pulled out her phone and while she was scrolling through, Owen snagged Abi's gaze, leveling her with a *be careful* look. She one-upped him with an *Or what?* shrug.

His eyes heated and roamed down to her breasts and back up. She gulped because she knew exactly what he was thinking about. She'd been thinking about it nonstop since she'd left his place earlier that afternoon.

"Here, dear," Margo said to Abi, and Owen lifted a shocked brow at the endearment. She patted Owen's arm. "Take this to Abi so she can see."

His eyes locked on Abi, Owen walked around the table and she could practically smell the heat wafting off him. He handed it over and she grinned up at him.

"Here you go, *dear*," he whispered the last word.

"My superpower, remember?"

"I remember everything you say," he said lowly.

It was hard to break eye contact, but the entire table sat rapt, watching the exchange. Abi looked down at the photo and her breath caught. "It's beautiful."

"Isn't it," Margo said. "He came up with the concept and painted it freehand. He's my most talented son."

He gripped the back of his neck. "I don't know about that. I mean you have a Super Bowl champ and Grammy-winning artist."

"And not a one of them can paint worth a damn."

"And not one of them is you," Abi said just for his ears. "Your talent takes my breath away."

"Oh, I know," he said flirtingly.

"Don't do that," she said. "Don't downplay it. You are amazing."

Something flickered in his gaze, something warm and real, something that touched her deep down inside. He was showing a side she'd never seen. A vulnerable and open side he usually camouflaged with banter.

Don't fall or you'll get hurt, she told herself. But it was already too late. No matter how this ended, friends or enemies, she was going to be heartbroken.

"You okay?" he said so quietly she barely heard him.

"What? Me? I'm fine." To prove it she smiled. Smart guy that he was, he wasn't buying it. But before he could probe any further, Margo interrupted.

"Shoo." She waved a hand at Owen. "Your lady friend and I have a tournament to win."

"When there's a break, I need to speak with my lady friend. I'm having an issue with, uh, inputting something."

Abi laughed and he grinned. As he took the phone back to hand to his mom, his fingers purposefully grazed hers. The simple contact was like a match to a powder keg.

The round seemed to take forever. Abi and Margo were cleaning house, but Abi kept thinking about Owen's hands on her. By the time she could excuse herself, her body was so primed her skin felt too tight to contain itself.

She made her way down the hallway toward his office but before she reached it, someone grabbed her and dragged her into the storage closet. Then his mouth was on hers, his hands tangled in her hair, her back pressed against the wall.

Owen.

It took her a scant moment to catch up, but once she did it was like a wildfire. He kissed his way down her neck, tugging her shirt collar off her shoulder and down went the bra strap.

"Mmm," he hummed against her skin. "So soft." His hands roamed all the way down her back to slip into the back pockets of her jeans. "Feels even better."

Careful not to wrinkle his shirt, she slipped her fingers beneath the waistband of his jeans and tugged him against her. He slid his thigh between hers and pressed, putting pressure on her favorite spot. She moaned, her head falling back to thunk on the wall.

"Owen," she breathed.

"Is this where you like saying my name?"

"This is where I remind you your mom is on the other side of this wall." He looked up at her, his eyes heated and dark. "What are you doing?"

"I'm taking advantage of the time that's been freed up by my new staff and managerial guidelines."

Chapter Twenty-Seven

Happy Things:
Brotherhood

Owen spent the first part of his morning making Abi scream his name, then making her breakfast, before he made her scream his name all over again on the upstairs deck. He'd considered skipping the gym, but his brothers would pummel him if he missed their weekly session of beating the crap out of each other again. Not that it mattered, his head was spun to the point of distraction. So much so that Rhett was able to get in a couple of cheap shots—costing Owen two hundred bucks. Not that he cared.

Thinking about Abi naked in his bed was worth the black eye.

"I'd kiss it and make it better, but it looks like someone beat me to it," Clay said, putting his boxing gloves into his gym bag.

Owen looked in the mirror and, sure as shit, there was a hickey on his shoulder. There might have been a little bite mark too, which made him smile.

"You constipated or is that an actual smile?" Gage said, slamming his locker door.

"I think it's a smile. Yup, a stupid-looking, deer in the headlights grin. I recognize it well," Rhett said, then gave a self-deprecating laugh. "Then again, it's been so long, maybe I don't."

Owen looked at his brother and noticed just how wrung out he looked. His eyes were bloodshot like he hadn't slept in weeks, his scruff was too long to be intentional and too short to be a beard. Then there was the devastated flicker in his eyes before he looked away.

"How are you doing with things?" Owen asked.

Rhett just looked at him as if he was an idiot. "All you have to do is pick up a magazine to know my life is a complete mess."

Divorce was hard enough. Going through it while every devastating moment was criticized and scrutinized and laid out for the world to see must be hell. Rhett had wanted to fight for the marriage, but his wife hadn't. It pretty much boiled down to that they wanted different things—like a family.

After two years of hectic and conflicting schedules, Rhett was ready for the stability of a home base, cutting back on his tour to make room for the marriage and eventually kids. Then last year, Steph said she wasn't ready to give up the lifestyle and dropped the bomb that she didn't think she wanted kids—ever. A statement that was in direct opposition with what she'd said prior to the wedding, where she'd gone on and on about wanting a family the size of Rhett's.

Steph did a complete flip-a-roo. Most of the brothers thought it was because being married to a guy like Rhett was good for her career and once she'd hit enough followers she wanted out. Owen wanted to give her the benefit of the doubt, but the way she was handling things made it hard.

"According to the tabloids you're seeing—" Clay said some famous actress's name.

"The only thing I'm seeing is that I have two months to move out of the house and no prospects on where to move. I have the condo in LA but at some point I'm going to nee my own place here in Portland to establish residency or the IRS will have my ass."

It wasn't as if Rhett could just buy a regular house in a regular neighborhood. With his fame, he'd need the right kind of property if he expected to have any kind of privacy. And there weren't many of those in Portland. Los Angeles, sure. But when Rhett wasn't on the road or in the studio he needed to be around family as much as any of the brothers.

"Funny, since last week you were seen leaving a certain pop star's hotel room," Josh said. "You aren't wasting any time getting back out there."

"Nothing serious. Just a night here or there," Rhett said.

"Any more nights and you're one step away from the guy who had a date for every day of the week."

Before Rhett met Stephanie, he'd been the playboy of the family, playing it fast and loose with the ladies. It seemed like old habits died hard, and Owen was afraid that his kid brother would wind up with a string of one-night stands and nothing to hold on to.

Owen knew firsthand how lonely that kind of life could be, and he didn't want that for Rhett. Hell, he didn't want that for himself. But putting your heart on the line was harder than his other brothers made it look. For them love seemed to come easy. Sure they'd all had their fuck-up moments, but in the end they'd all found love.

"Seriously, how are you doing?" Clay asked Rhett, his assessing eyes seeing everything. He might be the baby of the brothers, but he was the most levelheaded and introspective of the group. He also had the most accurate BS meter. When he was assessing, he was sniffing out exactly how bad things were. So when Clay's face went grim, they had their answer.

"It sucks. The whole thing sucks. The tour, writing music, my life. It's like one giant dumpster fire. Maybe it's time to take a break, find some simple in my world." Rhett shook his head. "Who am I kidding, that part of my life makes my world turn. And a lot of other people's too."

Like Owen, Rhett had a lot of people riding on his success. If Stout closed, his employees would lose their livelihood. With Rhett, it was ten times the pressure. Then again, wasn't that what Abi had given Owen—something simpler? A chance to gain some of his life back? Important parts that he'd thought long lost?

"There's more to you than a guitar," Owen said and clapped his brother on the shoulder. "A lot more."

"Truer words have never been spoken," Clay chimed in. "Giving up my place in Seattle to be here with Jillian when I'm not on the field was the best decision of my life. *You* get to choose your lifestyle and you've never had more options than right now."

Rhett seemed to consider this, then asked, "Have you convinced Jillian to marry your stupid ass?"

Clay's answer was a smile. A special kind of smile he gave whenever he spoke of his girlfriend and her son. "Life is perfect as is. I'm big on her and she's not big on marriage. After what her ex did to her, I wouldn't expect her to want to jump into another one. I don't need a ring to know that she loves me." He looked right at Owen. "Love might not have worked out with Elena, but it's worth it to give love a second chance."

Abi wasn't Elena. Nothing she'd said or done was remotely Elena-esque. She was honest and thoughtful and slowly opening up to him. Maybe a second chance was worth it. Maybe with Abi, it was worth potential heartache.

"Her last shift at the tea shop is on Thursday, then she leaves at the end of the week." Travel bound, starting in Thailand and moving her way around Asia teaching English is what she'd told him last night when he'd asked what came next for her.

"How do you feel about that?" Clay asked.

Owen sat down on the bench. "Confused." More than confused. The whole situation didn't sit right. Even the idea of her getting on some plane had his chest in knots. "I was the one who insisted on keeping things simple. No string, no ties, nothing remotely complicated."

Which, looking back, was stupid because even though he hadn't been willing to admit it, he'd known that giving them an expiration date was a shit move. When he told her a week was all he could handle, he'd unintentionally solidified her belief that she was temporary goods.

Even though she'd disagree, nothing about her said temporary. Abi was the kind of woman who deserved more than a tumbleweed of an existence. After a lifetime of being shoved aside, it was time someone showed her just how amazing she was.

"How's that working for you?" Clay asked.

"It's not."

"Then if I were you, I'd give her a reason to stay."

Chapter Twenty-Eight

Happy Things:
Naked Twister

Mother Nature was showing off. The spring night was crisp and welcoming, with a gentle breeze that rustled the maple trees lining the street. The fresh scent of wet pavement and cherry blossom filled the air and the warm sensation of Owen's hand in hers made the evening all the more special.

They'd just come from a romantic dinner at what was becoming their favorite Indian place. Even the idea that they had a favorite anything was enough to make her belly zing. Though it had only been five days, to Abi it felt as if they'd known each other for five years.

They'd spent their nights in tangled sheets and their mornings talking on the patio while sharing one of Owen's delicious breakfasts as the sun came up.

He would go to work at Stout and Abi would do her shift at the tea shop. They'd sneak away for a midday lunch, which usually involved tearing each other's clothes off. They'd both end their day at six and then make dinner together, where Owen cooked while Abi sat on the counter drinking wine and distracting him. Sometimes with her hands, other times with her mouth.

What started as a completely physical agreement had turned into so much more. At least on Abi's side. She had zero clues as to where his head was at. She knew he felt something for her, something that went beyond their time in bed, she just wasn't sure if it was enough to carry them through the looming deadline.

"Where are we?" she asked, looking up at the dark storefront. The historic, brick-fronted building was sandwiched between two brownstones and had a massive red-trimmed door with a half-circle glass panel above that took up the majority of the entry. Located a few blocks from Stout, it had the same upscale modern feel as the rest of the neighborhood, with high-end boutiques and dining below, and residential on the upper floors.

To the right sat a community park with an open, lush green space, a giant dogwood tree in full bloom and a small pond that reflected the silver moon above. The setting was as romantic as Owen was nervous. She could tell by the way he tightened his hands around hers that he was battling uncertainty. So she gave him a little reassuring squeeze.

He looked down at her and smiled, his eyes soft and warm.

"You brought me into your world, I wanted to bring you into mine," he said.

Owen took out a set of keys and unlocked the door, guiding her inside and flicking on the overhead track lighting. The space was masculine and luxe, with the original small checkered-tile floors and modern slate walls with a patina ceiling of copper tile. Lining the side of the room were three tattooing chairs with frosted glass accordion doors separating each station.

"Is this where you used to work?" she asked.

"It's where I currently work."

"Currently work?" As in he'd been tattooing again? As in the last good deed Abi had on her Owen list. A complicated mix of excitement and devastation rushed through her. Excitement for Owen and his new venture. Devastation because it was a reminder that her time was really up.

"I haven't spent much time here, just a couple of hours last week, but it was more than I've been here in months and it felt good." He shrugged like it wasn't a big deal, but she knew it was.

"Which one is your station?"

"Up here." He led her to a curved staircase that was made of hammered steel and dark wood. The upstairs was just as stunning. Modern and masculine with bold lines and a variety of textures. In the corner sat a black chair that she knew was Owen's.

"I'm really happy for you." She wrapped her arms around his waist and kissed him. He kissed her back until she was a big ball of goo. "You know, your dad would have been proud of you."

He didn't respond but he didn't need to. The emotion was there in his eyes.

"I want to show you something. And before you ask, no, it's not in my pants," he said. She knew he was downplaying the moment, trying to make what was a huge deal into a passing conversation.

She laced their fingers and walked them the rest of the way to his station. On the counter was an open portfolio. "May I?"

He nodded and she flipped through the book, stunned at the detail and quality of his designs. "These are amazing. Are they originals?" she asked even though she didn't need to, she knew he'd painstakingly designed each and every one.

"Most of them are from when I used to tattoo in Austin, but there are a few new ones."

"Show me."

He came up behind her and turned the pages to the back of the album. There sat a piece of contact paper with a single design on it. She could tell that his nerves had him second-guessing showing it to her.

"This is my most recent one. It's still not completely finished, and I'm open to changes and, well, this is it."

She looked at him over her shoulder. "I'm sure it's beautiful." It was more than that. It was stunning. "What is this?"

His gaze locked on. "It's you."

Abi's throat closed with emotion. "It's me?"

"When I look at you, this is what I see," he whispered, and her belly did a little flip. "It's bold." He softly kissed her lips. "Delicate." Her jaw. "Feminine." Her neck. "Unexpected." Her throat. "And beautiful." He nudged the neckline of her shirt down with his nose and placed his last kiss on her shoulder.

"And where do you see it?" she said breathily.

He slid the shirt off her shoulder and nuzzled the scar from the metal rod. "Right here."

Meeting his gaze in the mirror, she lifted her shirt over her head and let it drop to the floor. She touched the same spot. "Here?"

He groaned. "Or maybe here." Coming all the way up against her back, he slid his hand down her neck, her chest, her stomach, which was quivering with anticipation, and right beneath her waistband to caress her hip bone. "Or here."

"I think I want you right here." She shifted so that his hand was exactly where she needed it to be.

"I think you're right." He ever so slightly brushed her pleasure button, making her moan. He did it again and this time she jerked forward to meet his hand.

"Slowly," he murmured, sliding his other arm around her waist. He held her tightly to him while he tenderly, but thoroughly, began to take her apart with his fingers. He strummed her in a practiced, purposeful way that was exquisite torture.

Her pulse raced and her heart pounded as he continued to tease.

"Owen," she moaned, pressing all the way into him.

"Have I mentioned how much I love hearing you say my name?"

"If I say it again, will you move faster?" she asked, yet he still, *still,* teased until she was unable to hold her head up, letting it drop back to rest on his shoulder.

"Look up, Angel. I want you to watch to ensure I get it in the exact spot you have in mind."

She opened her eyes, watching as his hand disappeared further beneath her skirt, his fingers moving all the way down.

"There," she sighed, but if she thought he'd pick up the pace, she was wrong. He took his sweet time, rubbing back and forth, creating a friction that had her body trembling.

He set the pace slow, trailing his free hand up her stomach and back down, on the return trip cupping her breast, lifting it and rubbing it until it puckered painfully hard. His fingers hadn't stopped, teasing her with feather-light touches, until finally—*here we go*—finally upping the ante. Those touches became not so light and oh so delicious before disappearing inside of her.

"Owen," she groaned and watched him smile in the reflection. Watched how flush she was, practically glowing, how entranced she was—and how happy she was. So happy that the broken woman from the accident had vanished, leaving behind the Abi she remembered.

She'd come to Portland to make Owen's life better but in the end, he'd done the same for her.

Emotion bubbled up, filling her body and warming her chest until she felt it radiate from inside her. Need and terror fought for superiority. She wanted him like she'd never wanted another human being and that kind of want terrified her.

And challenged her. Oh, how she liked to be challenged. Especially by the sexy man who had her on the brink of falling.

There was something about watching his hand move up and down, in and out of her skirt, building her up to what she knew was going to be an epic explosion.

"Faster," she moaned.

"Like this?" Not only did he go faster but he also pushed harder, curling his finger to hit that special spot. "Eyes on me," he reminded her. She hadn't even realized they'd slid shut from the pleasure.

And when she locked on him in the mirror, what she saw got her so hot and heavy, her body grew tighter and tighter while the raw need in his eyes grew hotter and hotter. And when she couldn't hold on any longer, she cried out his name and pressed against his hand, her body flushing hot. She felt light-headed and clear-minded all at the same time.

When she came back to earth, Owen was stroking her stomach in soothing patterns, a smug smile on his face.

"Don't get cocky yet, the night has just begun." She stepped out of his embrace and unbuttoned her skirt, sliding it down her legs and stepping out of it. Then she did a little shimmy number, sliding her thong down her legs until she was completely naked and vulnerable. But Owen was looking at her with something similar that made her giddy and nervous.

Abi turned in his arms and pulled his mouth to hers, kissing him. Long and hard and filled with all the emotions she felt but was unable to express. When she pulled back, neither looked away.

Owen's hands spanned her bare back, moving up and down, from her neck to her thighs and touching everywhere in between. "This is my favorite outfit."

"I wore it especially for you."

"Lucky guy."

"Lucky indeed." She walked him back into the tattooing chair and nudged him down, then went about climbing on him like he was her new pleasure seat. And if he moaned when she straddled him, he out-and-out groaned when she wrapped her legs around him. He lent a hand, placing them both on her bottom and tugging her fully onto his lap.

"Now, where did we leave off?" She unbuttoned the first button of his shirt revealing a tattoo at the base of his collarbone. "Oh, that's right, we were here." She undid another, revealing a second tattoo, and another until his shirt parted right up the middle showing all the tattoos. And what an impressive display it was.

So was the bulge in his pants.

She hummed in approval as her hands roamed over his upper torso. She didn't think she'd ever tire of looking at him. "Nice."

"I hope it's better than nice."

"It is. I just don't want to give you a big head."

"Then we have a problem," he teased, and she laughed. They both did and, man, he was handsome when he smiled.

"You should do that more often."

"Get a big head?"

"No." She ran a finger down his abs to the little treasure line that was a map to the promised land. "Smile."

"You keep doing that and you'll get more than a smile" He went serious, so serious. "You make me smile, Angel. Being around you, talking with you, dancing with you, spending my mornings with you. Notice a theme there? It's you."

She swallowed past the rising sadness. "Then my job here is done." Even though her tone was light, she felt anything but because he'd become so much more than a name on a good deed to be granted. He'd become a part of her life—some of the best parts—and tomorrow, after the party, her job was indeed done.

Biting back the tidal wave of emotions, she focused on her hands as they made a journey up his body, from belly button to his neck, then over his shoulders and down his arms until she reached his biceps. She went for the shirt, but it was too tight to budge. She tried again to push the sleeves down his arms, but he was flexing—on purpose.

"Off."

"Yes, ma'am," he said in his best Texan impersonation, then in a move so manly he tugged it from behind with one arm and it went sailing over his head.

"That's better. Except for…" She rocked against him, pressing hard against his erection and making him moan. Groan really.

"That a pretty great except," he said huskily, his breath cut short when she did it again.

"How about a pretty great one." This time instead of rocking, she leaned back enough to unbutton his jeans, and slid him to freedom.

"I guess I'm not the only one going commando around here."

He picked her up by the waist, adjusted himself slightly, then sat her back down. They were skin to skin and she felt her breath catch.

Lowering his head, he took one breast into his mouth, then the other, teasing her with his tongue, his teeth, nipping and sucking until her body was quaking. Needing an outlet for the building pleasure, she squeezed her legs and he released a giant rush of air. She met his gaze and grinned, then moved up the outside of his length and slid back down.

"That's not playing fair," he said.

"Where does fair factor in?" She squeezed, pushing up with her thighs, and by the time she slid back down, her body was trembling with sweet, sweet pleasure even though he wasn't yet inside her. She did it again. Squeeze, push up, slide.

Squeeze, push up, slide.

Owen's head rolled back on a threadbare groan, but not so far that he broke eye contact, which he held the entire time. It was hot as hell.

He ran his hands down her back, urging her chest to chest, then took charge, lifting her by her hips and back down.

Squeeze, up, slide.

Squeeze, up, slide.

She'd never been so turned on in her life. Her head dropped to his shoulder and by the next round his face was pressed into the curve of her neck. She got the squeeze and up, but before she could slide, he held her in place.

"One more and it's game over." He pulled back. "And, Angel, when that happens, I'm going to be inside you."

How he managed to pull a condom out of his back pocket while she was riding him like a pony she'd never know, but he was wrapped by the next squeeze, up, slide, so he slid all the way home.

She gasped for air, but her lungs had stopped working and she was pretty sure she'd lost consciousness for a moment.

"You're fulfilling one of my fantasies," he informed her, his hands doing naughty things to her body.

"A teenaged fantasy?"

"Hell no. A *you* fantasy. And I've been thinking about this at least once a minute since we walked in. Although in my fantasy we started in the tattooing chair, not my swivel chair."

"We can move."

"We'll see where the night takes us," he teased and then kissed her silly. Then he kissed her again and again, ten times over and when she thought she couldn't be any more turned on, Owen's hands were once again at her waist. His forehead was pressed to hers, his eyes locked on as if they were about to pay witness to what was to be the greatest sexual duet of all time. She quivered just thinking about it.

Then they were on the move again, with him doing most of the heavy lifting—mainly because he turned her body to mush. He was calm and steady, practiced as he took over. There was no teasing or taking things slow. They did the exact opposite of slow. Going from zero to blow-your-mind in under two squeeze-up-slides.

He held her as if she mattered, and kissed her as if he couldn't get enough, as if he never wanted this to end. She was on the same page.

For once, just this once, she wanted to pretend that their week wasn't almost up. She wanted to know what it felt like to be cherished, treasured, and needed—and not worry about what came next.

Rocking into him, she matched his rhythm the best she could. Being on his lap made it difficult but, not being a slacker, Owen made up the difference. Taking over, taking her with him—taking them both to the point of sheer pleasure.

"Owen," she cried out his name, and he whispered hers back. Not Angel or Abi, but her real name.

"Abilene," he whispered again and there was something to his tone that had her heart pounding with hope. Hope that there was enough between them to carry them through the roughest of patches. To carry them through the minefield ahead.

Their pace picked up, almost frantic as he drove into her and she pushed down. Even if she wanted to slow down, she couldn't. They were already committed—to the moment and to each other.

He pulled her to him, their chests pressed together, their bodies slick with perspiration. Her fingers clung to his biceps, his hands grasped her hips, her legs strangling his waist, all the while their lips devouring one another. It was the build-up of all build-ups, the orgasm that would forever change the course of her sexual existence.

"Now," she begged against his lips.

The tiniest of smiles curved his lips. "Now works."

Needing to maintain perspective, she slid her arms around his neck, forcing her to rest her head on his chest and her gaze away from his because she was pretty sure that she was building up to something beautiful and right, but something that, in the real world, had a zero percent chance of taking hold. So she did the best she could to guard herself from his always assessing gaze and all-knowing looks.

But somehow the disconnect took the genuineness away from their time together, cheapened what they'd shared.

What were the odds that two personal and private people had found each other and shared their deepest darkest secrets—secrets that could never be taken back. Things that led naturally to a cherished friendship that felt invincible. But suddenly friendship wasn't enough. The way he held her against him made her want for things she best not want for. But she couldn't fight the way she felt, the scariest of emotions had quietly grown inside to the point that her chest burned with something akin to love—a love that was unlike anything she'd ever experienced.

He'd brought her here tonight, designed the perfect tattoo of her—took time and care planning out this evening to show her, without words, how much he'd come to care for her. How he valued her opinion and her honesty.

She told herself to stay detached, but she felt the way she felt and tonight she wanted to feel it all. She was more afraid of missing out on the what-ifs than living a lifetime of safety.

He tilted her head up. "Stay with me. Right here." He took her mouth in what had to be the gentlest kiss in the history known to mankind. "Whatever it is we can fix it, okay?"

Even though she knew there was no fixing it—her life was soon to be in Thailand, fulfilling the trip she and Jenny had planned—she found herself giving a watery nod.

Bodies pressed together so tightly even a coaster couldn't fit between them, they rocked and moved, so hard that Owen had to wheel the chair back against the wall to gain the proper traction necessary. They landed with a thud and they both laughed, breaking the seriousness and bringing them miles from the doubts and back to the moment.

"God, your smile does it for me every time." He kissed her. "Every time."

"Everything about you does it for me."

With a groan he spanned his hands up her back, running them everywhere all at once. From there, all it took was one well-timed motion and they both went off like rockets, the sensation going back and forth between them, until it was all too much to contain. He whispered her name and she bit down on his shoulder—hard.

And sometime later, when she woke up and found herself wrapped around him like a pretzel—she sitting on him, he sitting on the chair, the chair slightly spinning—she realized that this was a defining moment in her life.

The moment she'd fallen in love. And she'd fallen hard. So hard that when she'd finally pull herself up, there'd be floor marks from when she'd landed face-first. So she clung to him so that she didn't fall any further.

Because falling wasn't the scary part. It was realizing that the other person in the equation didn't acknowledge that falling was an option.

"Were I a lesser man I might take offense to you being able to think so hard after that," he teased.

Tapping into the lighter part of her, she said, "I think we've already established just how much of a man you are."

She kissed him. It was meant to be a quick kiss, but he took it further, longer, and languid and stripping away any last pretense she was desperately clinging to. He cupped her cheeks and studied her eyes. Whatever he was looking for he found because his face became serious. "You okay?"

"Just catching my breath," she lied.

"Remember your whole poker face being shit?" he said quietly.

"That's just you who thinks that. And that was just…"

"Yeah," he said, and that simple agreement helped erase some of the reasons that were building in her mind as to why it would never work.

Afraid he'd see even more, she dropped her gaze. "What do they mean?" She ran her hands slowly up his arms, over the collection of tattoos, paying special attention to each one. Unlike most people, he didn't have tattoos scattered all over, each individual tattoo played a part in creating a single work of art.

She stopped on his bicep where there was the logo for his bar. She traced it with her fingertip.

"I got that the day after my father died." He took her hands and slid them across his chest to the other side, where there was a kanji symbol. "The rough translation is beloved brother. In memory of Kyle. He chose to live a complicated life, then left it full of painful complications for those around him, but I still miss him."

"We all make mistakes. It doesn't mean he was a bad person, Owen," she whispered.

"He was selfish and robbed my family of a lot. He cheated on his fiancée, chose his mistress over Darcy, even knowing she was pregnant. She left him at the altar and he hit the closest bar. Thankfully, he was the only one in the accident."

She cupped his cheek. "It doesn't make the pain any less."

He turned his head and kissed the inside of her wrist. "I'm not an easy guy, Angel. My life is crazy."

Her heart lurched. "Is this a reminder that all you can give is this week and it's nearly up?"

"This is my way of letting you know that my life is more packed than my body has tattoos."

"A full life doesn't need to mean a bad life or some kind of albatross. You get to choose what's important to you, not the other way around," she said, tracing one of the lines that tied all his tattoos into a single, beautiful piece. "Some people would love to have those kinds of connection."

"Is that what you're looking for? A connection?"

She gave a deceivingly noncommittal shrug. "Aren't we all." Not willing to talk about things that took them down a long and painful road, she said, "I love your tattoos. It's the story of your life."

"Which is full and complicated," he repeated like he was trying to warn her.

She worked hard to keep the sadness from her eyes. "I love how important your family is to you and how you care for them. I love how you treat your employees and work hard to keep your dad's bar open. I love the way you make me breakfast and the way you make me laugh. Mostly, I love how you make me feel." She cupped his face. "There's a lot about you that I love."

Sweet Lord above, what had she just said? What she felt and what she wanted him to know were vastly different things. Dammit, her eyes were going a little blurry and it was incredibly hard to breathe.

"Hey." He held her cheek in his hand. "You have me slayed. Every part of you."

She swallowed hard. "If I'm not careful I might just fall for you."

"If I'm not careful I might just catch you."

Chapter Twenty-Nine

Happy Things:
A roadshow starring
Christian Grey & Mr. Darcy

After two months of good deeds, Abi's time as Portland's professional Good Samaritan was coming to a close. Not that she was going to give up good-deeding forever, she still had a long way to go to make amends, but now that she'd come clean with Owen, she was giving up the official title.

Owen had a full life now. Or at least he was headed in the right direction.

She'd played an important part in capturing Owen's new freedom and happiness—and he was happy. The real kind of happy that ate away at the weight he'd been carrying. He was letting people in, delegating responsibility, and reclaiming parts of his world that had been lost when his father had passed.

She'd been a part of that transformation, and that knowledge brought her joy. But tonight was their last night of bliss because it would mark the end of their agreed-upon week.

She wasn't sure how tomorrow would play out, but she had faith that things would go how they were meant to. And if that included Owen wanting to abide by their agreement, then she'd grant him that last wish. Even though it would wreck her heart.

Abi smoothed her hands down her dress—the red dress she'd spent an hour rustling through Dotti's closet to locate and three hours convincing her sister to let her borrow. The dress that made her waist look tiny and her boobs busty. She'd even managed to iron it without Lemon-Marie *swoosh-swish*ing grape juice all over it.

Giving herself one last glance in the mirror, Abi opened the door, prepared to go downstairs and find Owen. Only when she stepped onto the landing there he was, looking handsome in a gray suit with blue shirt and tie, casually leaning against the railing. Legs crossed at the ankles, one hand in his pants pocket, the other holding a box.

"What are you doing here?"

"Waiting for you."

She looked at her watch, a delicate, vintage watch from the thirties that her grandma had left her. "But I'm fifteen minutes late." She'd been at the senior center, leading her final book club, where the month's pick was *Fifty Shades of Grey,* and the topic of conversation quickly turned to who would be the best in bed, Christian Grey or Mr. Darcy. It ended with Darcy winning nine to one.

His eyes tracked her from head to toe and every place in between, lingering every so often. Her body zinged in his wake.

"It was worth the wait." He pushed off the railing. "You're worth it."

Unable to resist, she walked right up to him, slid her arms around his neck, and gave him a kiss. A long, deep, lingering, this-is-a-proper-date kind of kiss that kicked her hormones into hyperdrive.

Arms around her waist, hands resting indecently low on her back, he tugged her to him and—*sweet Lord above*—talk about leaving her breathless.

"I missed you," he whispered against her lips.

"I just left your bed a few hours ago."

"A few hours is too long."

She had to agree. Mr. Darcy didn't have a thing on Owen Easton.

He looked at her for a long moment. "I have something for you. I don't know if it's old fashioned or if you'd even like it. But if it's not your thing I won't be offended."

She loved this shy and vulnerable side of him. It was the same boyish charm she'd felt at the tattoo shop. She tightened her arms around his waist. "I already know I'll love it."

He stepped back and opened a small white box and Abi's breath caught. Inside was a stunning corsage made from red dahlias, just like the ones at Lauren the birthday girl's house, that she'd listed as one of her happy things. He slid it on her wrist and shoved his hands in his pockets, nervously rocking back on his heels.

She brushed a finger over the petals. "Owen, it's beautiful."

"My dad used to give my mom a corsage whenever he'd take her on a date." He shrugged. "My dad was a pro at making my mom feel special, so I figured I'd take a note from the old man."

"Thank you," she whispered, completely taken aback by the gesture and by the sentiment behind it. She meant enough to him that he'd kept the family tradition alive for her. She took his hand in hers and placed it over her racing heart. "You make me feel special."

His hand slid up her neck, his fingers cradling the base of her neck. "You are special. To me, you are becoming more and more special as each day goes on." He went quiet, completely still as if he was weighing something in his mind. "Stay with me."

She had to take a beat. "Tonight?"

"For a start," he said. "But I meant tomorrow night and the next."

"What happened to only a week?" Her heart thumped in her chest as she waited for his answer.

"I was an idiot," he said, running his thumb over her lower lip. "An annoyingly smart man recently told me that if I didn't want to lose you, I needed to find something to make you want to stay." He laced her arms around his neck, sliding his hands down to her hips. "I know you want to travel, just like I know that I'm stuck here at the bar, which sometimes I love and other times I resent. I'm a workaholic, grumpy, unwavering, and usually stubborn as hell."

"You're selling points are really hitting home," she teased. "How long will you want me to stay?" *How long will you want me?*

"How long would you want to say?" he asked, achingly quiet.

Forever. If Abi had it her way she'd stay forever. Forget Thailand or Bali or any other place she had on her itinerary. Adventure wasn't really an adventure unless you had someone to share it with.

"What if you decide I've given too much?" The sound of her heart beating thrashed in her ears. "I'm a lot, like *a lot,* and, even though I don't mean to, I end up making a mess of things, which sometimes hurts those closest to me. When I get scared, I take the easy way out. And I'm not adventurous like you think, it's just when things get hard, I bail."

"That's okay because when things get hard, I dig in." She nodded but couldn't look him in the eye for fear that he'd see the panic his proposition brought on.

She wondered just how far he'd dig in when the honeymoon phase ended or if it would become another catch-and-release kind of situation that she'd become so painfully familiar with.

"Before I can even consider it, I need to know that if you change your mind, we still part as friends."

Her answer hurt him, she knew it. It was there in his eyes, hidden beneath the hope. "Then we part as friends."

What was she even saying? This was what she'd been dreaming about—more time. So why was she so scared? "Then yes!"

"What about Thailand? And the teaching job?"

"What about Thailand? And there's no reason why I can't teach here. With you."

He kissed her gently, then took his time looking at her, really looking. She wasn't sure what he saw—the fight-or-flight instinct thundering through her or the brave woman who had faced down her demons and was ready for something lasting.

She looked down and fiddled with the corsage. "I didn't get you anything."

"Oh, you get me, alright," he said in the light flirty way that implied he was giving her the space she needed to respond. "You get to me in your jeans. And those red boots. You, in this dress, gets to me." He let out a low whistle taking in every inch of her. "Damn, you're beautiful."

A shyness crept over her at the way he was looking at her. Like she was the most stunning thing he'd ever seen. "It's the dress."

He tilted her chin up. "It's you, Abi. Your laugh, the way you look in the morning, the way you feel in my arms." He leaned in and kissed her. "The way you taste. The way you say my name. I love the way you say my name." He kissed her again. "I'd like to cash in that rain check."

"What rain check?"

"The one I just made up to get you to go back inside with me."

She considered it for point-one seconds, then imagined Margo tapping her watch, counting down every minute Abi made Owen late for her party. "No way. Not with your mother just downstairs?"

"We're going to find a reason to leave early or we're going to need to find a closet." She laughed, but he remained serious.

She kissed him gently and took his hand. "Ready?"

He wove her arm through his, resting his hand over hers. "More than ready."

She was glad one of them was. As far as she was concerned, now that she was there, she could avoid seeing Margo for the next five thousand years. She wasn't sure if Owen had talked to her or not. But she knew that when it came to the Eastons, they stood as a unit.

They entered through the back of the bar and Abi took in a nervous breath. The place was packed. There were enough button hats and lace gloves to double for high tea with the queen herself. Then there were the men. *Woo wee*, those Easton men. Big, built, and one more handsome than the next, with Owen leading the pack. If someone had told Abi two months ago that she'd be in love with an edgy tattoo artist, she would have laughed in their face. Abi didn't do edgy or artists—tattooed or otherwise. She did logical, practical men who offset her spontaneous and emotionally driven side.

But Owen seemed to offset her perfectly. For a time, Jenny had been the most important person in Abi's entire life. Owen was quickly coming to fill that empty hole that was left behind at the crash site, which made Abi wonder if there was some validity to destiny and divine intervention. She'd had Jenny in mind with every step she'd taken and yet she'd landed here, at a party with a man she was completely smitten with.

"Don't you look handsome." Margo preened like a proud mother.

"You look great, Mom." Owen leaned down to kiss his mom on the cheek. "Happy birthday."

"And you," Margo said, turning to Abi. Her mind must have been in overdrive because it almost sounded like an accusation. "Let me get a look at you. Red is your color."

Abi let out a breath and smiled a real smile. "You look beautiful in that pantsuit." Which was the truth. No one could rock a pantsuit quite like Margo Easton.

"Who all is here?" Owen asked. "I want to introduce Abi to Darcy, Jillian, and Piper." He leaned down to whisper. "There's strength in numbers."

"Nonsense, Abi and I will be just fine on our own." She looked at Abi. "Won't we, dear?"

Abi wasn't so sure about that but when Owen gave her a *You okay* look she nodded. This time when she turned to Margo, the woman's face had hardened.

"Why don't we go over here so we can have a bit of privacy?" Without waiting for Abi to join, Margo walked to the back corner of the bar.

"I forgot to wish you a happy birthday," Abi said brightly as she fell into step with the older woman.

Margo studied her with a sour look on her face. "I'm not quite sure how to proceed."

"Proceed?" Abi asked, her stomach roiling.

"I nearly lost two of my sons because I was judgmental and overbearing. I'd like to think I've grown since then, which is why I'm not here to judge, I just want answers."

This was it, the moment that Abi had been dreading had finally come. She'd come clean with Owen, but admitting her role to Margo would be a completely different beast, which was why her plan had been to avoid the matriarch of the family for as long as possible.

Abi felt her face heat and her head go light. Margo was sharp and informed and would never make a move unless she knew the outcome. The tempered censure in the older woman's eyes had Abi's palms sweating.

"Did you grow up here in Portland?" Margo asked politely, her hands going to her pearls, her fingers running rhythmically back and forth along the strand.

"No, ma'am, but I did spend summers here with my grandma."

Margo didn't say a word, just made a sound of disapproval and Abi had a feeling, deep in her gut, that the jig was up. Margo knew. Abi didn't know if Owen had already told her, but the woman had put it together.

"And the lawsuit against my husband? Were you a part of that?"

Abi's knees went weak, and a painful lump formed in her throat. "I want to say no. I wish I could say no, but I can't."

"And the testimony that won over the grand jury? Was that you?"

When Owen told her that she wasn't the only minor involved, Abi had assumed that she wasn't the only one who testified. "I was deposed, and that went to the grand jury.

But I wasn't aware that my testimony had much effect on the outcome."

"It was the backbone of the district attorney office's case." Instead of flaming with anger, Margo's eyes went still with sadness. A bone-deep sadness that came from wading in enough grief to take one under. "Even though it never made it to trial, that case derailed my family's life."

"I know."

"In part, your testimony was the reason Owen came from Austin to help his father with the bar."

Abi had taken a lot of blame for a lot of people's choices over the past few months and, at that moment, she realized that being sorry about something didn't make her guilty. "While I'm sorry how it affected your family, I only testified to the truth."

"And were you truthful with my son about everything?"

"Yes, ma'am." And all the lightness she'd felt after coming clean suddenly wrapped around her neck and slowly started to choke her.

Margo went silent, her lips pursing as if she'd come to some idea of who Abi was as a person. And she didn't think it would be all that flattering. "So did you come to work your way into my son's life out of remorse?"

Oh my god. She hadn't meant to but that's what she'd done. "It might have started that way but—"

"But what? You befriended my son, myself, and my friends by doing little favors to appease your own guilt. Is that what my son is to you?"

"No! It wasn't like that." But when she heard it said aloud, she knew it was exactly like that.

"How much of why you're in Portland does he know about?"

Abi closed her eyes and expelled a deep breath. "He knows that I came back to heal after an accident and to right some wrongs."

"Does he realize that he was nothing but a wrong to right?"

"I was going to tell him everything about why I came back to town tomorrow after your party."

"What were you going to tell me?" an achingly familiar voice said from behind. Then there were his hands, gentle and protective as they settled on her shoulders. As if she needed the reassurance.

"Mom," someone said from beside her. She turned to find Josh and his wife standing beside Owen. The eldest Easton brother was shooting Margo a look of warning that was tangible. Then his eyes locked on Abi.

He knew. She didn't know how he knew, maybe Owen told him, but he knew. Which made this moment all the more gut-wrenching. How many people besides Owen knew the truth? And how long had they known?

"He deserves to know," Margo said in a soft plea.

"But not like this," Josh said.

"Lies have ripped this family apart. I won't let it happen again," Margo said.

"Will someone tell me what's going on?" Owen asked.

Abi closed her eyes against the pain she knew was about to come. Even before she could open her mouth, she felt the emotion rise and pool on her lashes.

"Whoa," Owen said and, to make things worse, he slid his hand into hers and squeezed. "I got you."

"But you shouldn't." Unable to meet his worried gaze, she looked at her shoes. "This is a mess. A total and complete Impulsive Abi mess and I am so sorry," she began. "I was going to tell you. No." She lowered her voice and because he deserved to be looked in the eye when being delivered this blow, she met his gaze. "I should have told you."

"Take it slow," Owen said supportively. He searched her eyes and hers started to sting.

"Remember when I told you about buying beer from Brody?"

"We talked about this, and I told you it wasn't a big deal." He looked his mom square in the eye. "It isn't a big deal. So, she told the truth? So what?" Owen said, and Margo gasped. "It's the truth. She didn't force Brody, he did it all on his own."

"There's more." Abi took his hands. "The reason I came to Portland was that I made a promise to Jenny to make things right and you were the wrong I needed to make right."

She knew the minute Owen put the pieces together, could feel the way his body went rigid. "So helping my mom's poker team, hiring new employees and helping with bar, all the ways you immersed yourself in my life, that was because of some promise you made to a person I've never met?"

"Yes," she whispered, shame heating her cheeks.

"So you came here with an agenda?"

"Yes."

And that's when she felt it. Felt his grip loosen. The tighter she held on, the more he let go until he dropped her hand altogether. And his expression said it all—she'd made a mess too big to clean up.

"I asked you more than once if I was one of your do-gooder acts and you played it off as it being nothing more than a friend helping a friend. But you had an agenda before we became friends. If that's what we even are."

Panic wove its way around her chest and tightened like a vise. "But we are. Remember? That was the promise. We walk away friends."

"We'd have to have been legit friends for that to happen. Not some fabricated relationship."

"We are friends. It might not have begun like how normal people start a relationship, but we are friends. And yes, at first I just wanted to do a few things to make your life easier and maybe it was to make myself feel better, but then it changed, you changed me," she pled, needing him to believe her.

"Clearly not enough, since you've been lying to me the entire time."

"It wasn't a lie. I just didn't tell you—"

Owen took a step back, but it felt as if the Grand Canyon separated them. "So you came here, to what? Take me dancing and dog walking?"

"Partly. I came to see Dotti and I came to see how your family was doing. Then I saw how hard you worked to keep the bar going and make your family happy and I wanted to find a way to make *you* happy. Make *your* life easier, happier."

"Why me? Out of all my brothers, why me?"

"Because they were off living their lives while you were running a bar that you didn't seem to like. As if it was your obligation rather than your dream. I know you came back after the suit was filed and that you took over the day-to-day of running the bar when your dad fell ill. You didn't trust anyone because of me, put up walls around you because of me and the mess I helped create, so you decided to do everything all yourself. You took it on without complaint to help your family. You still do," she explained. "That's why I chose you."

"You chose me? Jesus." He ran a hand down his face. "You inserted yourself into my life under false pretenses and played me."

She shook her head fiercely. "I didn't play you."

"Did you purposefully leave out the details of why you befriended me?"

"You befriended me! In the parking lot," she said. "I was trying to maintain space, but you just kept—"

"What? I kept... what?"

"Being so nice."

He threw his hands into the air. "You say that like this is all my fault because, what, I'm a decent human being? Maybe you should come with a warning, 'Be nice and I'll screw you over.'"

She staggered back at the forcefulness of his statement.

"I should come with a lot of warnings," she whispered. "But with you, it should have said, 'Approach with care, damaged goods.'"

He didn't say anything, didn't even change his expressions which were purposefully schooled and, she was sure, cold to the touch. "You told me you loved me even though you were using what was between us to make you feel better about yourself."

"It doesn't matter how it started, it only matters that my feelings for you are deep and real."

He gave a hollow chuckle. "Hell, Abs, I told you that I loved you."

"You said you loved all my parts," she said, acutely aware that his family could hear every single word spoken between them. Even though they'd moved a short distance away to give she and Owen a little privacy, Margo's shoulders stiffened at Owen's declaration and his brothers huddled together in hushed silence.

Abi could barely register anything past the word 'love'. Or was it 'loved' as in he'd changed his mind.

Barely able to catch her breath through the anxiety, a thin sheen of perspiration coated her body and her vision turned spotty. "And this part is scared and cowardly and so incredibly sorry."

"I told you about how hard it is for me to trust people, how scared I am of getting played again, and you still chose to lie to me."

"I knew the second I told you my secret, why I was here, that everything would change and then I wouldn't be able to make your life better."

"Well, lying sure as hell didn't make it better."

"Owen," she said, and she no longer thought he liked the sound of his name on her lips. She swallowed down the rising fear.

Calm and tranquility can shove it, she thought. *Today it's about holding it together until you're alone, then you can cry it out. Give in to the darkness pushing in around the edges.*

"I just need some ..." He raised a palm but didn't finish, and what she saw in his eyes broke her heart. Then an absolute determination overtook his expression and Abi watched Happy Owen disappear, and World on His Shoulders Owen take his place. "I don't know what I need."

"This is where you dig in," she begged. She moved to take his hand again, but he pulled back. "This is about how I screwed up but you dig in, remember?"

He looked around as if just remembering that they had an audience. "It's my mom's party, there's a bar packed full of people. This isn't the right time."

Her stomach sank. She knew what came next. It was like an arrow through the heart. "I get that a lot. Seems my timing isn't all that great."

His face did soften, but it wasn't with concern, it was with disappointment. She'd done this and he was going to call her on it.

"It's just a lot right now."

And there it was, the final blow to her heart. She was once again too much. Words that were her cue to pack up and get the hell out of his life.

"Is that what you want? For me to go?" she asked, giving them one last chance.

Their eyes caught and hung but there was no warmth there. There was pain and anger and, worst of all, hurt. She'd set out to make his life better and somehow managed to hurt him.

"That's probably best."

Abi stopped breathing. It was a direct hit. Nothing about her, or her life, was easy. She knew this, but she was working really hard to overcome that. If she thought she was in pain a second ago, it was nothing compared to the deep ache which now burned so cold her body felt like it would crack.

Her heart caught and her skin felt too tight to contain the ache hollowing out a cavity in her chest. Her hands shook and those spots in front of her eyes grew until she was certain she was going to hyperventilate and pass out. Anxiety was threatening to take her down.

Something flashed in Owen's eyes that told her he noticed the signs. He stepped forward as if to catch her and she realized that she needed to learn to catch herself.

Starting now.

She wobbled backward, then straightened her spine and reminded herself that the key to survival was to stay calm and breathe through the pain.

"Jens, I need my wing girl," she whispered. Immediately the ambient song switched to Gloria Gaynor's "I Will Survive," and that's when she knew she wasn't alone.

Even though her heart was broken beyond repair, and she was one sob away from shattering into a million pieces, she did what she'd promised herself she'd do.

She granted her last Good Deed and walked away.

She was tired of fighting for things she loved, only to have them be taken. For once, she wanted someone to fight to be with her, to push through the pain and choose her. To tell her she was worth the mess and the crazy.

But he wasn't going to say any of those things, so she said the one thing she needed him to hear. "Whatever you decide, running the bar or opening your shop, I sincerely hope you find whatever it is that makes you happy."

She looked at everyone who was staring back, everything from anger to confusion in their gazes, but it was Owen she focused on.

"Goodbye, Owen," she said knowing that no matter how much she loved saying his name, this would be the last time.

Chapter Thirty

Happy Things:
Jeans that make your ass
look great

"What the hell did she mean when she said that you're not happy?" Rhett asked, leaning back in the booth seat, taking way too much joy in Owen's current situation. "Since when?"

It had taken him a whole ten minutes to realize he'd overreacted. Even less time to figure out he'd blown it with Abi. He'd known that the second he saw the anguish on her face. He'd reaffirmed her biggest fear, that she wasn't worth the time.

Owen sat at a booth in the back of the pub, tie gone, shirt unbuttoned, arms folded across the table. His head was pounding. The party was winding down; most of the place had cleared out, yet there he sat replaying every moment of the last few months. Trying to pinpoint a moment, any moment to contradict what she'd said.

"I don't know, a while."

He could feel his brothers all exchange worried looks. Hell, he was worried. There were a lot of things he'd been able to come back from—his dad's passing, Kyle's accident, even Elena's betrayal. But he wasn't sure how he'd come back from this.

It felt like he'd been blown open by a shotgun leaving his chest like Swiss cheese.

"Why didn't you tell us?" Gage asked.

"I'm a tattooist who runs a bar and doesn't drink alcohol!"

"It's called words, dude. Use your words," Gage said in that dad voice that grated on Owen's last nerve.

The moment Abi had walked out, his brothers had quietly ushered him to the back of the bar, then rallied around. Only instead of feeling supported he felt suffocated.

"You know what's really annoying?" Owen said. "Happy people who are always wanting to dole out advice that means jack shit to those of us living in the real world."

"In your real world, you just let your happy walk out the door," Rhett pointed out.

Yeah, he knew that. Knew that he'd hurt her. Badly. She'd finally allowed herself to let someone in, and he'd abandoned her at the first sign of trouble.

He closed his eyes, remembering the look on Abi's face as she asked him to dig in. Instead of holding on, as he'd promised, he'd let go—actually dropping her hand and leaving her standing all by herself, staring down the entire Easton clan. Yet, she hadn't buckled.

Nope, her shoulders had gone back, defiant even when she was one breath from a panic attack.

Jesus, he was an ass. He didn't even help her, just watched as she slowly spiraled on the inside. And that look of resigned devastation would haunt him forever.

She'd expected him to hurt her—which he had. She'd been waiting for the blow—which he'd so graciously given her. And he hated himself for it.

"What did she really do that was so bad to let her walk away?" Josh asked. He wasn't poking or trying to get a reaction from Owen, he was genuinely interested in Owen's answer. But he didn't have one.

"I don't know." Then Owen asked, "And how the hell did you know who she was?"

"Abilene is a pretty distinctive name. I remembered it from when I was going through Dad's case."

"Did you tell Mom?"

Josh shook his head. "She must have figured it out the same way." Josh paused. "Is it so bad that she came here to check in on you and when she saw you were drowning—"

"Something we should have taken more seriously," Clay added. "She did what none of us found the time to do—help you."

"She had ulterior motives," Owen said.

"You mean her good, sweet intentions?" Clay asked. "You waited on her doorstep to ask her to stay with you. You even brought her flowers hoping to persuade her to say yes. You stacked the deck in your favor to get the best possible outcome. How is that any different?"

"It's different," he said, and even he didn't believe it.

"You asked her to stay, then pulled a Kyle?" Rhett said loud enough for the entire bar to hear, then burst out laughing. "You are so screwed."

"How is this anything like what Kyle did?" Owen wanted to know. He loved his late brother, but he and Kyle couldn't be more opposite. Where Owen always put his loved ones first, Kyle had had a way of putting himself first.

"Rhett's right," Gage said. "You tell some chick you love her, ask her to commit to you, then she drops a bomb that complicates things and you say, 'See ya.' That's a move straight from Kyle's handbook. So the only question is: are you going to let her walk away and lose her forever or are you going to go after her?"

"Darcy's intentions were pure, Abi's weren't." Even as he said it, he heard just how lame his excuse sounded.

"She hurt your man-feelings, is that it?" Rhett asked.

"He does have an ego the size of Texas," Gage chimed in.

"Isn't that where Abi's from? Texas?" Rhett laughed it up. "You managed to find your perfect Southern girl and you chased her off."

"What do you mean, *chased her off*?"

Gage was as stupid as they came because he leaned forward, resting his elbows on the tabletop, bringing his face within smack-down reach. "Well, she was looking at you like she'd swim through lava for you, and you pretty much told her to take her sweet intentions and fuck off."

"She lied."

"I didn't tell you that those pants make your butt look big. Is that a lie?" Rhett asked.

Clay, who'd been silently watching the events unfold, spoke, "For the first time since Elena, you had a shot at something good and you'd rather piss it away than admit that maybe you're scared."

"No wonder you chased off the only good woman you've had in years," Josh said, and Owen felt his chest tighten.

He leaned back and rubbed his hand over the pain, trying to ease the raw ache that had been gnawing at him. It didn't help. Nothing he seemed to do helped. It just got worse, deeper, hollower.

He hadn't chased off Abi. What he'd done had been worse. After knowing her past and all the people who'd let her go, he'd stood by and watched her walk away—all by herself.

Rhett stared at him with so much sadness. "Do you know how many people would kill to have a person care so much that they'd put their life on hold to check in with someone from their past?" Owen didn't know what to say. "I'd kill for a woman like that."

The table went still, and Owen felt the weight of the situation. Felt his brother's pain and shared in his loss.

"My life didn't work out that way but yours could. All you have to do is take the first step," Rhett added.

"How do I get past knowing that it started on a lie?" Last time someone hid a lie, it broke his damn heart.

"Are you even listening to yourself?" Gage asked. "My bet is that you're using this as an excuse to push her away because you're scared of getting hurt again. She's not Elena."

Owen's posture dropped as he considered what his brothers were saying. Maybe they were right. Maybe he was backing off because he was scared. What had Abi really done? Gone out of her way to make him smile? To make his life a little better?

Hell, she'd made his life a whole lot better. Just thinking about her made his heart skip a beat.

"What are you so scared about, man?" Rhett asked.

"Isn't it obvious from his face?" Josh asked.

Owen shot him a look that would have had most men wetting their pants. Josh just laughed. "What does that mean?"

Rhett leaned in. "Think about it, bro. Why are so you set off by one little omission? And before we go through this again, it was a harmless, from-the-heart omission."

On paper it seemed harmless, so then why did it feel anything but. His stomach was in knots, his gut was swimming with all the things he should have said, and his head was filled with the tears she'd worked hard to hold back. Even at that moment, he'd wanted to pull her into his arms and tell her that she wasn't in this alone.

"You said you love her, was that the truth?" Clay asked.

"Yes." He did love her, more than anything. That's why this was all so confusing.

"You've said the three words, which is the hardest part. And If I understand correctly, she said it back."

He looked up. "So?"

"So, love isn't concrete, it's always changing and moving. Either you change with it, or you lose it," Rhett said. "I wasn't willing to change and I lost my shot. How is your story going to end?"

"Not like this." Owen pushed out of the booth and stood.

Not only did he love her, she owned his heart. She had from the moment he'd seen her in those clown shoes. And he couldn't imagine not having her in his life. She was his life.

"I blew it."

"No shit," Clay said.

"I gotta go."

'Yeah, you better before she realizes what an idiot you are."

Chapter Thirty-One

Happy Things:
Love

Knowing that a single sob would release the floodgates, Abi hurried through the back door of the bar and up the steps to the apartment. She clutched a hand over her heart to make sure it stayed in one piece while she packed up her belongings.

In a daze, she left the key by the front door with a note scribbled on the back a coaster:

For me, it was all real.
Especially the love part.
~Abi

She secured her bag to her basket and went on autopilot until she found herself pedaling up to her sister's house. She raced through the pouring rain, up the steps and banged on the front door. Only instead of finding Dotti in her usual outfit of leggings and an inspirational T-shirt, she was dressed in a pink silky dress.

"Are you going to prom?" she asked.

"It's date night. And you're the one wearing a corsage," Dotti said, her eyes turning hard. "Are you standing in the rain in my save-for-an-important-event, back-of-the-closet, when-I-lose-the-baby-weight, red designer dress?"

"I'll buy you a new one." Which would clean her out she was sure, but money didn't matter when one died of acute onset heartbreak.

"I don't want a new one!" Dotti looked closer and concern laced her face as she stepped onto the porch and into the rain. Abi watched the drops speckle her sister's dress and soak into the silky fabric. "What's wrong, Abs?"

The sound of her childhood nickname released the first sob, which rolled through her chest and exploded free. It was quickly followed by another, which wracked her body. By the next, she was pouring herself into her sister's arms until they were both sitting on the wet concrete.

"I need Jenny," she choked out, and Dotti's face went still because it was the first time Abi had mentioned Jenny to her sister. Or to anyone other than Owen. "I need her so much right now and she's not here."

"I know how much she meant to you and that you two were like sisters," Dotti whispered, and Abi could hear the longing in her sister's voice. "I'm sorry she's gone."

"It's like with Mee-maw. I thought it would get easier. I thought that maybe someday it would simply be a happy memory. And sometimes it is. Like I'll see a ladybug fly by or a deer in the park, and I feel like they're right there with me. Then other times, the grief is so strong it drags me to my knees and I'm right back there in the bus where everything is scary and out of control."

"You're not on the bus, you're safe at home. And you've got me to lean on."

She rested her head on her sister's shoulder like she used to when they were younger and Abi'd had a bad dream. Only this dream was her reality.

"Am I? I'm not on the bus but I don't feel safe or like this is my home. Well, I did." With Owen she did. "But I don't feel safe anymore. All I feel is loss, never-ending, excruciating loss."

"Oh, honey," Dotti cooed. "I know I'm not Jenny, but I'm your sister and I'd like to help." Abi looked up to find that Dotti was crying too. "How can I help?"

"Can I have a hug?" she said in choppy breaths.

"You can have all the hugs." Dotti pulled her closer and Abi buried her face into her sister's hair. She smelled like apple juice, hair spray, and days of childhood past. Abi's body wracked with sobs, so hard that it felt like her chest was cracked. "Do you want to talk about it?"

Abi shook her head. "If I do, I'll start crying."

"You're already crying, so you might as well get it all out." Dotti went quiet. "What happened?"

"I friended him for selfish reasons and then he told me I was too much."

Dotti pulled back. "He told you that? What a dick!"

"Well, not those exact words. Okay, not those words at all but he did say that it was a lot right then."

"Maybe that was all he meant. That he was a little overwhelmed by how it went down."

"It doesn't matter how he said it, he let me walk away," she said miserably. "He told me he loved me, then promised he was the kind of man to dig in, then he told me to leave." Abi sucked in a shaky breath. "I don't get it. No matter how hard I try, I'm either too much or not enough. All I want to be is someone's just right."

"You're my just right." A pair of dress shoes came into view, so Abi closed her eyes and wished him to go away. "In fact, you're so damn right it scares the hell out of me."

She looked up and the familiar, handsome face swimming before her eyes made her breath catch. Owen had lost his jacket and tie, his clothes were soaked through, his hair slicked back. She looked past him. No truck at the curb.

"Did you walk here?"

"I ran. Nineteen blocks in dress shoes. Nineteen blocks with the fear that I blew the best thing that ever happened to me."

"Um." Dotti looked between the two of them. "This is my cue to leave."

"What happened to having my back?" Abi asked, clinging to her sister's hand for dear life.

"It might not seem this way right now, but I promise I have your back."

Her sister leaned in and kissed Abi on the cheek, then whispered, "This is what Jenny would do." She got up and walked into the house.

When the door clicked shut, Abi turned to sit on the first step and stared at her open-toed heels, which she'd also "borrowed" from Dotti, who was going to kill her when she saw how scuffed and torn they were from the bike chain.

"I should have told you the truth that first moment in the parking lot," she said to her feet. "But you promised me that, no matter what, we'd walk away friends. You lied to me too."

"I did," he said.

She felt him sit next to her on the stoop. She looked over, not bothering to hide her crying. "And you told me you loved me and then told me to go."

He brushed a tear away with the pad of his thumb. "I did."

Now the hurt was turning to anger. A hot, from-the-depths-of-her-soul anger that had her hands shaking. "And for what? Maybe I wasn't upfront but all I wanted was to make your life better and you acted as if I kicked Waffles."

His lips quirked. "Waffles?"

"The dog you're going to buy to bring more joy into your life." She opened her mouth and then closed it. The hurt was back. "You broke my heart, Owen," she whispered. "Broke it so thoroughly I can't even feel all the pieces." Embarrassment crept in all over again. "Why am I so hard to love?"

He cupped her jaw. "Loving you is the easiest thing I've ever done." He turned to face her and took her hands in his. They were both wet and chilled, but at the contact a warm glow flickered inside.

"I have something for you." He reached into his pocket and pulled out a wet piece of paper and hand it over. Uncertainty rushed over her as she opened it. Was this his official resignation from being her friend?

"What's this?" she asked.

"A job posting I wanted to talk to you about."

"At the bar?" She'd already filled that position, then quit. Just like he'd quit them.

"That one's already taken," he said. "This is for another job."

Not sure how to take that, she lifted the paper, but she was shaking so badly it was impossible to make out anything beyond a few words like *pillow* and *spoon*. "I don't understand."

"I'm a big spoon looking for my little spoon. She's about yay high." He held up his hand to right above Abi's head. "Got this sweet Southern accent that gets to me, loves ice cream, doughnuts, the feel of the sand in her toes, and litters of puppies. She is also kind and strong and the most amazing woman I've ever met."

Abi's eyes filled but for a whole other reason. "I may know of someone, but she's kind of a bed hog and has ice-cold feet."

"Good thing I run hot." He waggled a brow and she burst out laughing, which was more of a sob-laugh combo. "Now that." He kissed one hand. "Right there." Then the other. "Is the best part of my day. You get to me, Abilene Woods. For me, you're it and if you let me I promise to show you every day that you are enough. More than enough." He kissed her lips gently. "More than I deserve, which is why I promise I'll put you first. Above work, my family, even above my own stupid fears and insecurities."

She paused, thinking back to what he'd first said. "I scare you?"

"God, yes. The way you make me feel, the way you look at me, the way you say my name. I'm not scared now, and I intend to spend the rest of my life proving it to you."

His words reached her in places she'd thought were buried so deep they'd never see the light of day, but she couldn't ignore it anymore.

"You don't scare me. You make me feel safe. And it's because that's what love does. It makes all the bad things seem manageable."

He rested his forehead to hers. "When I saw that your stuff was gone, I thought I'd lost you forever."

"I'm right here." She wrapped her arms around his neck.

"Does this mean you're applying, because you should know this is a forever kind of job."

"This little spoon would accept no less." The drizzle picked up and, when she looked at the sky, the rain was falling like a million twinkling stars around them.

"Do you know one of my happy things?" he asked. "Kissing you in the rain."

Epilogue

Happy Things:
Puppies named Waffles

Six weeks later…

"That right there is the sweet spot," Owen said. "Hit that every time and she'll purr like a kitten."

Heart racing, palms sweating, Abi pushed down on the clutch and shifted into second gear. Today was her third driving lesson and she'd finally moved up from first gear. And she hadn't cried once.

The truck pushed forward at a steady eleven miles per hour as she did her first circle of the parking lot. She rounded the pylons Owen had set up, slowly weaving in and out of them like some kind of geriatric NASCAR driver.

"What do I do when I get to the end?" she asked, panicked. She'd never made it to the end. Yesterday's record was a whopping three pylons before killing the engine. Then she'd accidentally flooded the engine, cutting their lesson short.

"Just slide into that spot right there." Owen pointed to a parking slot that butted up to the back wall of Stout.

"What if I hit the wrong pedal and drive through the bar?"

Owen slid his hand on her thigh, giving it a supportive squeeze. "Then we redecorate. But it won't come to that since you're going to nail this."

"Why does everything you say sound like an innuendo."

"On average, men think about sex once every hour and a half. Around you, my average is much higher."

She snorted and downshifted without instruction, then smoothly pulled into the spot and sputtered to a stop. "I did it!"

She slid across the bench and gave Owen a big smack to the lips. And then because she was already there she crawled onto his lap and gave him a long, slow kiss that had them both breathing hard.

"You did it," he said against her lips, delivering one last panty-melting kiss.

She pulled back. "You're thinking about doing *it* again, aren't you?"

His fingers dug into her hips as he held her tightly to him. "Like I said, my batting average is impressive around you. But before we go there, I want to show you something. Close your eyes and don't peek."

"Now that you said not to peek, all I want to do is peek."

"And ruin the surprise?" He set her gently back in the driver's seat, then took both her hands and rested them over her eyes. "Don't move."

She felt his lips brush hers, then he was gone. The door opened and she felt the warm summer breeze fill the car. She strained her ears, trying to hear what was happening but there was complete silence.

"Is this some kind of hazing?" she called out.

Nothing.

So she opened one eye and found Owen sitting next to her with a big grin. "Cheater."

She shrugged, uncaring that she got caught. Then she saw a big box with a giant red bow on top. He placed it on her lap.

"What's this?"

"Happy things."

She looked up at the man she loved and her heart skipped a beat. "But I already have my happy thing. You."

"This might top me."

"Nothing could ever top you," she assured him. Then the box moved and a little *grrr* came from inside. "Oh my goodness." She took off the lid and staring up at her was a golden retriever puppy with the biggest brown eyes and a little wet nose.

Yip.

"This totally tops you," she whispered, lifting the puppy into her arms. His tail wagged so hard it moved his entire backside. With a bark, he licked her face making her laugh. That's when something shiny caught her eye.

Around his neck was a blue collar with a gold tag dangling from it. Abi read the inscription. "You named our puppy Waffles?"

"Only the second-best food on the planet, besides blueberry cake doughnuts," he said. "There's more. Look closer."

Abi did and her mouth fell open. Attached to the collar was a stunning diamond ring. "Is this what I think it is?"

"If you think it's me asking my little spoon to be my wife, then yes."

"I didn't realize that that particular job opening was going to happen so fast." Nerves coursed through her body as she said, "I'm an as-is kind of girl."

"I love every bit of your as-is."

She slid the ring on her finger, held it out, and gave a little wiggle. "It's perfect."

He chuckled. "Is that a yes?"

"Yes! That's an absolutely, positively yes!" The moment she said those words a feeling of rightness came over her. She'd waited her entire life to be chosen for exactly who she was and looking into the eyes of her perfect man, she decided it was worth the wait.

THE END

Thank you for reading!

Make an author's day and consider leaving a nice review! Reviews help authors like me find new readers and gain advertising. If you enjoyed the read, tell a friend!

Review it now!

Want more Eastons?

Turn the page to check out Jillian and Clay's story, *Summer Affair*, a sexy, feel-good friends to lovers romantic comedy!

Chapter One

Resolutions from Jillian's Journal
Rename Resolutions to Recommendations
so that one could, at any time,
ignore them without a trace of guilt.

Jillian Conner was naked.

Not entirely naked, but her teeny-weeny teal bikini didn't leave much to the imagination. With a few scraps of material held together by a series of tug-and-they're-gone straps, she was living on the edge, about to do something thrilling—and so out of character—even if it could constitute a public indecency charge.

She tightened the silky belt of her robe and looked out the kitchen window to the pool. A giddy excitement rushed through her. The last time she was this naked outside of her bedroom or en suite was when her son was in diapers. It was only a matter of time before the homeowners' association added a new regulation prohibiting skinny-dipping in one's own yard. She could practically hear the wildfire of gossip from the local mill and see the write-up in the Forest Park Newsletter: Local Cake Goddess Turned Moon Goddess in Nude Pagan Ritual.

While her backyard was open on all three sides and butted up to twenty acres of state-protected forest land, her side yard had no gates, no fence, and no privacy, leaving her exposed to any passersby. But those concerns were for another time because tonight Jillian was about to embark on something so rare and extraordinary she could scarcely believe her luck.

Me time.

An uninterrupted, unsupervised, unadulterated kid-free night. She'd heard of this white magic whispered around playgrounds and in local mommy-and-me circles. Tales of sleep-through-the-night, wake-after-noon, no sugar-induced tantrums kind of affairs. Once upon a time, she'd been one of those carefree non-moms who frequented happy hour, spent weekends with the girls, and enjoyed a good romp with a handsome man.

Ah, sex. It seemed as foreign a concept as window browsing. And while there wouldn't be browsing or sex on tonight's menu, there would be chocolate cake, a bottle of wine, and a nice dip in the pool.

To most, a little skinny-dipping wouldn't be considered bold or even pushing the envelope, but when one's envelope had been stamped Sealed until further notice, tonight's agenda was the equivalent of streaking at the Super Bowl. Especially when Jillian was a by-the-book advocate and follower. She brushed and flossed after every meal. Always used her signal, never hit snooze on her alarm, and found lists relaxing. Her hall-monitor status was strong, forged from a place of necessity.

It took a fair-weathered fiancé, a Ponzi schemer, and a forensic accountant of a husband—who forensic-ed her right out of her alimony—for her to admit the cold, hard truth.

Jillian's picker was a lemon. An honest-to-god, Cupid-phobic, unwilling doormat, lemon of a picker who always picked the wrong pecker. Sadly, according to her divorce attorney and a circuit judge, bad pecker-picker lemon laws were not recognized in the state of Oregon. Which left her with one solution.

Absolutely, positively no men. No charmers, sweet talkers, bad boys, pretty boys, GQs, lumberjacks, or jack-offs. And especially go for the "nice guys," who hid their dine-and-dash tendencies that, in her experience, unmistakably went hand in hand with a certain appendage.

She'd seen her two best friends find their person and fall in love, and she was elated for them. But what were the odds of a third unicorn in their tiny state?

Sadly, there was a list of dine-and-dashers throughout her thirty-plus years, with her most recent breaking her heart and her bank—making her a five-time loser when it came to the game of love. But she wouldn't let that rob her of her deep and unwavering affair with all things romance and weddings, which was one of the reasons why she'd started Cake Goddess. The other was to keep the power company happy.

Jillian was a special-occasions cake designer, whom the *Portland Tribune* called one of the premier pâtissiers in Portland. She specialized in classic, couture, and edible happily ever after. What had started as a small home business to supplement her income had turned into a cake company that sold decadent desserts all up and down the west coast. The demand was almost more than her kitchen could handle. Between being a single parent and a mompreneur, nights like tonight were a rarity. She loved her son, Sammy, but was desperate for some time to focus on herself.

Which was why, last week, after her birthday celebration, Jillian had signed up for *Hear Me Roar,* a podcast designed to help single women get their groove back. To resuscitate the bold, fun-loving, adventurous side that divorce and dating had annihilated. Tonight's session was titled *Get it, Girl,* where she'd explore a series of resolutions that she'd painstakingly compiled to help bring some much-needed fun back into her life. Between baking and being Sammy's whole world, Me Time was hard to come by, but since it was his dad's week, Jillian had a whole seven days to herself.

And she knew exactly where she wanted to start.

Grabbing a bottle of wine and a glass, and her TODAY YOU ARE AN EAGLE AND YOUR WINGS ARE MADE OF AWESOME journal, Jillian headed next door to the main house for her skinny-dipping, date-of-one, middle-of-the-night adventure. With three years between her and her divorce, this was her way of shedding the past and arising from the water a new woman.

Jillian cinched the belt of her white, silky robe with the kissy-lips print and walked barefoot from her little cottage, where she and Sammy lived, to the main house she rented out as a vacation destination to help cover the cost of the two dwellings and six acres of property she'd inherited from her grandmother. Tomorrow, she was expecting a tenant who'd rented out the main house for the entire summer. He was a rather famous musician, and her best friend's brother-in-law, who needed a quiet place to unwind away from the spotlight. But for tonight, the entire property was hers to enjoy.

She walked across the small bridge separating the two houses, scattered pine needles and damp soil pressing into her feet. The June air was crisp and still, the sky so clear she could see a billion stars twinkling overhead. There couldn't have been a more perfect setting to begin her journey into a sexy, single, and capable woman, who lived life to the fullest.

She'd decided to leave the pool and porch lights off—she wasn't that bold—to camouflage her courageous first step from potential peepers. Enjoying the night surrounding her, and sipping her glass of wine, she sat on the edge of one of the padded loungers, pulled her small journal and a pen from her pocket, and pressed Play on the latest episode.

Welcome back, you're listening to Hear Me Roar, *a psychological look into the world of dating, and I'm your host, Dr. Claire,* the podcast began. *Today starts your new journey and I'm here to tell you that Single-Girl Anxiety is real. From check-one invitations to the singles' table, and well-meaning family members who invite you to dinner and fail to mention the balding, middle-aged neighbor who works at the button factory and is waiting just for you. You can stop the crazy and take back your life.*

I know what it's like to be that single girl in a sea of penguins. Being single in the city isn't always easy, but it can be fun. But this isn't only a course in being single, it's a course about finding love. Self-love, familial love, and, yes, even the kind of love that comes when you find your person. But to find that forever love, first you need to remember how to love that scared, scarred girl deep inside who looks for validation over value.

Jillian had made that mistake once and vowed never to do it again, which was why her list was so important. Red flags, gut instincts, different ideals—these were things that would make up her manifesto.

After watching her friends find love, Jillian was starting to wonder if maybe she was missing out on something. She wasn't looking for her penguin, and after three generations of lemon pecker pickers, she didn't even believe in marriage, but a date here and there wouldn't be so bad. Neither would an orgasm. All she wanted was a small taste of that fancy-free, single-girl life she'd lost.

You can be single and happy without suffering from Single-Girl Anxiety by taking stock of your life and building a place where you get back in touch with you, that bright, confident Girl on Fire who reveled in her freedom, flirted with strangers for flirt's sake and wasn't afraid to get a little burned because she knew that the safe path wasn't always the fun path.

Jillian's heart picked up, and an empowering flutter warmed her chest. That's what she wanted. To remember how to love herself. To fill up her passion cup so that she didn't start her day depleted. She was even open to some adult fun with no strings, but mainly she was on a mission to find her inner Girl on Fire.

Now, I want you to pull out your Get it, Girl *list. Look at it and let your brain absorb each and every resolution.*

Jillian smoothed a hand down the paper and looked at her list. It had exactly twenty items that she'd compiled earlier that day. She'd settled on twenty because it was an even number and divisible by two, five, and ten.

Now, I want you to turn to a clean page and at the top, under the first item, I want you to write: One—Stop making lists. If it's important, you'll remember it.

Jillian hit Pause. "What kind of list asks you to abandon the list?"

She could scarcely remember to put on underwear, let alone an entire list of to-do tasks. It would be like going to the grocery store and saying, *Okay chips and powdered-sugar doughnuts, come jump in my cart* and then forgetting the kale.

If Jillian was going to take the time to write a list, then everything on said list was important.

Hoping Dr. Claire was joking, she hit Play.

I know for most of you, that's a hard thing to wrap your brain around. But the only way you are going to get in touch with...

Fftt...

Fftt...

Fftt...

Jillian fast-forwarded to the next step.

I want you to go back a moment, to when I asked you to abandon your list. How did that make you feel?

"Like this is a stupid podcast and I'm wasting my time," Jillian said.

I often get words like empowered, alive, ready for anything that comes my way.

"Then they're liars," Jillian announced.

Fftt...

Fftt...

Fftt...

Now for number two. I want you to really think about what your second resolution would be. It can be one from your discarded list or one that stands out in your mind. Without peeking, I want you to envision it.

Jillian chose to quickly write her next rule, then read it back to herself. "Rename Resolutions to Recommendations, so that I can, at any time, ignore them without a trace of guilt."

And because she felt that was more of a guideline and she made her own rules, she wrote down another resolution. A real make-change, show-what-you're-made-of kind of resolution that would take her from frazzled single mom to sexy, proud-to-be-single woman.

Taking a fortifying-sized sip of wine, Jillian walked to the pool's edge and dipped her toe in—just one. Then, with her confidence boosted, she submerged her entire foot before stepping on the top step.

The pool was set to a balmy eighty-seven degrees, and she could see the steam rising off the surface. Feel the nerves floating up in her belly like helium balloons. Hear that Girl on Fire telling her to jump without a life preserver.

Closing her eyes, she undid her robe, letting it slide down to her elbows and reveal her bikini, and jumped. Well, slid down to the next step and said to the stars above, loud and proud, "Lose the negative whispers and lose that suit."

"While I'm in strong favor of both those statements, you might want to wait until I turn my back," a very low, very unexpected voice said from the abyss at the deep end of the pool.

Jillian squeaked. Panic rose and grabbed her by the throat, and every horror movie she'd ever watched came flooding back. She moved backward, her robe's belt catching between her legs, yanking the silky cover-up and sending it into the water, where it slowly sank to the pool's bottom, leaving her in three scraps of material with teal strings.

Telling herself it was the wine, she closed her eyes and whispered, "Your imagination is working overtime, and you are dreaming."

"It bodes well for me that you imagine me in your dreams."

Recognition hit hard, and her eyes snapped open. It was not the wine. She was not even a little tipsy. She was stone-cold sober, and swimming over to her was an Easton, the youngest and sexiest of the brothers—and the only one

Jillian let herself fantasize about because, with their age difference, *that* was never going to happen.

Clay, who lived in Seattle, was way too young and therefore had an expiration date—which was why she'd allowed her fascination to only morph into an embarrassing crush. So when he stood, arising from the now waist-deep water that sliced down his body, her mouth went dry.

Like some Greek god, his hard chest glistened with moisture in the moonlight, and a thin patch of wet hair trailed down the plains of his flat stomach, disappearing beneath the water. His hair and lashes were spiked, and his lips were turned up into a grin that had her bathing suit nearly melting off her body.

"Clay?" she asked, squinting her eyes to ensure it was the Seahawks running back swimming in her pool. She gulped. There he was, in only the night's air and steaming water. "What are you doing here?"

"Waiting to hear what number three on your list is. Number two was a showstopper," he said, his gaze flickering with amusement and something a little more dangerous.

Interest. Even worse, it was clear that Clay of the chiseled abs and bulging biceps was teasing in a very flirty way.

"If you'd waited another minute, you would have seen the real showstopper," Jillian flirted back in that flirt for flirt's sake way Dr. Claire spoke of.

Clay took another step toward her, revealing a pair of board shorts that hung indecently low on his hips and matched his cobalt-blue eyes. "My loss."

A wave of single-girl anxiety washed over her, causing her to fold her arms across her body—at least concealing the top half of her bikini.

"Why are you here?" she asked.

"Going for a swim before I turn in," he said. "It seems you're doing the same."

"I was actually just—"

"About to lose your suit?"

"Not expecting Rhett until tomorrow," she finished, referring to his older brother who was her renter.

"I'm not expecting Rhett at all," he replied, amusement thick in his tone.

"I don't understand." Although, her gut understood perfectly. "You're my new tenant?"

With a mischievous grin, he walked toward the stairs, every step revealing more of his delicious body until he was within reaching distance and the water only hit his thighs. He reached out and she took a step back—up the stairs and out of the pool.

He froze, and that grin turned into a smile as he scooped up the robe and held it out to her. "Disappointed, Jillian?"

And that's when she saw it. The knowledge in those deep, blue eyes. He knew about her little crush. A silly—but very real—schoolgirl crush that caused her to blush whenever he so much as looked her way. Heck, every time she was within the same square mile as him, she stumbled over her words or gawked at him.

Like she was now. And here, all this time, she assumed she'd played it cool. It was clear she had not.

"What? No." She was in trouble, that's what she was. She took the robe, which was dripping wet, and used it as a shield for her body. She shivered at the warm water on her chilled skin. Or at least that was the story she was sticking to. "Sorry, I'm just a little confused. You're Darcy's brother-in-law who rented my place?"

"Is that a problem?"

A gigantic one. "No, but I'm still a little startled." She was also panicked and thrown and incredibly turned on. "When Darcy called last week, saying her brother-in-law needed a quiet place to decompress, I thought it was Rhett, because of all the craziness surrounding his separation. I didn't even look at the signature on the lease. I just assumed..."

He lifted himself out of the pool, water sluicing down his body, and she forgot what she was talking about.

"You're probably one in a handful of women in the world who wouldn't check out the famous Rhett Easton's signature. The rest of us only share his last name."

She shrugged, then grabbed the towel she'd intended on using and held it out for him, quick to pull her hands back when he took it. "More of a country fan myself."

"I'll add that to the list of things I like about you." He towel-dried his hair in a way that was all things manly, then wrapped the towel around his waist. It didn't help, his chest was still bare, his shoulders glistening in the moonlight. It was his smile. That genuine and warm smile that always made her nervous. Because smiles could be deceiving.

"We barely know each other, so it must be a short list," she said.

"It has more than three items. Yours?"

She ignored this. "You weren't supposed to come until the tenth. Today's only..." She silently counted off all the activities she had accomplished this week and grimaced. "It's the tenth. I am so sorry. I lost track of the days. Well, not the days, because Sammy and I are practicing days and he wakes me up every morning to tell me what day it is, but we haven't reached actual dates yet, which is why I'm here dressed in this, interrupting your swim."

"You aren't interrupting. In fact, the pool's a bit lonely with just me and my thoughts," he said. "You're welcome to join."

"Oh, I couldn't." She pulled on the robe, tightening the belt and sending droplets of water splashing on the concrete. "The pool is part of the rental. It's for you. For the summer." God, every time she was around Clay she came off as having an IQ equivalent to a pack of gum.

His eyes locked on hers and held. It was the kind of stare that told her he was making a conscious effort not to look down. The kind of stare that made her nervous. She shivered again—but for a whole other reason.

"Are you aware that the robe is sheer when wet? And, um, clingy?"

"Oh my god." Her robe was more than sheer; it made a wet T-shirt contest seem tame. She had almost shucked the suit altogether. At least she'd kept on a bikini—a teeny-weeny bikini that she only wore when alone. The last thing she'd ever want was Clay comparing her to the cleat chasers in triangles and dental floss he was usually seen with. Then again, a muffin top might be less embarrassing than being caught in a swim-dress her grandmother would have worn.

"Are you saying I can't invite friends?" he asked.

"Of course not. It's your place to do whatever you want with whoever you want and, wow." She closed her eyes. "I just said that."

"You did."

Great, now she was sweating in uncomfortable places. "I meant that the pool is all yours. I already talked to Sammy about how we aren't to bother you while you're here. And if my uncle hounds you to join his poker night, he's trying to fleece you."

"I'm a pretty good player."

"He cheats. Sleight of hand, card counting, stacking the deck. He was a professional hustler in New York before moving here. Some people call him a crook."

"What do you call him?"

"Uncle Eddie." That earned her a smile. "He's at the back room at the senior center, likely cleaning house. He's been banned from the VFW hall. Six times."

"I'll keep that in mind." He sounded as if her warning amused him. "As for the pool, I'll only need it early morning and at night for PT. Doctor's orders."

"Darcy told me about your surgery. How are you feeling?" Last winter, Clay had torn his ACL, taking him out for the rest of the season.

"Better by the moment."

She swallowed. "Let me know if there's anything I can do to make your stay easier."

"That's the plan." He pointed to his lower leg, but her gaze stopped much higher. "Not sure what you're offering to help with, but the surgery was on my knee."

Realizing she was staring, Jillian jerked her gaze upward, and when she met his eyes, he winked. *Oh boy.*

"What time do you want to eat breakfast?" she asked.

"Is that an invitation?"

"No. A home-cooked breakfast is part of the package. You just tell me what time you want it, and I will make sure it's ready."

His smile increased ten-thousand watts at her comment.

Oh my god, everything she was saying sounded sexual. "Where do you want to eat? Patio? Kitchen?"

"Kitchen's fine."

Why was she so ridiculously ruffled? She was too old and too tired to experience tingles. But there they were, zinging north and south of the equator.

Her phone rang and she checked the screen. It was Dirk.

She'd bet a pile of dry, non-see-through towels her ex was calling because of a problem with Sammy. "Excuse me, I have to take this." Clay walked over to the table to gather his things and turned away. "Is Sammy okay?"

"You need to get over here right away."

Continue *Summer Affair*

Want more Eastons?

Turn the page to check out Darcy and Gage's, *Chasing I Do* **a reluctantly funny, feel-good enemies to lovers romantic comedy!**

Chapter One

Darcy Kincaid had dreamed about this day since she was six and uncovered her mother's stash of Southern Wedding magazines in the basement. After a lifetime of planning, handpicking two thousand of the palest of pink peonies, and her entire life savings, she was about to pull off, what she believed to be, the most romantic I Do in history. The sun was high, the sky was crystal blue, and a gentle June breeze carried the scent of the nearby primrose blooms and ever after.

Today was the perfect day to be married, and the rose garden at Belle Mont House was the ideal backdrop. And Darcy wasn't about to let a tail-chasing wedding crasher ruin her moment. No matter how charming.

Not this time.

"Nuzzling the bride's pillows before the wedding will only get you escorted out," Darcy said to the four-legged powderpuff in matching pink booties and hair bow.

The dog, who was more runway than runaway, dropped down low in the grass, eyes big black circles of excitement, tail wagging with delight—her jewel-encrusted collar winking in the sunlight.

Darcy squinted, but could only make out the first word. "Fancy." The little dog's ears perked up and her tail went wild.

"Such a pretty name," Darcy cooed, taking a cautious step forward. "I'm Darcy; it's nice to meet you. I'm going to come a little closer so I can get a better look at your collar and find your mamma's number. Is that okay?"

With a playful snort, the animal's entire body was wiggling as if so excited by the idea of making a friend she couldn't hold in the glee. Darcy reached out to ruffle her ears, and Fancy, confusing Darcy's movement for time to play, snatched up the pillow and gave it a good shake.

"No!" Darcy cried, halting in her tracks while little bits of stuffing leached into the air, causing perspiration to bead on her forehead.

Fancy, on the other hand, wasn't worried in the slightest. Nope, she gave another rambunctious whip of the head before jumping up and down with the pillow as if this were all fun and games.

Sadly, this situation was about as close to fun and games as natural child birthing. Not only was the vintage silk pillow, a family heirloom passed down from the bride's great-grandmother, in danger of becoming a chew-toy, but the bride's ring was swinging dangerously from the aged ribbon.

And this wasn't just any bride. Candice Covington was the former Miss Oregon, a Portland mover and shaker, and the first bride to be wed at the newly renovated Belle Mont House. Candice was already in the bridal suite, her beloved in the tower room, and two hundred of their closest friends and family were set to start arriving in just over an hour—and the dog looked content to nuzzle the pillow all afternoon.

With its teeth.

"Stop!" she said in her most authoritative tone, putting her hand out.

To Darcy's surprise, the dog stopped. Her snout going into hypersniffer mode, she dropped the pillow to the grass and rose up to smell the air. Seemed Fancy had caught the scent of the prosciutto-wrapped figs sitting on a chair that Darcy had been tasting, and she stood up on her hind legs, then walked around in three perfect circles.

"Someone's got moves," she said. "Not bad, but mine are better."

A decade of planning events for Portland's pickiest clients and four years in the trenches as a single mother had taught Darcy the art of positive redirection. She'd lasted through potty training, teething, and chickenpox. This stubborn ball of fluff didn't stand a chance.

Eying the flower arrangement on the closest table, Darcy grabbed a decorative stick and gave it a little shake. "Want to play with the stick for a while?" The dog sat, eyes wide, head cocked to the side in an explosion of cuteness. "We can switch toys before you destroy the pillow, okay?"

"Yip!"

Tail up like a heat-seeking radar, the dog hit the fetch-and-retrieve position, pointing her nose toward one of the open fields.

"Ready?" Darcy wiggled the stick again for show. "Go get 'em!"

The stick flew through the air, going as far in the opposite direction as it could. Darcy released a sigh of relief when it cleared the fountain and landed in the middle of the field.

A low growl sounded, followed by a blur of white fur that bolted past.

Those little legs working for the prize. A position Darcy could relate to.

Located in the prestigious West Hills, Belle Mont House was three stories of Portland history with extensive manicured gardens, six bedrooms, a grand salon, and captivating views of the city and Mount Hood—all of which needed to be meticulously cared for. And Darcy was the sole caretaker.

She had driven by the old property a thousand times over the years. But she hadn't really recognized its potential until after her world had fallen apart and a heartbreaking betrayal had left her life in tatters—much like the foundation of this forgotten house. Unable to watch something so beautiful and full of history crumble, she'd saved it from demolition, then spent every penny and waking moment renovating it back to its original grandeur. In return, Belle Mont had given her something even more precious—a future for her and her daughter.

Today marked Belle Mont's first day in operation as the year's "Most Romantic" wedding destination in the Pacific Northwest and Darcy as its planner extraordinaire—according to the editor at Wedding Magazine, who'd left a message earlier about sending a high-profile couple to check out the location.

A couple so hush-hush, the editor refused to give the name for fear that the press would show. But if they decided that Belle Mont was their dream wedding venue, and Darcy could accommodate them with the last Sunday in July, the only date that worked around the couple's hectic schedule, then Belle Mont would land a huge spread in the August issue.

The endorsement alone was enough to make her say yes on the spot. Not to mention the profit for hosting such a lavish event would go a long way toward helping pay back all the money she'd invested into the renovation—and secure her future in Portland.

A future that now resided in the jaws of a dog that could fit in her pocket.

Fancy snatched the stick and darted across the lawn toward the twinkle-lit and peony-covered gazebo in record time—all with the pillow still in its jowls.

"Hey," she called out, "we had a deal!"

The dog's tail went up as if flipping the bird at their deal before she ran beneath a row of chairs and struck a different kind of pose altogether. A move that showed enough doggie bits to prove that under that pink bling, Fancy was all male. And about to shit all over Candice's perfect day.

A situation Darcy knew all too well.

"Had I known you had a stupid stick down there, I wouldn't have bothered trying to reason with you."

In Darcy's experience, men loved the forbidden almost as much as they loved their stick. So she fumbled with her skirt, pulling it above her thighs, and gave chase.

Fancy took off, and man, those toothpick legs could fly. Ears flapping behind him, butt moving like lightning bugs in a jar, the pooch headed straight for the rose garden, which lay directly across from the aisle runner that had Candice and Carter spelled out in the palest of pink peony petals.

"Not the runner!" she cried, only to watch in horror as Fancy raced up the center of the white pillowed Egyptian cotton, his legs pumping with the speed and grace of a cheetah in the wild, leaving a few dozen miniature muddy paw prints and a tornado of petals in his wake.

"No, no, no!" she called out. "Not the rose garden."

Terrified of the damage he could do to the roses and the pillow, she picked up the pace and rounded the white iron fencing, gravel sliding under her heels as she burst through the gate and snatched the pillow right before the Fancy dove his fancy-ass—and Candice's ring—into the fountain.

"Got it!" she yelled, but the celebration quickly faded as her momentum carried her forward—and right into the stone cherub boy's watering hole.

"Oh god, no!" Darcy yelped as water exploded around her.

Having landed ass first, she felt the cold wetness seep through her silk skirt and slosh into her shoes. Her brand-new designer shoes she'd found at a consignment store and purchased especially for today. "Please, no."

She clawed the edge of the fountain and pulled, mentally willing herself out of the fountain—but she couldn't gain any positive momentum.

No matter how hard she tried, she just couldn't pull herself out.

Refusing to give up, she looked around for Fancy, hoping to either send him to find help or pull him in with her. But he'd vanished, right before the wedding, leaving her waist-deep in his mess.

The situation was so painfully familiar, Darcy wanted to cry. Then devour the entire wedding cake in one sitting.

"Are you okay?" a husky voice asked from above.

"Thank god you're here," she said, pushing her hair out of her face and looking up, expecting to find one of her kitchen staff.

But instead of a clip-on tie with a comb-over, Darcy's unexpected hero looked like an underwear model in a dark blue button-up and a pair of slacks that fit him to perfection. And his arms—oh my, those arms—were impressive, perfect for helping a lady in need.

Although Darcy had worked hard to not be reliant on others—a lifetime of letdowns could do that to a girl—she knew that sometimes it was okay to take an offered hand. And those hands were big and solid and— whoa—reaching forward to wrap around her hips and easily lift her out.

Her feet hit the ground, and she did her best to wring out her shirt. "I'm sorry if I'm getting you all wet."

"You never have to apologize to a man for getting him wet." He chuckled, and Darcy, realizing how that had come out, went to move, but his arms tightened, stilling her. "Make sure you're okay first. You were moving pretty fast when you dove in."

Not as fast as her heart was racing.

Closing her eyes, Darcy took stock. Her chest tingled, her head was light, and a wave of delicious thrill jump-started parts she'd long believed dead. In fact, she was as far from fine as a woman who had sworn off men could get.

"I'm good. Thank you," she lied, trying to gain some distance without falling back into the fountain, which was not an easy task. He was so big, he filled the space, leaving nowhere for her to go. She brushed off her elbows, which were scraped up, but she'd live, then started to straighten when a big hand appeared, Candice's ring resting in its palm.

"I believe you lost this."

"Thank you," she whispered, a wave of relief washing over her. "You have no idea how—"

Darcy looked up, and the words died on her lips and dropped to the pit of her stomach, where they expanded and churned until—oh god, she couldn't breathe.

Her unexpected hero wore slacks and tie fit for Wall Street, a leather jacket that added a touch of bad boy to the businessman, and a pair of electric blue eyes that she'd recognize anywhere. They'd always reminded her of a calm, crystal clear lake. Today they were tempestuous, like an angry spring storm.

The change wasn't a surprise, given the last time they'd seen each other. But the deep ache of longing it brought on was.

"Gage," she said, her heart pounding so loudly she was certain he could hear it thumping in her chest.

It was the first time she'd seen him since the funeral, a thought that brought back a dozen memories—some sad, some of the best moments of her life, but all of them a painful reminder of what had been lost.

"Hey, Pink," he said in a tone that implied that had he known it was her he would have let her drowned.

She swallowed back the disappointment, hoping he didn't notice that she was shaking. "What are you doing here?"

"It looks like I'm helping you find your wedding ring." He took her hand in his and slid the ring on her finger. The sensation was so overwhelming she jerked back.

Gage Easton was over six feet of solid muscle and swagger. He was also sweet and kind and, at one time, one of the few people she thought she'd always be able to count on. If things had gone how Darcy had dreamed, he would have made for one heck of a brother-in-law.

An even better uncle.

A swift shot of guilt mixed with the swelling panic in her throat, her reckless secret pressing down until she was choking. But Darcy swallowed it back and refused to shoulder all of the blame.

Life was filled with hard choices. While Gage's twin had chosen to be unfaithful, Darcy had chosen their daughter's happiness.

She would always choose Kylie.

Gage looked at her bare feet, then aimed that intense gaze her way. "I would have thought that after jilting Kyle like you did, you'd have started wearing running shoes to these kinds of events."

Although Gage had a big heart, he was still an Easton. And when someone messed with one brother, they messed with the whole clan. The only way to survive was to hide your fear and never stand down.

Shoulders back, chest slightly puffed, Darcy made her body appear bigger, the way she had when she'd been a young girl and encountered a stranger at her breakfast table. She'd walk into the kitchen and pretend she was big and strong—someone not to be messed with.

Her mother had a thing for rot-gut whiskey and bottom-shelf men—and made a habit of bringing both home. Sometimes they stayed the night, sometimes they stayed the year, but Darcy never knew who—or what—she'd encounter in the one place that should have felt safe.

But this was her home now, and she'd do whatever was necessary to protect it.

"After five years, I would have hoped you'd realize your family wasn't the only ones who were hurting," she said. "I may have walked out on your brother, but I wasn't the one who let him drive that night."

Gage Easton felt the truth of that statement hit hard, the power of it nearly taking him out at the knees. Darcy wasn't a confrontational person by nature, but she knew how to stand her ground. No doubt a trait she'd picked up from dealing with his family.

He hadn't seen her since the funeral. Nobody had. Not that he'd blamed her. His family had still been reeling from the aftermath of the wedding that never happened, when tragedy struck again, tearing a chasm between Darcy and the Eastons that could never be fixed. His brother, Kyle, was gone, and with the overwhelming and sudden grief that had been thrust upon his family, most especially his mom, a lot of the blame had been unfairly placed upon Darcy.

There were so many times he wanted to reach out, make sure she was okay, but he'd spent the majority of their relationship keeping his distance, certain that no good could come from letting himself get too close. And he wasn't looking to test his theory.

Not today.

"Are you okay?" he asked, waving a hand to her elbows, which were scrapped and he was certain smarting.

"Nothing that won't heal," she said, and he knew she wasn't talking about the gravel burn. "I just have to change my skirt and shoes."

"You might want to change the top while you're at it." He grinned. "Not that I mind the view, but it might cause some heart problems with the older guests."

Darcy's gaze dropped to her shirt and the two beautiful buds peeking through the translucent fabric, and she gasped. Hell, Gage was in his prime and her top was causing some serious gasping and heart palpitations on his end.

"Don't worry, I didn't peek. Much." He leaned in and whispered, "Although, if you know you're going to take a swim, you might just consider skinny dipping. You'd get the same effect, only you wouldn't have to hang-dry your lace bra and panties."

"You can't see my panties."

No, he couldn't, but she didn't need to know that. The narrowed eyes and pursed lips were enough to tell him that she was ticked just thinking about him seeing her panties.

And that was a far better state than the tears that had been threatening a moment ago.

"Look," she said pointedly, crossing her arms over her chest, which did nothing except pull the fabric tighter. "I'm grateful that you found the ring and helped me out of the fountain, and I have no clue as to why you're here"—her tone said she didn't care to find out either—"but I need you to leave."

"Don't worry," he said. "I didn't come to ruin your big day. I'll get out of your way as soon as my meeting is over." And he found the abomination in bows he was stuck dog sitting.

"Oh, it's not my big day," she clarified. "I'm the planner for the wedding that is supposed to start in less than an hour."

He looked at her outfit and, while cream in color, it wasn't bridal attire. The skirt, the buttoned silk top, even her hair said professionally elegant. Not bride-to-be.

A heaviness that he didn't even notice he'd taken on lifted at her admission, and he wanted to kick himself. She wasn't getting married? So what? It didn't matter. Kyle was gone, Gage was still struggling to make peace with things, and Darcy would always be off-limits.

No matter how great she still looked. Even scratched up and sweaty, she was as gorgeous as ever.

"Well, if you'll just direct me to the manager's office," he asked. "I'm late, and don't want to keep him waiting."

She looked at her watch and froze, an expression of resignation washing over her.

"Actually, you're early," she said, so full of dread she felt sweat bead on her forehead. She stuck out her hand. "Darcy Kincaid, owner and exclusive planner for Belle Mont House.

I believe the editor from Wedding Magazine said you'd be dropping by tomorrow."

Continue *Chasing I Do*

Want more Eastons?

Turn the page to check out Piper and Josh's story, ***Definitely Maybe Dating,*** **a hilariously smart and tender opposites attract romantic comedy!**

Chapter One

Piper Campagna knew better than to tempt fate.

Acting as the Ansel Adams of love for even a single wedding was as risky as blow-drying her hair in the shower. It wasn't that she didn't love the idea of love or even dream about seeing something so beautiful aimed her direction. Once upon a time, Piper had given up everything in her quest for unconditional love only to wind up broke, homeless, and completely alone.

Nope, as far as she was concerned, happily ever after was about as realistic as Prince Charming riding in on a Pegasus.

She'd been to exactly five weddings in her lifetime. All her mother's. And all but one ending before the photos were developed. Making Piper the last person on the planet to take a resident photographer position at one of Portland's up-and-coming wedding venues.

Yet there she was, about to shoot a highly publicized engagement party for a local celebrity family—acting as if she were the right person for the job. As if she truly believed in something as laughable as forever. She wasn't sure what that said about her, other than she was willing to do anything to land this job, even if it meant faking it.

Piper pressed the palm of her hand to her forehead and groaned loudly. She hated fakes.

Apparently, Fate agreed because just as the fairytale of a wedding venue started to come into view through her cracked windshield, a guttural groan rattled the car. POSH—her Piece of Shit Honda—was telling anyone who'd listen that she needed more than duct tape and prayer to handle the steep hill and hairpin turns.

"Come on, girl, don't fail me now." Piper lovingly rubbed the dashboard.

The engine gave a low hum as it downshifted, pulling through the worst of the bend, handling the tight curve like a pro. POSH might have a junkyard past, but she was scrappy as hell and had an aftermarket gear-shift knob that was shaped like brass knuckles. When shit got real, POSH rallied. Break-ups, break-downs, let-downs, broken promises, and even a handful of impulsive decisions that nearly broke the bank, that car was the most reliable thing in Piper's life. Over 150,000 miles of shared history.

150,000 miles of survival.

When Piper spotted the minefield of potholes ahead, her first reaction was to slam on the brakes. As a former rebel, she might do a little roaring and rumbling when cornered, but she knew when to push forward and when to concede. Yet as the steering tightened beneath her hands, jerking the wheel hard to the left with a force equal to Goliath playing the Hulk in a game of tug-of-war, with POSH acting as the rope, Piper's stubborn side kicked in.

"Not today, Fate. Not today!" Pulse accelerating, hands slick with perspiration, Piper slammed on the brakes and tried to strong-arm the steering into submission. She'd had plenty of experience with strong-arming, which was likely why she was still single.

"Shit!" Her hot-headed impulse backfired, and instead of breaking on a dime, POSH, with her thread-bare spare and duct-taped chassis, broke traction. The back tires lost grip, spinning and kicking up gravel and dust, the car fish-tailing into the oncoming lane.

Thankfully, there were no other cars on the road. Just narrow and windy with nothing but dirt and gravel to slow her down. And trees. Lots and lots of trees. Big ones, little ones, enormous ones with trunks the size of water towers.

She skidded off the road onto the shoulder and on a direct course with a pothole the size of the Death Star. There was a large white oak, its gnarled branches swaying in the wind like a bat rhythmically swinging before a grand slam.

Ignoring her rising panic, Piper reached beside her for the e-brake and, channeling the tough-girl attitude that had helped her survive her teen years, she lifted the lever, smooth and steady. POSH released a loud pop, followed by some rhythmic thumping that beat hard in tempo with her heart. The car slowly decelerated, rolling off the road, finally coming to a stop inches from the oak tree, so close the leaves scratched back and forth across the hood.

She closed her eyes and dropped her forehead against the steering wheel, no longer judging Snow White for her hysterical reaction to trees. Allowing exactly one minute to collect herself, she took in a deep breath.

It took an additional three for her hands to stop shaking, but that was from frustration. At least, that was the story she was sticking to.

Ignoring the stench of singed rubber and desperation filling the cab, she popped the hood then opened the door. Even before she got out of the car, she knew the power steering was shot. Confirming her suspicions, she let out an impatient sigh and made her way to the trunk, grabbing the tire iron, because the belt was the least of her problems.

POSH was sporting a blown back tire and, while she could technically drive the last mile uphill without power steering, no amount of tenacity could make up for a flat tire.

As if her day wasn't challenging enough, Fate sent in her official RSVP to the party, by way of a streak of lightning which cut through the inky dusk sky.

One Mississippi. Two Mississip—

The ground rumbled under the boom of thunder. The wind picked up, plastering her dress against her legs and whipping her hair around.

"Is that all you got?" Piper hollered, waving the tire iron at the sky, which was turning all different shades of furry and brimstone.

Suddenly, it stopped and an eerie stillness moved in, surrounding her as static crackled in the evening air. Thunder and lightning she could handle. It was the quiet before the storm that was the most unsettling. Knowing it was only a matter of time before the drops began to fall, she grabbed the tire iron and went to work on the lug nuts.

Ten minutes, three grease stains, and a few choice words later, she succeeded in loosening half. The other half were stubborn little assholes that wouldn't budge.

"I'm small, but I'm scrappy," she said, shucking her impractical shoes to stand on the tire iron. She gave a few bounces, willing it to budge, when another streak of lightning reached across the darkening sky, exploding so close to her car that every hair on her body became electrified.

"Lightning doesn't scare me!" she shouted over the rustling trees.

Neither did Fate. Piper had taken on tougher and survived to tell the story. Plus, fear clashed with the ball-buster vibe she'd worked so hard to perfect. Not to mention, too much was riding on tonight for anything to go array.

The beautiful bride-to-be wasn't only Piper's new boss, but her fiancé was an agent to the stars. So the guest list read like a Who's Who in Portland—the exact kind of people Piper usually went out of her way to avoid.

However, circumstances had changed, and Piper needed to adapt, so she went back to work on the flat. Within minutes, stray strands of hair clung to her skin, and smudges of break-fluid covered the hem of her dress.

She was an utter mess. And no closer to changing her tire.

Refusing to give up, she removed her blazer and placed it gently inside the car, then propped her knee against the fender and shoved. Up and down and back and forth. She worked the tire iron as if more than just her pride depended on it. And she was making headway, creating a good rhythm for herself when she heard a loud sound rip through the air.

"Shit!" She shot up, her hands going to cover her backside, her mouth gaping open.

She didn't need to look to know that she had blown the back out of her fitted "wedding photographer approved" work dress. Praying the draft made it seem worse than it actually was, she glanced behind her.

"Shit, shit, shit!"

It was bad. Pink silk with black hearts bad. And the zipper looked like it had jumped the track and split from her lower back to right below the lace waistband of her panties.

She reached behind her to unzip the dress, hoping she could somehow fix the rip, but the zipper was stuck. She tugged. And when that didn't work, she tugged while hopping around.

"I get it!" she yelled at the sky. "Message received. Now go away so I can make my own destiny."

Destiny. She snorted. Yet another thing she didn't believe in. Every decision she'd made up to that point had been hers and hers alone. Something she normally prided herself on. But today, it left her feeling vulnerable and alone. And as she took in the grease stains on her hands and bare feet, Piper knew she needed help.

Admission was the hardest part.

But with three months' rent on the line, Piper was willing to do just about anything. Even if it meant phoning in a favor.

She dialed Jillian Conner, wedding cake designer extraordinaire, the person who helped Piper land this job, and the only soul she knew at the party besides the bride-to-be.

Jillian answered on the first ring.

"Piper, oh my God, where are you?" Jillian's voice came through the phone in a hushed whisper. "The mother of the groom has been asking for you."

"I'm almost there." Piper peered over the hood of her car to the historic mansion perched on the hill in front of her.

Located in the prestigious West Hills, Belle Mont House was three stories of Portland royalty, with extensive grounds, five large entertaining rooms, including a grand salon and conservatory which captured some of the most captivating views of the city and Mount Hood. It was a premier destination for weddings, cooperate parties, and highbrow events.

No family was quite as highbrow as the Eastons, who Groom Gage, along with Bride to Be Darcy, were the couple of the night.

"Like at the door almost?"

Piper hadn't known Jillian all that long, but she could tell the woman was beyond stressed. "Like my tire blew out at the bottom of Belle Mont Drive."

"This is bad. So, so incredibly bad. Most of the family has already arrived, and Margo is demanding to know when pictures are going to begin."

"The party doesn't start for another hour," Piper stated, but a bad feeling began to grow in the pit of her belly. She had met the matriarchal dictator of the Easton family once, at her initial interview. Getting struck by lightning would be less painful that going head-to-head with Margo Easton.

"The guests arrive in another hour, but most of the family is already here."

"You've got to be kidding me!" Piper looked up at the sky and squinted at the tiny molecules of rain flittering down. A drop landed on the tip of her nose.

She gave Fate a little wave of the finger—her middle one.

"Not even one bit." Jillian lowered her voice to a bare whisper. "Margo went over Darcy's head and told the family to get here an hour early. Darcy wasn't even dressed when Margo busted in with her closest friends in tow looking for tea. Now the woman is ranting about taking a picture of the entire family in the rose garden to use for this year's Christmas card."

Rain dotted the windshield and ground, and that bad feeling grew until Piper could feel it pressing against her ribs. "She does know that a storm is coming, right?"

Jillian laughed. "I don't think Zeus himself could take on Margo when she's like this. So please tell me you're going to arrive before she begins aiming her death glare my direction," Jillian begged. "With everything Darcy and Gage went through to get here, today has to be perfect. And that means keeping Margo appeased and away from Darcy. And since Darcy's my bestie, that task apparently falls to me. When I volunteered to be Margo's keeper, I had forgotten what nightmares are truly made of."

Piper had firsthand experience with nightmares who walked in the daylight. She wasn't scared of a five-foot-nothing sourpuss in pearls. "She isn't that bad."

"She is. Which reminds me, are you wearing the dress?" she asked as if Piper had a choice in the matter. Which she most definitely did not.

She looked down at the designer dress Jillian had made her try on—then buy. It was a little dustier—and a whole lot draftier—than it had been earlier, but with a few safety pins, a wet wipe, and lint roller it would do. "I'm wearing the dress."

"Thank god. Margo told me everyone needs to be in appropriate attire, even the staff."

"My closet was filled with appropriate photographer attire. Some of it is even press-core approved. Yet, I'm dressed as if I'm going to high tea." She tugged at the neckline and signed. "Or the Queen's funeral."

"Yeah, well, if it goes with pearls, it's Margo approved," Jillian said. "She's driving me crazy. So when I say I need you here now, I need you here *now*."

Piper took in the tire iron extending from a lug nut, then the tempest on the horizon. She calculated that she had less than fifteen minutes before the late summer drizzle turned into a Portland downpour. "I can fix the tire, but it will take time. Can you come get me? I'm just at the bottom of the hill."

There was a long pause, long enough that perspiration beaded down her spine.

"God, I wish I could. But today, of all days, my son decided he's scared of dogs and one of the brothers brought his wife's dog, who peed in my purse. Not on it—in it. And I still have one hundred twenty-six mini cakes to frost before Margo decides my dessert isn't quite right and does it herself."

Piper eyed the distance from her car to the top of the hill. It was like being stuck in the middle of the ocean in a life raft with only a whisk to paddle to shore.

Suck it up, buttercup.

"I'll figure it out. I promise."

"Before the storm hits. God, Piper, please tell me you'll get here before the storm hits."

It would be close, but she could make the hike.

"Fate herself couldn't stop me." Especially if it meant disappointing Jillian.

The two had met at the community park over the summer, during team pictures for the local Tiny Tikes football league. Piper had been conned into taking the team photo, and Jillian had volunteered enough cakepops to feed a small army. They'd bonded over the coach being a ginormous prick, which lead them to the conclusion that all men were ginormous pricks, and—several cakepops and a juice box later—they'd cemented a budding friendship.

A friendship Piper had come to treasure. She didn't have many friends growing up. Especially ones like Jillian, who not only had her life together but also cared enough about Piper to stand in her corner if the need arose.

That's because you're difficult, a little voice said from deep inside. A voice that sounded a whole lot like her mother.

Driven, Piper corrected. *Okay, stubborn.* Two qualities that had saved her life more than once.

With an unpredictable alcoholic for a mother and a chaotic childhood, Piper was wary of people's intentions. Moving from town to town, her mom burning through husbands like most people went through chips—you can't just have one—it made it hard to cement connections. Even harder to trust that the relationship could go the distance. So, she built walls. Big, impenetrable walls that were nearly impossible to scale.

But while she might be afraid to let people in, a little thunder and lightning didn't even rank on her list of things to run screaming from. If she had to trudge up that hill to get to the party on time, then trudging she'd do.

Piper opened the back door and pulled a pair of black combat boots off the floorboard and slipped them on. She grabbed her blazer, back up clothes—just in case the dress didn't make it—and was reaching for her camera bag when Jillian squealed. "Oh wait! I forgot. One of the brothers took an Uber from the airport and the driver just left. I can have him double back to pick you up."

Piper dropped her coat back in the car and climbed inside to avoid the rain. "You are a goddess. Tell him if he gets to me before the ground turns to mud, I'll double his tip. And Jillian, thank you. I so owe you."

"Friday night is girls' night. No excuses this time, and the first round is on you."

"Done and done." Piper disconnected.

Minutes ticked by with no sign of the hired car.

"Depending on a friend is not the same as being dependent," Piper said aloud then pulled out a tub of emergency peanut butter from her purse. Because if there was ever an emergency, pink silk with black hearts was it.

And—*ah* man—just the crinkling of the cellophane wrapper was enough to send all kinds of good feels to the brain. And then, because a jar of emergency peanut butter deserved some chocolate, she dusted off her hands and grabbed a fist of candy kisses from her camera bag.

The savory smell of peanuts and salt filled the car as she dipped the first kiss in and popped it in her mouth.

"Oh my gawd!" She sighed, closing her eyes to savor the momentary bliss. She hadn't eaten since breakfast, and it was fast approaching dinner time. With the setback of the flat and the lack of an assistant, her next meal would likely be well after midnight.

When she ran out of kisses, she dipped her finger in the jar and scooped out a mouthful, then licked it off.

She was on her third pass when the sound of gravel crunching under tires came up behind her. Piper turned to find a sleek black car headed her way.

"Thank you, Jillian," she whispered because help had finally arrived—and in Piper's world, that wasn't always the case.

With one last dip of the finger, she hopped out of the car and into the rain. Raising the jar in greeting, she gave an embarrassed little wave. The car got closer, and she sucked the remaining gooey goodness off her finger and stepped toward the road when—

"Holy shit!"

The sedan roared right past her with all four hundred of its horses powering at full tilt and nearly taking her out in the process. The car was so close it created a wind tunnel intense enough to rip the jar right from her hands. And cover her from head to toe in a fine speckling of mud.

"What the hell?" Piper yelled as the break-lights blared a steady red and the car skid to a stop a few yards ahead in the middle of the road.

Piper grabbed her blazer and tied it around her waist, then ran to the car. She'd barely reached the driver's side when the window slowly rolled down, exposing the driver within.

He was big and muscled, his body filling all the space in the car. Under the dome light she could see that his suit was freshly pressed, his dark wavy hair carefully manicured. He had the look of a man who controlled his world.

And he was gorgeous. The kind of gorgeous that made people want to stop and stare. Not that Piper was staring. Nope. She didn't do gorgeous. And she most certainly did not do suits who nearly ran her over.

"Are you okay?" he asked, his voice low and gravely.

"Do I look okay?" she asked because he looked as if he was about to climb out of the car and see for himself.

"You look like someone who was standing in the middle of the road during a storm, at dusk, wearing black," he said. "What? Were you playing chicken or staging a car heist?"

"No, I was waiting for you."

This seemed to amuse him. He looked at her over the rim of his wraparound sunglasses and grinned—a big, smug grin that pissed her off. "You were waiting for me?"

"Don't flatter yourself," she said, wondering how he'd managed, in sixty seconds, to get under her skin. "Just looking for a ride."

"Well, hop in."

"Gee, thanks."

"I did nearly run you over," he said, a humor to his voice saying he'd purposefully chosen to ignore the purposeful lack of gratitude in her words.

"You might not want to admit that," she advised. "Some people are jerks and would use it against you."

"Are you one of those people?"

"A jerk? Usually." She made a big show of dusting off her dress, which only made a bigger mess. "But life is too short to deal with lawyers."

His lips twitched. Not quite a smile, but enough to let Piper know it was at her expense. "Noted." His voice went soft. "But seriously, are you okay?"

His genuine concern deflated any hostility she'd been clinging to. She held her arms out to the side and when she looked down she nearly laughed. "Well, my dress is ruined."

He took off his sunglasses and—sweet Mary mother of God—his eyes were the exact color of the sky, a deep stormy blue with bright specks, like the lightning moments ago. Then there was the carefully crafted five-o'clock shadow.

"And yet, you're smiling," he said.

"My usual MO would be to swing the tire iron in your direction."

That twitch was back, and this time it exposed two double-barreled dimples that sparked all kinds of tingles. Their eyes held for a long moment as if he was trying to figure out what to do with her. It was a look she was used to.

"I guess today's my lucky day."

"Mine is looking up," she said. "If you hadn't stopped, I never would have made it to the party on time."

"You also wouldn't show up looking like your dress fell victim to a finger painting drive-by."

"Who doesn't love a good finger painting?" She lifted a single, sexy brow.

"I guess it depends on who's the canvas."

Not sure how she felt about that or the growing tingles, she said, "I'm Piper. And I'm late."

"I'm Josh, and I guess I'm your driver." He reached out his hand. "You headed to the party?"

"I'm shooting it." She lifted the camera bag, then looked at his still outstretched hand. "I would shake, but my hands are covered with—"

"Peanut butter," he said, and something playful lit his voice. "I saw."

Well, wasn't that embarrassing. She wondered what else he'd seen. The way his eyes held steadfast, almost as if he was fighting the urge to veer south told her he'd most likely seen some pink and black silk.

Oh, lucky day!

"I'd offer you some but..." She pointed over her shoulder to the peanut butter-sized roadkill on the ground.

"You're mourning the peanut butter but not the dress?"

"I have other clothes in my bag. But that was my emergency peanut butter," she said.

"That would make me the jerk." He rested an arm on the window and smiled. At her. As if their meeting was serendipitous. "How can I make it up to you?"

"How good are you with zippers?"

Continue Definitely (Maybe) Dating

About the Author

Marina Adair is a *New York Times* and #1 National bestselling author whose fun, flirty contemporary romcoms have sold over a million copies. In addition to the Easton series, she is the author of the When in Rome series, the Heroes of St. Helena series, the Sugar, Georgia series, and the St. Helena Vineyard series, which was the inspiration behind the original Hallmark Channel Vineyard movies: *Autumn in the Vineyard, Summer in the Vineyard,* and *Valentines in the Vineyard.* Raised in the San Francisco Bay Area, she holds an MFA from San Jose University and currently lives in Northern California with her husband, daughter, and two neurotic cats. Please visit her online at MarinaAdair.com and sign up for her newsletter at www.MarinaAdair.com/newsletter.

Sign Me Up!

Printed in Great Britain
by Amazon

11369197R00192